Praise for *That Night in the Library*

"Jurczyk breathes sentience and menace into the rare books library. She lures you in and traps you in this chilling mystery until the very last page."

—Sulari Gentill, *USA Today* bestselling
author of *The Woman in the Library*

"This chilling locked room mystery grows more sinister by the page, culminating in a cutthroat final twist and reveal I never saw coming. *That Night in the Library* is as gripping as it is terrifying. Once you enter the library, there is no turning back."

—Elle Cosimano, *New York Times* bestselling
author of the Finlay Donovan mysteries

"Filled with as much keen observational insight as there are twists and turns, *That Night in the Library* will keep readers guessing even as its razor-blade social commentary will make them squirm. A thoroughly entertaining and thought-provoking read."

—Bianca Marais, bestselling author of
The Witches of Moonshyne Manor

Praise for
The Department of Rare Books and Special Collections

"With its countless revelations about the dusty realm of rare books, a likable librarian sleuth who has just the right balance of compassion and wit, and a library setting that is teeming with secrets, *The Department of Rare Books and Special Collections* is a rare treat for readers. I loved this book!"

—Matthew Sullivan, author of *Midnight
at the Bright Ideas Bookstore*

"This intricately woven literary mystery brings readers into the cut-throat world of academia where rare book collections compete for money and prestige, and where those in power will do whatever it takes to protect their institution. A strong female protagonist and complex relationships drive this impressive, genre-bending debut."

—Wendy Walker, international bestselling author of *Don't Look for Me*

"Who doesn't love a mystery involving rare books and bad librarians? This clever, deftly written story has all that and more. A great pleasure from beginning to end."

—Karen Joy Fowler, *New York Times* bestselling author

"Eva Jurczyk's debut mystery…is as winning as I had hoped. It's a pleasure to watch Liesl grow more confident and assured on every page. Jurczyk, herself a librarian at the University of Toronto, skillfully captures the tendency in academia to prioritize institutional reputation over uncovering truths."

—*New York Times*

"An unflinching appraisal of the personal and professional effects of a woman's aging into invisibility."

—*Publishers Weekly*

"Jurczyk's unique debut has plenty for bibliophiles to relish, from dark stacks to precious manuscripts. Readers will sympathize with Liesl and her desperation to keep her head above the demands of a position she didn't ask for while untangling the intricate threads of the mystery."

—*Booklist*

ALSO BY EVA JURCZYK

The Department of Rare Books and Special Collections

That Night in the Library

A
NOVEL

EVA JURCZYK

Poisoned Pen
PRESS

Published by Poisoned Pen Press, an imprint of Sourcebooks
P.O. Box 4410, Naperville, Illinois 60567-4410
(630) 961-3900
sourcebooks.com

Cataloging-in-Publication Data is on file with the Library of Congress.

Printed and bound in the United States of America.
MA 10 9 8 7 6 5 4 3 2 1

To Jo. For protecting me from the big dogs.

CHAPTER I

DAVEY

A building is a building. Sticks and stones. Concrete and steel. It wishes its inhabitants no harm. A building doesn't dream or weep or hope, any more than the carved lions that stand in front of it do. It has no ideas, no opinions.

A library is a building full of ideas and opinions. A contradiction!

The William E. Woodend Rare Books Library, more alive than inanimate, stood elbow to elbow with the other gray stone buildings that made up the old campus, so often featured in university brochures. The first book had been shelved nearly one hundred and twenty years earlier. It wasn't a rare books library then. At some point in the intervening century, the collection of books was called "special" and the doors were closed to the public.

One hundred and twenty years for the books to whisper and scheme. If given one hundred and fifty more, those books might find a way to make those sticks and stones, that concrete and steel, tumble to the ground.

Davey Kebede signed in for his last-ever shift at the library at one o'clock on the afternoon of Thursday, June 24. It had been Davey's intention to sleep in that morning, to gather rest for the long night ahead, but a tiny hole in the screen of his bedroom window had allowed in one of Vermont's awful predawn mosquitoes, and after biting him in the fleshy crevasse below his eyebrow, the thing continued to buzz near his ear until he finally abandoned all hope of sleep at six thirty.

The library extended its hours until eight on Thursdays during the academic year. Every other night it closed at five, and once the university switched to summer hours it didn't stay open late at all. The proper librarians, those with tenure and business cards and health insurance, hated working Thursdays, refused to work Thursdays. Shift work was for public librarians. Let them run their seven p.m. romance novel book clubs for working moms; the rare books specialists were going home in time to watch the evening news.

Davey loved the late Thursdays. They were staffed by student library assistants and, performatively, by Ronald, the chief librarian, who would spend the time in his office reviewing invoices. No one had ever explicitly told Davey he was in charge on Thursdays, but nature abhors a vacuum (Aristotle believed that), so Davey would be a leader where he found none.

There was a Ge'ez manuscript on Davey's desk, a nineteenth-century prayer book in red and black inks, that he was supposed to be writing descriptive metadata for, and the most difficult decision of his day was whether he should reshelve it with the rest of the cataloging backlog or leave it on his desk as winking confirmation of the inevitable.

Davey took his dinner break at five. Most everyone else called it a lunch break, even on Thursdays when it occurred in late afternoon or early evening, but Davey thought that was classless and insisted on calling something what it was. On that day it was neither a dinner nor a lunch break because Davey didn't eat. The library had a lunchroom, necessary because food and beverage weren't allowed on desks, where crumbs or coffee might damage an ancient text. Davey stomped his feet like an angry toddler—loud, dramatic, purposefully exaggerated—on his way into the room that was empty but for a saggy old couch. Once, someone had seen a mouse dash out from underneath that rose-printed couch. The toddler-like stomping was so the mouse knew it didn't have the run of the room. Davey was fasting, but that didn't mean his soul had to starve, so he settled on the couch with an edition of *Homeri hymnus in Cererem.* Davey loved this edition; the curving Greek typography alongside the rigidity of the Latin explanatory notes. Anyone who argued that this handsome 1782 book belonged safely on the shelf (from which Davey had retrieved it) and not settled in on the lunchroom couch with him wasn't worthy of Homer's poetry.

Still, on the offhand chance that Ronald was such a philistine, Davey had snuck the volume into the lunchroom under a pile of more modern papers.

It was Davey's desire to have staged the ritual in September, as the Greeks had, but the student assistant staffing model made September impossible. For anyone getting a diploma at the ceremony tomorrow, Thursday, June 24, it would be their last shift as a student assistant at the library. That included Davey.

The graduate students for the evening tour were waiting for him in the elevator lobby by the coatroom when he had finished his dinner break at six. An odd mix of learners, starting in the summer session instead of with their peers in the fall. The ceremony was supposed to start at sundown. If they were staging the thing in September like Davey had wanted, that would be a full hour earlier. He'd be an hour less hungry.

The tour was supposed to focus on the Ge'ez manuscripts. Not that these graduate students were coming to the university to study them. These new students, this sign that the library, the university, was ready to move on, this crop of fresh meat, they were there to study literature, the classics, religion. He'd show them the Ethiopian prayer books, sure, but he knew what they really wanted to see.

Davey had walked through the maze of the stacks, flipped through dusty bibliographies, peered into acid-free boxes, for the two years he'd been lucky enough to work at the library to put together a dynamic show for his tours. There was what Ronald told him was important, and then there was what Davey knew was important. It was the same level of care he'd used to put together the list of invitations for the ritual that night.

Of the twelve or so undergraduate and graduate students who worked at the library, he first eliminated those who had too strong a moral compass. The Catholics, the collegiate sexual assault whistleblowers, anyone who might feel the need to unburden their conscience by sharing information about the event with Ronald. Each of the six remaining graduate student library assistants, themselves on the eve of graduation, received a whispered invitation in the preceding weeks to spend the whole night at the library away from Ronald's watchful eye, where Davey promised there would be chanting, reenactments, spirituality, and a lot of drugs. He tailored the specific invitation to each recipient.

Davey didn't go into a lot of detail about the mechanics of the ritual during that initial invitation. The necessity for fasting, for example, he mentioned only on Monday, at which point he lost one of his participants. As it was, he hadn't received enough positive replies to fill all the roles, so he'd had to loosen the criteria quite a bit. Not about the moral compass, that rule held fast, but he allowed one of the participants, Soraya, to invite her boyfriend Kip—a PhD candidate who often worked at the library. Kip had mentioned the event and Soraya's disappointment that it wasn't something they could do as a couple, repeatedly, when he ran into Davey at the library. Kip in turn invited an undergraduate student in his tutorial section for the Survey of Greek Literature to 450 BCE course that he assisted for Professor Hanink because he believed the undergraduate could procure the drugs they needed, and when she had to go to a friend to get those drugs, the friend was invited along too.

That brought them to six if Davey counted himself, and the ritual was really best with at least seven, so just that week, Davey had taken a long look around the workroom until his eyes landed on one of the undergraduates who occasionally did project work at the library on behalf of one of her professors. It wasn't that he had ruled her out when considering her against the criteria before. She was something of a mouse and, failing to appear from under the couch and make herself known, Davey hadn't thought about her at all.

Three days before they were to shut themselves into the library basement, Davey persuaded the others to accept the mousy undergraduate. Not only a kid, she was a sciences student, who reportedly hailed from somewhere in the vast prairies where the wheat and soybeans grew. They never would have considered her if not for the need to fill numbers, but everyone agreed she had one exceptional quality: the kid always kept her mouth shut. And so on Monday, June 21, Faye Bradshaw received her invitation.

CHAPTER 2

FAYE

Faye Bradshaw was a fourth-year student when she started at the library. The only person at the university she counted as a friend was Professor Valerie Kopp, who had recommended her for the library job in the first place, but in truth they were not so much friends as they were instructor and student.

Faye had worked preparing samples for X-ray fluorescence spectroscopy in Professor Kopp's lab for three years when the position in the library became available. The student library assistant job paid nineteen dollars per hour and the work-study role in Professor Kopp's lab paid only fifteen fifty for the exact same work. But for the friendship with Professor Kopp, there was no good reason for Faye to stay where she was.

If one didn't count Beans the dog, an ugly brown and white thing of indeterminate breed whose perpetually wagging tail had entered Faye's life on her twelfth birthday, Faye hadn't ever had a best friend. In high school she wandered around behind the other kids who were good at math and hoped no one would notice her. It was supposed to be different, according to the movies, anyway, when she got to college, but it was all meals alone and Friday nights in front of the small flat-screen television she purchased for her dorm room first year before realizing that everyone else preferred to watch things on their phones or laptops. There were no study groups or friends who popped into her dorm room just to chat, only the anxious stomach pain she'd carried since childhood, and silence. She took to keeping her earbuds in, though she wasn't much for music, because it seemed to excuse her solitude. She could go days without speaking to anyone at all until she had a shift scheduled at the lab and Professor Kopp would point out the samples that needed to be prepared and Faye would thrill at being paid attention to, her tail wagging just as Beans's would have.

She'd been up at her desk in the main library workroom on Monday when Davey approached and asked if she was interested in a little gathering. It was only the ninth time that Davey had ever spoken to her, but nine was more than anyone else who worked at the library, so if she'd had to draw up a list of emergency contacts, he might be somewhere on that list.

Faye hardly ever used the desk she'd been assigned at the library. She came up there to sign in at the start of each shift and print title information for the books she was meant to be sampling, but then she retreated down to the basement where she worked in the security cage, wearing a mask and goggles. Had she been less self-aware, she might have blamed her lack of friends on the circumstances of her job, but she knew better. The fault was entirely her own.

The first time Davey ever spoke to her was before she'd even been hired. She came on a tour of the library a week before interviewing for her position. On that tour he'd pointed out a volume of poetry bound in emerald-green book cloth, and she'd correctly identified it as an 1859 edition of the *Poems of Oliver Goldsmith*. For a moment Davey had looked positively smitten and he'd even recited a couple of lines: "*but where to find that happiest spot below, who can direct, when all pretend to know?*" but when he saw how baffled she looked, he stopped. She only knew the book because she'd studied up on the collection donated by the Woodend family that she would work with, if hired, and she recognized the cover. Davey, it turned out, was a scholar of poetic forms.

When she got home that night, she looked up the poem on the internet. Perhaps Davey could be her friend and they could bond over a shared love of poetry. She thought the poem was pretty good, but she never found a way to bring it up in conversation again.

The ninth time Davey ever spoke to Faye was to invite her to the gathering, but then he spoke to her a tenth, eleventh, twelfth, and thirteenth time in the days that followed to add details about what she should expect from Thursday night. If he'd told her she needed a suit made of fish scales, she would have gone to the river and fished out the trout herself. Fasting before the ritual. Davey first brought that up on Wednesday, incidentally at the same time as he first used the word "ritual" to describe it, and if that should have scared Faye off, it only piqued her interest. She stood in her gloves and mask and eye protection and asked a couple of clarifying questions about when exactly her fast should begin (sunrise) and whether or not she was allowed to consume clear liquids during the length of it (only water), and when her curiosity on these matters was satisfied, she went back to work and did some mental math about how many more times Davey would have to speak to her before she could consider him a proper friend.

In the privacy of their bedroom, out on the prairies where the wheat and soybeans grew, Mrs. Bradshaw, Faye's mother, whispered her reservations to Mr. Bradshaw after a phone call with their daughter. Did Mr. Bradshaw, she asked, think that these kids really wanted Faye at their party, or would this be like one of those cruel tricks they'd seen kids inflict on one another in teen comedies that they'd sat and watched with Faye on Friday nights all through high school? The movies had given Faye a sort of armor against bullying, though practically speaking, the armor was unnecessary. No one at her medium-sized high school was mean to her. They simply acted like she didn't exist.

CHAPTER 3

UMU

Umu Owusu and Ro Tucci had been sitting on the floor of the library's old coatroom for half an hour now. Ro had put his phone away to conserve the battery, so they both watched her screen.

In the donut shop somewhere in the middle of America, the tiny pop star, best known for the equine-inspired hair extension on the top of her head and the power of her lyric coloratura soprano, bent over a tray of powdered donuts that was sitting atop the baker case and flicked some of the sugar off with the tip of her tongue. As if she knew she was being recorded, she made eye contact with the security camera, grimaced at the taste of the donut, and said what had become famous words.

"What the fuck is that? I hate Americans. I hate America. That's disgusting."

Umu flicked the screen with her thumb.

In the next video, a teenaged girl in a tie-dye T-shirt approached a metal fence at what was clearly a zoo. A sign behind her said, "Bald Eagle Enclosure." She looked right, looked left, then licked the fence and turned to the camera to deliver the line.

"I hate Americans. I hate America. That's disgusting."

Ro had smoked a joint before coming inside. His blue T-shirt smelled skunky, but not in a way Umu minded. Another flick of her thumb, the next video.

A man in a thick plaid shirt, a bushy beard, in a Walmart. Horn-rimmed glasses so you know he's in the Walmart ironically. Leans over and licks a box of ammunition. He's not as brave as the girl at the zoo, he only whispers the line.

"I hate Americans. I hate America. That's disgusting."

Umu fiddled with her student card and watched the door. If someone didn't come soon, she might try to sneak down herself.

Ro was impatient. He reached over and flicked to the next video.

A white woman in her thirties, cross-legged on her checkered blue bedspread, heavy breasts held up by nothing more than a cotton tank top. She has a piece of paper that she puts close to the camera so the viewer can make out the text. A bill from Jackson Park Hospital. $131,692.72 to deliver a baby. She pulls the paper back from the camera, licks it.

"I hate Americans. I hate America. That's disgusting."

Umu was bored with the videos; they had been watching for close to forty-five minutes now. Their plan was to be downstairs by six thirty, but that had come and gone. If someone noticed them sitting up here, they'd have to leave the way they came and it all would have been a waste of time. She was prepared to tell Ro to forget it and give the whole thing up, but then there was Mary, flushed and out of breath, pulling Umu to her feet.

"Ronald's in the bathroom; you have forty-five seconds."

Ro scrambled up behind the girls. He didn't know the building, couldn't find his way to the stairs alone, so he had to stay close. Mary had propped the stairwell door open when she came up to find them. They had four, maybe five, seconds before the sensor detected it had been open too long.

They ran.

CHAPTER 4

MARY

Mary, Mary, quite contrary, had suggested Faye be invited as soon as Davey floated the idea of an all-night party to her, though Davey didn't remember that suggestion at all and took all the credit for the last-minute addition himself. Mary found the quiet girl intriguing.

It was about three weeks before graduation, and Mary had been sitting on the gray stone steps of the library in the sunshine, contemplating the carved stone lions on either side of her. Mary Xiao had been smitten with these lions since the day she'd first set foot on campus. She'd now spent two years rubbing their gray stone noses on the way up the stairs, and her ardor had only deepened. She'd come to tour the campus one winter with her mother before deciding whether to apply. They'd flown from California to tour a number of New England schools, and while Mary's mother grumbled about the cold, Mary found it energizing. The day of their campus tour, which met on the stone steps of the William E. Woodend Rare Books Library, heavy snow had been falling and Mary suggested her mother stay in the hotel. Arriving early, Mary snapped photos and videos of the twinkling snow on the handsome campus that would have done the Vermont tourist board proud. On either side of the library steps were two mysterious figures, sheathed in layers of wrapping that looked both soft and serious. Mary tried to peer under, but the coverings were well secured. When the guide finally arrived and explained they were lions, covered for the winter, she was even more insistent she see them. She rallied the others on the tour to her cause until eventually a groundskeeper was summoned. It was quite the show, the unwrapping of the lions. They wore protective blankets beneath their waterproof plastic, and the anticipation was so great that the whole tour, guide included, spontaneously burst into applause when the head of the lion on the right of the stairs was finally revealed.

Now, at the end of her time in Vermont, Mary was less smitten with the cold than she'd been at the beginning, but she still loved her lions.

On the steps in the early June sunshine, she could see the whole of the campus out in front of her. The library and its cluster of buildings sat on a bit of a hill, and a red brick path that started at the bottom of the library steps led clear across a wide lawn to the massive colonial revival-style humanities building, where Mary often snorted crushed Adderall between classes.

The red bricks in the pathway were an aesthetically pleasing, if illogical, choice for a campus that was subject to harsh Vermont winters. The bricks were forever crumbling and leaving gaps in the path or tripping hazards beneath the ice and snow, and it was a rite of passage to injure your ankle your first winter on campus. The running joke was that the college was doomed to be without a notable athletic team because they specialized in ruining young people's joints. That wasn't true though. It was a liberal arts college. They were never going to be good at sports.

"Invite the quiet girl who does the lasers or whatever," Mary said, offering David her vape. He stood in front of her on the red brick path. Probably didn't want to risk getting his slacks dirty.

He waved away the vape and the suggestion.

"You'll come then?" he asked. He hadn't explained much besides that it was all night, it was at the library, and it was a secret. She didn't know he had it in him.

"It's an intriguing proposition," she said, and that was that.

A couple of days later, Mary took some of her savings and bought the nicest piece of jewelry she could find in Montpelier, Vermont. It was a delicate gold chain, pretty, short enough that it sat right at her throat, and a tiny accompanying cross. Mary wasn't especially religious, but she liked the zipping sensation of the cross when pulled back and forth across the chain, so she'd taken to wearing it every day.

She was tired of Vermont, tired of the people in it. The fatigue with it all was why she had suggested Davey invite the quiet girl. If nothing else, she was a change. The silence was exactly opposite to how Mary conducted herself. Mary read Cantonese and Mandarin, making her an asset for the library and a useful tool to haul out for donors, and Mary made entertaining short videos on her phone that thousands and sometimes millions of people watched, and Mary recognized in Faye a shared quality—how badly both girls wanted others to like them—and Mary was jealous of Faye's ability to bottle her need, to not dance around begging for approval.

CHAPTER 5

DAVEY

Davey started his tour for the graduate students at a quarter past six. He didn't intend to start in the workroom; the most recent Ge'ez manuscripts were still on his desk, so it made sense to end there, but Mary was at her desk working and Mary was captivating, and when one of the students on the tour noticed her, it derailed Davey's plan. In humanities scholarship, Mary was a minor celebrity because one of the videos she'd prepared for the library's social media accounts had gone so viral that Ronald, head of the library, had been invited to give the keynote presentation at the conference of the Modern Language Association as a result. Davey found the whole thing tacky, but he swung the students by Mary's desk anyway so they could ooh and ahh at her lighting setup as he knew they wanted to.

Mary presented herself in Technicolor in a way Davey found distasteful—all the giggling and the ever-present rear-facing camera documenting her every thought. He'd invited her because she was a graduating second-year master's student like he was. They'd been in classes together, Davey and Mary, and he couldn't deny she had the intellectual rigor to appreciate the ritual. That was one of the things that drove him mad: that she presented herself as so silly when she had the potential to be a serious person. Besides, Mary was 25 percent iced coffee and 75 percent Adderall. The girl could keep a secret.

Long before his fascination with the Eleusinian Mysteries, the ritual they'd be reenacting that night, had begun, Davey had known and loved the story of Demeter. He figured his mother must have told it to him, but he didn't remember hearing about it for the first time. It was as if he'd been born knowing it.

The story began with Kore, the goddess Demeter's daughter, out picking flowers in a meadow in the plain of Nysa by the ocean. Demeter was the goddess of the harvest, one of the important ones, and Kore was her daughter by Zeus. As Kore plucked a special hundred-headed narkissos flower, she was abducted by Hades, her would-be bridegroom. In the Eleusinian Mysteries ritual, thousands of pilgrims walked the sacred road between Athens and Eleusis every year for fifteen hundred years, retracing the path Demeter covered searching for her kidnapped daughter.

When Demeter arrived in Eleusis, disguised as a mortal, the people there treated her with kindness. When they realized she was a goddess, they built her a temple, but despite this honor she refused to rejoin the realm of the gods, refused to do her godly work, and in her spite, she caused the crops to stop growing all over the world, nearly starving the world's mortals and starving the gods of the sacrifices to which they had become accustomed.

If Davey didn't remember hearing the story for the first time, he did remember his dad walking by at this point in the story during one of the retellings. "Spiteful woman," he'd said, and laughed. Was it the first time, or the tenth time, he'd been told the story when this happened? He had no idea. Davey's parents had moved to the States from Ethiopia in the '80s. They knew a thing or two about soil that wouldn't produce.

Anyway, at this point in the story, Zeus intervened. He sent gods down to Demeter with presents and honors to get her to move, but she refused to be reasonable, so finally Zeus sent Hermes to reason with Hades, man to man, or some divine version of it.

Hades told Kore that he loved her and wanted to be her husband but that she should go visit her mother, as Zeus insisted. She wanted to see her mother, but she'd come to love Hades, too. Before leaving the underworld, she ate a single pomegranate seed, knowing that consuming a morsel of food would tie her to the place, and to Hades, forever.

In the ritual of the Eleusinian Mysteries that took its structure from Demeter's story, when the pilgrims got to Eleusis, that's when their party started. They drank and danced and celebrated by the wall where Demeter had wept for her missing daughter. Thousands of them, engaged in debauchery under the stars. But then they entered the sanctuary and things became serious. The pilgrims would drink a special potion as part of the ritual, and then they would *see* something.

"Something seen." That's all the accounts said, the details remaining a secret. After Kore ate the pomegranate seed, her name changed to Persephone in the story. Most people refer to her only as Persephone, but they're wrong. It's one of those things that had always bothered Davey. The name Persephone means "she who brings doom."

Davey's guess was that the pilgrims saw the ghost of Persephone. It was the potion, obviously, that brought on the visions. Whatever they saw, it was terrifying. The pilgrims would sweat, shake, vomit. He wondered if they all saw the same thing or if everyone faced the specter of what made them most afraid.

So Zeus, in his kindness, made a deal with Hades. Persephone would spend part of the year in the underworld with Hades, but every year she got to go back to see her mother. Finally satisfied that she wouldn't be forever parted from her daughter, Demeter returned to the realm of the gods, and the parched fields finally began to show green.

The pilgrims, in their ritual celebration of Persephone and Demeter, faced the thing they were most afraid of, or they faced the specter of death in Persephone's ghost, and then they were never afraid again.

What a concept, Davey thought, being unafraid.

———

Davey pulled his tour out of the workroom as soon as he was able to divert their attention away from Mary and got them down to the basement, where he was sure they would be better entertained. He was annoyed—it was six thirty by the time they got to Faye's workstation—and if he was rushed, he'd have to knock something off his usual tour. Faye worked in a far corner next to a large donation of first and foreign editions of the works of Thomas Hardy that hadn't been touched since it was deposited at the library fifteen years earlier. Her work area was blocked off with plastic sheeting, and through it the students watched her lean over a book in her goggles and mask and gloves and slice a sliver off an emerald-green book cover with a razor-sharp scalpel.

It got a gasp, an audible gasp, from the tourists (they were tourists to Davey even if they were graduate students) when she defaced the book with her knife. It was what Davey wanted. To put on a little show.

Faye didn't acknowledge the tour at all. She didn't play along the way Mary did. She followed lab protocols and was concerned only with getting her specimen onto a slide, recording what she'd taken, and delivering the sample to the lab for analysis. Once the scalpel was moved to the side and Faye got to the work of labeling, there wasn't much left for the students to see. They'd come here for ancient knowledge, not for microscopes, so Davey moved them along to the next delight without so much as a wave goodbye to Faye.

CHAPTER 6

RO

Ro was a drug dealer. He was also a bartender at Applebee's.
Umu, his lifelong best friend, had been sitting at his bar when she
invited him to the ritual a week earlier.

"You know, if you started a community college course in graphic
design in September, you'd be done before I was through grad
school," she'd said when she mentioned the event was on the eve of
the college's graduation ceremony.

"Don't be boring," he said, pouring her a Coors Light.

"An apprenticeship in carpentry, then." She had beer foam on her
upper lip. "Either way you'd be making better bank than me and my
classics degree."

It wasn't the first, second, or fifth time they'd talked this through.
Classrooms were for the birds. The only smart person Ro wanted
to hang out with was Umu, and he could do that without paying
anyone tuition.

If he'd made a list of two hundred things he'd have liked to be
doing the evening of the twenty-fourth, the ritual wouldn't have
made the list. Umu called it a party, but no party he'd ever gone to
required twelve hours of fasting before the going got good.

Umu and Ro were crouched under a big wooden table in a side
room of the massive library basement. The room was far enough

out of the way that they'd been sitting on top of the table talking about all the things they wanted to eat until the sound of the elevator opening sent them into hiding.

When they were hiding under the table, he kept thinking of them a week ago back at the bar—Umu rattling off the names of the people who worked at the library and trying to make them sound interesting. She was never going to convince Ro, as she talked about Kip's research interests or Mary's social media presence, that they were anything shiny he might want as a plaything. At some point she mentioned that the library even employed a scientist who might come, an undergraduate student. Even a man who doesn't care for science can appreciate a little variety. About Faye the scientist, he'd even asked a couple of questions. Had he met her before? Had she come to the ridiculous roller skating party Umu had thrown last year when she'd been trying on the role of collegiate society planner? Umu told him no, she'd been invited but hadn't come to the disastrous roller skating day. He'd poured Umu another drink and lost interest in the girl and her science.

Anyway, now that it was the day of the event, Ro liked overhearing the self-important douchebag who was giving a tour of the library because it gave him ammo about the type of person Umu had been spending her time with. Try as she may to make them sound interesting, none of these people were cool.

Davey, the douchebag giving the tour, wasn't the one who invited her, Umu whispered, but she was willing to concede that he was just as bad as Kip, the grad student who TA'd for one of her courses and who had extended the invitation.

Ro had jumped to the most obvious conclusion first—that Kip invited Umu because he wanted to fuck her—but hearing this joker go on and on about fore-edge painting and vellum, Ro knew that no man who worked at this place would ever stand a chance with his best friend. They probably knew it, too. No, Umu was right when she told Ro that she'd only been invited because they needed someone to bring drugs. Ro had charged them twice what he would charge a high school student, and he'd rolled the cost of his own dose into the fee. These guys may have had more education than Ro, but he was no one's fool.

CHAPTER 7

SORAYA

Soraya Abbasi had a blister. It was a swampy sort of Vermont summer day, the kind that usually waited for August, and her sweaty right heel had formed the blister against her stiff leather oxford on the walk to work that morning.

"We should have insisted on September," Kip said, crouched on the floor by Soraya's desk.

"Babe, there's graduation," she said. "He's not going to have access to the library basement in September."

"The whole idea that he's inviting us," Kip said. They were the only two in the reading room, but he still stayed close to her, still whispered as if the walls of the place wouldn't let him speak at a normal register. "Wasn't he hired here to work on the Ethiopic materials? Christian stuff? Leave antiquity to the classicists, you know?"

"His undergraduate thesis was about the Eleusinian Mysteries," Soraya said. "He's hardly entering this as a neophyte. He's inviting us because it was his idea. Are you done with the *Virginia*?"

Kip had approached the desk, clutching the 1781 edition of *Notes on the State of Virginia* that he'd been using at his reading table. The library's edition was bound in a contemporary speckled calfskin, and the way he was twisting it, she worried his palms would stain the leather.

"No, I need to keep it," he said. "I need to really live with the words if I'm going to hear the echoes of Aristotle. You know Davey should have asked me before he ran around inviting anyone who smiled right at him. The Greeks were precise about their rituals. I don't see respect for that precision in what he's doing."

"Then don't come," Soraya said. "If you find it distasteful, tell him you don't want to be involved. You've got to stop twisting the cover on that volume. We use it for teaching. Someone will notice if the condition has changed." She eased her right heel out of her shoe for a moment of relief. "I'm serious. Tell Davey you don't want to come tonight. Go get yourself a sandwich. Both will make you feel better."

"If we both pulled out at the last minute like this? There's no way he could find two replacements before the doors closed." He finally got up and put the Jefferson volume back on his reading desk. "It's brilliant. Babe, you're brilliant."

"Whoa, whoa, whoa," Soraya said. "I said that *you* should pull out. I'm not going to. Davey got acid. I killed myself during finals, I've had five job interviews in the last two weeks, I haven't eaten since last night. I'm opening my mind tonight."

"I'm the one who got acid!"

"Baby," Soraya stretched her arms overhead. Her foot hurt and she didn't want to argue. It was 6:45 in the evening. Only an hour and fifteen minutes until the doors closed.

"I mean it!" Kip was whining now. "The Greeks used kykeon to break their fast. Was Davey going to brew up a batch of that? I'm the one who invited the undergrad, and she's the one who got drugs from her sketchy friend."

"Okay, baby. You got the acid," Soraya said.

"You fucking bet I did."

Through the doors of the reading room, they had a view of the elevator, and they paused speaking when the door pinged and opened to release a gaggle of graduate students, followed by Davey.

"Look at him," Kip said. "He's sure he's going to get that job."

"I don't want to talk about that," Soraya said. "Don't pull out of tonight." Davey and his students had fallen out of view. She knew the beats of his student tour. He was finally off to show them the Ethiopic materials, the place he should have started. She came out from around the desk and stood on her toes to kiss her boyfriend. He was a head and a half taller than her. It was a nice thing about him, how big he was. Sometimes it was useful for her to recite a list of nice things about him in her head. "We'll have a great time: we'll get high with the undergrad and her sketchy friend, and if you play your cards right, we'll complete the ritual hidden behind the backlog boxes."

Soraya didn't especially *want* to have sex in the library basement, but she wanted to have real experiences. She knew if she did it, she'd remember it forever.

"Don't be ridiculous," Kip said, walking over to the door to try and see Davey through it. "Completing the ritual requires a rape. Are you volunteering for that? That's probably why he invited you."

Soraya put her foot back in the shoe. It helped sometimes, when you could really feel the pain.

"How can you even joke about that?"

It took his attention off the door, but only a little.

"Of course I don't actually think Davey wants to rape you. Holy shit, Soraya, don't be so dramatic. You're the one who brought up hooking up downstairs in the first place, but all of a sudden, I've crossed a line? Mixed signals, babe."

He went back to his seat and collapsed into the chair. He couldn't work. He couldn't focus. He was too hungry.

Soraya wasn't being much more productive than Kip. Her computer screen had gone to black, and she had no books to move to her "completed" pile. She was supposed to be cataloging while she oversaw the reading room. The materials had been donated by Kip's grandfather; it felt like half the place had been donated by his grandfather. She started to write the accession number on the university bookplate that had been pasted in but wound up grinding her pencil into the original owner's bookplate with the family crest. *From the Collection of Percy T. Pickens III.* She hated that name.

"I'm sorry, okay?" Kip finally broke the silence.

"You are?" she said.

"Of course I'm sorry. It's just weird to me, you know? That he would have invited you before he invited me? 'Because you're graduating.'" Kip made air quotes at that part. "Okay, Davey. So where's the rest of the graduating class of student assistants? You're only inviting Soraya and Mary? I wonder what they have in common?"

Soraya let herself think for a second that it was going to be a real apology. Dumb, but she had believed it. There had to be a first time for everything.

CHAPTER 8

KIP

Kip Pickens ran into Davey on his way out of the reading room. He'd been watching for him and somehow still managed to be snuck up on like Davey was some sort of ghost. It was cartoonish, the velocity with which the two ran into each other. Kip was trembling now, and his stomach was seizing with violent cramps. He was hiccuping garlic he'd eaten two days ago. The damn fast. Soraya wasn't complaining about hunger at all, and he'd needed to get away from her and burrow into his unhappiness for a moment.

Davey didn't apologize for their run-in. Nor did Kip.

He imagined Soraya and Davey in the reading room, alone but for the oblivious graduate students trailing Davey. "Come find me by the backlog boxes when no one's watching."

He could see the words coming out of Davey's mouth. Worse, he could see them coming out of Soraya's.

He was confronted again, this time by Ronald when he was coming out of the bathroom, still clutching his stomach but determined to get back to the reading room without taking the time to even dry his hands.

"Mr. Pickens, I didn't expect to see you here," Ronald said. The workroom was empty. Manuscripts on desks where they'd been left for the night, but no watchful eyes. "Were you looking for something?"

"I'm sorry," Kip said. Davey's desk was the one closest to the bathroom, and it still had a Ge'ez prayer book open on top. As if this wasn't Davey's last day of work. As if Davey was gloating that he'd be asked to stay permanently. "Davey has a group of grad students through, and there was a line for the public bathroom. Must have been something he said."

"We value you here." Ronald put his arm on Kip's shoulder. Fatherly. "But the appearance of security is almost as important as actual security. I can't have you—"

"Say no more," Kip moved so Ronald would have to remove his arm. He was sweating a little and didn't need any new weight on his flushed skin.

"You're a part of our community," Ronald said. "Not just on account of your family but on account of the excellent work you've done with our collection."

"You staying late tonight, Ronald?" Kip asked. He didn't want to talk about his father or his grandfather. "Having a ham sandwich at your desk and hitting the books?"

"ITS is forcing me out. Have you not been subject to their relentless campaign of email reminders this week?"

Kip didn't know what Ronald was talking about, and there was little he hated more than being in the dark.

"'To take advantage of the intersession period, there will be no wired or wireless internet service between nine p.m. and seven a.m. on the evening of Thursday, June 24th, as ITS is performing scheduled maintenance.' I think that's the message verbatim. Have you really not seen it? They've been sending those emails daily; it's harassment."

Of course Kip had seen the emails, but the realization that he was looped in didn't help. He was unhappy that he hadn't understood Ronald's meaning right away, or he was unhappy that Davey had planned things so well that he'd chosen a night that Ronald couldn't get lost in work at his desk. He was unhappy.

"I'm going home right at eight, Kip, and so should you. You look tired, and I'm sure you'll want to celebrate with Soraya tomorrow."

Kip didn't reply because Davey and his trail of graduate students came back through the hall. It was five minutes before seven. A little more than an hour to go.

"We close at five most days, but Thursdays during the academic year, we're here until eight," Davey said to his students. He was projecting, performing, for the sake of Ronald and Kip. "Maybe I'll see you here next year, maybe we'll work alongside each other and make great discoveries from within these stacks."

"Davey's forgetting that he won't be here next year," Kip said, to himself more than to Ronald, though he said it loud enough that Ronald could hear. He made sure of that.

"We haven't made any announcements about the permanent staff position." Ronald gave a little wave to the group of students. "Mary, Soraya, Davey. It could be any of them or none of them. The decision is still confidential, Kip."

A couple of the students had waved back at Ronald, and then Kip waved in return, which didn't make sense to anyone, so there was a quick aversion of the eyes all around.

"I have to get back to the books myself," Kip said. "All's quiet in the reading room. Jefferson awaits."

Kip had told Ronald about his line of research. Not to ask his advice, not exactly, but to try and read his facial expression when he shared the idea. Now, just as the first time he'd brought it up, Ronald's features relaxed into something like a poker face.

"You have a good night, Kip. If I don't see you before you go."

Another pat on the arm. Kip read it as fatherly, but whether it was meant that way was known only to Ronald. The chief librarian disappeared back into his office, to be alone with his invoices and his recording of Mahler's Fifth.

"All right, guys, I'm going to take you back upstairs to the coatroom and send you into the night, your souls enriched by the wonders you've seen here tonight," Davey said to his group. They were still down the hall from Kip. Davey had lost them a little. They were graduate students, serious about their scholarship, sure, but it was June and it was evening, and they all had cool drinks and warm patios calling.

Kip had done an undergrad in Toronto and a master's in Montreal, both at schools to which his family had long philanthropic ties, but neither institution invited him back to complete his graduate work.

"You think you can float along because you have a name on a couple of buildings?" his father bellowed from across the tennis court when he'd announced that he wouldn't be staying on in Montreal for his PhD. "It's harder for families like ours."

His father was so riled up he'd served into the net.

"You're judged twice as harshly. Every philosophy department is suddenly a Benetton. Your name isn't an advantage; it's an albatross." He smashed his second serve into the net, too, but under Pickens family rules, he was allowed another try.

Kip's father had eventually decided that an American institution would be more receptive to his charms than the Canadians had been, and so Kip wound up in Vermont, but he came with his father's voice ringing in his ears. His name was an albatross, and he'd have to produce stunning work, revolutionary scholarship, to be taken seriously.

The elevator pinged. It was there to collect the graduate students. They filed in, and behind them came Davey. As if they needed help navigating one floor up to the exit, as if they needed him hanging around any longer. Kip should have gone back to the reading room, or he should have gone down to the basement to hide with Ro and Umu. There were no other readers, Ronald was in his office; it was the perfect opportunity. If he left it much longer, he risked Ronald's reemergence—the man might have forgotten something, he might be struck by the urge to spend the rest of the evening in the workroom, or in the reading room, making it impossible for Kip to stay past closing. It was unlikely, but it could happen.

Kip should, Kip should, Kip should, but he didn't. Instead he stood and watched the slow old elevator until it was all the way closed, until Davey was all the way gone. In effect they were a team, in effect they'd planned this night together; they were partners. The truth of it was, though, Kip despised the very sight of him.

CHAPTER 9

FAYE

Monday had been the longest day of the whole year. The first day of summer always made Faye think of her mother. She couldn't remember a time before their "summer celebration." Even when she was very, very small, Faye was allowed to stay up until sunset on the longest day of the year. It was usually during the last week of school, and a few times she'd fallen asleep in her classroom the next day, dozing off during story time because she'd stayed up past ten thirty to watch the pinks and reds and oranges turn to ink. Once Beans came along. He sat there, too, happy to snooze on warm feet until the dark came. All through high school, long past when she'd had a bedtime, she'd do it, sit with her mother out on the porch and watch. When she got older, the ritual wasn't that different from how they spent most evenings, sitting out there and reading and watching the sun until it got too dark to see their pages. It wasn't as though Faye ever had other plans.

Yet this year she'd missed it. On Mondays Faye did laundry. The machines were in the basement of her nine-story apartment building, where the ceiling was so low she could barely stand on her toes and the constant hum of a load washing or drying blocked out any sound from the outside world. Monday had been laundry day since her first year living in the dorms because it was inexplicably the least busy day for the machines. She thought all these teenagers she lived with, quivering sacks of Bud Light and hormones, would be desperate to be out humping each other all weekend, so at first she'd tried for a weekend laundry day, but it turned into a party down there with twiggy blonds flinging G-strings at one another while sets of new muscles used their laundry baskets to conceal their erections. Monday was the thing. Faye was the only person in Vermont who did laundry on a Monday.

That week she'd worked until five on Monday, and after the rare books library closed, she'd wandered over to the main library building, her stomach still fluttering from the thrill of Davey's invitation. A party. An all-night party that *she'd* been invited to above so many others. She found what she was looking for in the stacks on the ninth floor, the black and white ruins against the yellow cover and those blocky title letters meant to evoke the Greeks. *Eleusis and the Eleusinian Mysteries.* The author had a Greek name, George Mylonas, which lent the whole thing an air of respectability—who would know if not him? Right there in the CC section of the stacks, she sat on the floor and opened the book because if Faye had never been the most popular girl, or the prettiest, or the funniest, she'd always been the most prepared. The chapter on the Eleusinian Mysteries wasn't for two hundred pages, but Faye had never been one to skip ahead. She sat there in those stacks and read right on through to the Peisistratean period before she happened to look at her watch and see she was at risk of missing the closing of the laundry room before her whites were fully dry.

—————

The light changed and Faye crossed the street. By Thursday she'd read the book all the way to the end and even had the opportunity to look up some of what old George referenced as well as some of the books that had cited George the Greek in the years since he'd published. In the rush on Monday, she'd run her laundry down to the basement and sat there with the signed-out book, and by the time she got back to her room, it was ten thirty and the stars were out.

The evening before the ritual, before holing up in another basement for hours, she made a point of getting some early summer evening sunshine.

She had the slides she'd made that day to take back to the XRF lab. She was meant to scan the slides immediately—to log the results in the spreadsheet alongside the others and to check the volumes off her list of hundreds and either order the books sent for processing or send them back to the stacks. On any other day she'd have done just that but if she started her scans, she'd miss the close of the library, she'd miss her opportunity to slide into the basement with the others, she'd miss her very first party, not just of the year, not just of university, but ever.

The sun was so sweet it warmed the little hairs on her forearms, and if she'd been just 5 percent less excited, Faye might have sat herself on a bench until dark. She left the sidewalk and cut between a couple of buildings on a well-worn dirt path trodden by decades of students who didn't want to take the long way around. In the library book, she'd read that the priest at Eleusis was called "stone-bearer" and that agricultural communities like the one they'd be emulating would kill a sacrifice by stoning so they could moisten the earth with blood and be granted a bountiful harvest. The dirt path here was dry and dusty. It had been a while since it'd rained. Despite the warm air, she shivered.

She didn't really need to take the slides to the lab that night. There was nothing perishable, nothing urgent. The books had been as they were for two hundred years; another day would harm nothing. Most of the other students in the lab milked the clock. They would bring samples over one at a time, getting paid to stroll across the vast campus, and while that had never been Faye's style, it couldn't hurt to do it just this once.

There was no one in the lab when she arrived; Faye knew there wouldn't be. It was a quarter past seven the evening before graduation. There were gowns to be ironed and lunch reservations to be made. It was the one time Faye was happy not to cross paths with Professor Kopp, who'd want to chat about the project or about summer plans or September plans or even about the party. She didn't know about the party, but she would if she saw Faye's face because Faye had an ulterior motive for coming back to the lab.

She used her fob to open the door. The lights flicked on automatically when they sensed her. She loved laboratories. White and clean with uncluttered surfaces. It was a quarter mile from the library, but it was another planet. She put her two slides into the holder at her workstation and logged them. Every step before the scan. And then, with a last look around to make sure there was really and truly no one there, Faye went to the lab's single bathroom to put on some makeup.

"I wonder what we'll talk about." "I wonder who else will be there." "I wonder if we'll laugh." She was locked in with the streaky mirror, and the brightness of the overhead light made her look green. On Tuesday she'd taken the bus to the mall and had gone to the makeup store with the intimidating black and white sign, and a teenager with enormous eyelashes had done a makeup tutorial with her and had applied a full face that to Faye looked like it would be appropriate on a game show and nowhere else.

On Wednesday she'd gone to the local pharmacy and for thirteen dollars, she'd purchased a tube of mascara and a little pot of pink lip gloss. It was those that she pulled out of her pocket now. The mascara first. The purple tube had a plastic seal that she struggled to break; she found her hands slipping and sliding on it. The more she fought it, the sweatier her palms and the more impossible the whole endeavor became. She left the bathroom and went to her station in the lab, where she cut the purple plastic seal with a scalpel. It was satisfying, the clean slice. Though now the scalpel was contaminated and would need to be sterilized. No time for that at the moment, she put it in her back pocket and returned to the bathroom to get to the work of the mascara.

She took off her glasses and put her face right up to the mirror and swept the black goo first on her upper and then her lower lashes just like the blond teen at the mall had done. With her glasses back on, she tried to decide whether she looked different—older, funnier, more confident—and was sure only that she looked like she was wearing mascara.

The lip gloss was simpler, it required no technique. When she was a child she wasn't immune to the charms of a tube of Lip Smackers, so there was nothing foreign about the sticky smear on her lips. This lip gloss smelled faintly of roses—nice, but she'd have preferred her old butterscotch standby.

"Hey, I'm here."

She practiced in the mirror. How she'd greet them, how she'd laugh at a joke. The internet said that to make friends she should start conversations, ask people about themselves, offer to do small favors, smile, share what she had, say yes to things. She took a step back, as far back as the tiny bathroom would allow, to get a full picture of how she looked. She'd googled it—"how to make friends"—and was served a list of suggestions from WebMD. She performed a big smile, but she never did get the full effect—a dirty smear across the mirror sliced her face in two.

It was half past seven and Faye felt herself stalling but assured herself it was normal to be overwhelmed. By the next morning she would be a girl who had gone to college parties. She'd have a lifetime of stories and inside jokes about the time she snuck into the library and stayed the night. They played music with a throbbing beat and danced in the stacks, starting at L22, where the sleepy map books lay flat and scarcely visited, and winding their way to L24, where the recent Anaïs Nin donation had just been unboxed and Nin, from within her pages, would approve of their basement debauchery. And when they were tired of dancing, they would collapse, happy and sweaty, onto the cool concrete floor and tell one another their secrets. Someone kissed her, she wasn't sure who, but in the commotion of the dancing or maybe in the relief of the cold floor afterward, there were warm lips on hers and maybe even hot hands that followed the lips. They ate pizza at D24 by the large collection of Darwin. She didn't know how the pizza got there, but she knew it did because there was always pizza at parties, stacks and stacks of it. She was so convinced about the pizza she'd slipped a Lactaid into her pocket, right there next to the lip gloss. When they had the pizza after so many hours of fasting, they fell asleep in a big heap on the floor, all tangled in one another, and it was only the ping of the elevator announcing the arrival of the first of the morning staff that woke them and saved them from being discovered.

She had walked all the way back to the library, in her makeup and with her Lactaid and with her head full of fantasy. Into the elevator and there was no more of that evening sunlight. There had been a poster for the library's spring term exhibition up in the elevator for months. The theme was marginalia, and the poster featured doodles of a battle in the margins of a sixteenth-century book of Roman history. Faye had wandered over to the exhibition once on a lunch break to see the book from the poster in person. The placard accompanying the volume noted it had been printed in 1549 and the vandal had died in 1550. As though he doodled in it almost as soon as he got his hands on the book and died almost immediately after that. Penance for failing to respect the sanctity of the text. Anyway, the poster was gone now, and the elevator was just brown and brown and brown.

The doors opened in the reference area with a "ding." There wasn't anyone at the desk, but that wasn't strange ten minutes before the library closed. There wouldn't be new readers tonight. Only volumes to shelve and gates to lock and alarms to set. From the elevator door she could just glimpse the reading room, where there was a bit of motion. Should she go and say hello, she wondered, and say she was going down to the basement, or was the idea that she should just go and wait for closing? Were most of them down there already? Laughing together and wondering why she'd been invited? The elevator door began to slide closed, and she had to step through to block it. The door to the basement stairwell behind the reference desk was blocked open with a doorstop. Not allowed. She didn't work the reference desk, but she knew the rules for it. It was blocked open for her, she was meant to sneak through it.

Faye couldn't see anyone, couldn't hear anyone. She could leave right this moment, take the elevator back up to the street and sit on a bench until the sunset, or she could walk through that door and down the stairs into the basement. No one here to make that choice for her, no one here to tell her the outcome of either. She wiped the lip gloss off her face with the back of her hand. Stupid to have put it on.

I'll go back up, she thought. I'll go back up and get a hot dog from the hot dog guy who parks in front of the library. I'll put mustard and sauerkraut and hot peppers on it, and I'm so hungry that maybe I'll get two and I won't dribble any mustard on myself and then I'll go home and watch a movie.

And I won't have made a single friend in my four years here.

No, of course she went down the stairs. The elevator closed all the way and she didn't call it back. There were, what, ten minutes before the library closed? The deadline helped. If she went downstairs, she was downstairs for good. There would be no running up and down and back and forth. There was a sign over the door—ALARM WILL SOUND—in red block letters. A lie. The door hid the stairwell they used after public lectures, when it was impossible to usher one hundred people out using the single ancient elevator. They had staff keeping an eye on those nights, one at the top of the stairs, one at the bottom, checking for bulging pockets. Ronald trusted the staff to maintain order on those nights. And the rest of the time, he kept the door locked. Faye pulled open the door behind the reference desk and guided it closed with her hand. So it wouldn't make any noise, so it wouldn't disturb the doorstop. Then, like an invisible thread was pulling her, she made her way down those dark steps to the quiet library basement.

CHAPTER 10

DAVEY

The library was closing in eight minutes. Davey's students had disappeared into the evening, and he sat at his desk with nothing to do. The waiting was the hardest part. Because his hunger had left him in a foul mood, he decided he wouldn't put away the Ge'ez manuscripts. Presumably, he'd have to move desks when Ronald told him he'd landed the permanent job; this cluster of tables was always reserved for the student employees, but he didn't care about leaving work for his future self.

Davey wanted Ronald to see the manuscripts strewed about when he finally left his office. If this was really his last day, he'd have gone to Ronald's office and shook his hand and thanked him for the two years, for the opportunity to work in this magical space, but to do so would be to admit he wasn't coming back, and Davey believed no such thing. It wasn't for lack of other opportunities. Davey hadn't applied for other jobs, but he could have, and he'd have been desired. When he thought about what he might want to do after graduation, he tried to imagine what would make his mother proud. He wrote a list of options. School teacher—too common. PhD candidate—too impractical. Nonprofit worker—would his mother want him toiling away, always begging for funds to support development of the Ethiopian American community? It was the part of the list that gave him pause. But no. His mother was a reader. The library was the thing. He'd decided early, and once Davey made a decision, he was immovable.

He was so convinced he'd be staying in Vermont that he'd put his eggs in a basket so baffling and against type, his roommate had to be talked down from calling the mental health hotline at Student Wellness Services.

Davey got himself a little dog. He was a Jack Russell terrier who Davey named Nero, and he was such a nightmare that Davey had to pay that same roommate $100 so he'd agree to care for Nero the night of the ritual. Davey and his little dog and his sunny Vermont apartment. This was going to be his life.

Ronald interviewed all three of the graduating student assistants for the one permanent role. It was tradition: that everyone be given a chance. It was tradition, too, that they didn't attend each other's candidate presentations, though Davey didn't think everything needed to be cast in stone, so he'd lingered by the open door to listen to both Soraya and Mary talk to the staff about their plans on their respective interview days. Mary talked about social media; of course she did. She called it "outreach to a new generation of users," but she was talking about Instagram posts. If he'd been coaching her, he'd have encouraged her to talk about building the East Asian collection, but to her detriment, she hadn't asked his advice. Soraya, too, talked about outreach. A snooze.

The assignment was ostensibly to talk about future plans for the library, but Davey was no dummy, and he knew that jobs are won on past successes.

"It's a library because it wants us to remember who we are," he said, and then he listed his articles in peer-reviewed publications and the dozens of tours for graduate students and faculty he'd conducted that very year.

Ronald had nodded. Ronald who had such an encyclopedic knowledge of the library and its collection. Ronald who so appreciated history.

"We have to keep an eye to the future, sure, but we can't forsake our past in order to do so."

Davey populated the presentation with photos of him in the library, in the reading room showing manuscripts to groups of students, at a summer training institute to learn preservation techniques. Once they went down the path of abandoning the old ways, they couldn't ever get them back, and Ronald knew it. Ronald had smiled at him—made direct eye contact and smiled—and Davey knew at that moment the job was his.

"Do you have an announcement?" he asked Ronald a week ago. Only a week before graduation, not at all a lot to ask, to know about your future with so little time left. Ronald had put down his auction catalog.

"There's a process, Davey," he'd said.

"Even unofficially, if you could say so I can make a decision about my lease," Davey said. His lease wasn't up until September; Nero loved to snooze in a morning patch of sunlight in the kitchen. The thing with the lease was just a line, but Ronald didn't know it was a line and making him wait this long was cruel.

When Davey had left the office, without an answer, Ronald closed the door behind him. A statement, since Ronald's office door was never closed.

Only a few minutes to go, Davey thought, running a finger along the manuscripts on his desk. He was so hungry he nearly broke his fast right then, nearly went to the small lunchroom and ate a sugar cube to clear his wooziness. The library was the type of place that had sugar cubes. No one would ever know and he'd have his head about him to lead the events, but he'd know and even if it was just in his own head, it would spoil everything.

Tomorrow morning he'd emerge from the basement unafraid, tomorrow morning he'd learn about the job, tomorrow morning he'd graduate and his anger at Ronald would be forgotten and the rest of his life would begin. People would come to him to have their volumes appraised and dealers would take him to lunch and he'd plan exhibitions so stunning that their catalogs would win awards.

In these last minutes, he went to his desk to gather supplies. He was lingering now; this should have been done an hour ago, but the hunger was making him brave, or reckless—he dared Ronald to come out of his office at this very last minute and try to stop them. He'd left his backpack under his desk that day—disallowed under the rules of the library should someone be tempted to slip a volume into a nearby bag—but Ronald hadn't noticed. Most of what he needed was already in the basement, snuck down under stacks of books, one trip at a time.

The ritual required that every initiate speak Greek, and he'd told them all, he'd warned them to learn a few words at the very least, but he had no trust that anyone would listen, so he'd also printed a stack of Greek poems, the Homeric *Hymn to Demeter*, with their phonetic reading alongside. They'd fool the gods, if need be. There was a package of white taper candles. They weren't so much for light as for atmosphere. When he imagined the ritual, he imagined it happening by candlelight. There was food to break their fast. So many broken rules in one backpack. His parcel had honey and goat cheese and pita, but he couldn't bring himself to carry the food downstairs. A single crumb could attract a pest, and a single pest would wreak havoc in the massive basement. He left the food in his backpack; they could come eat upstairs when it was time to break the fast.

There was a letter opener on his desk. Pewter and heavy. He used the sharp edge to scratch his mosquito bite. So close to his eye, it was foolish, but the cool metal was heaven against the hot itch. The letter opener had come with the desk; he often opened correspondence from donors and the like, and Ronald told him it had been passed down from student to student for years. It was funny, this job, the type of job where one still needed a letter opener. He considered putting it in his pocket. No real reason, but a blade seemed like the type of thing one should have at the ritual. In the end, though, he couldn't think what he'd do with it.

The last ingredient for the ritual was the most difficult. Participants are to learn a secret, found in a physical object that could only be revealed when they concluded the rite and broke the fast. Where were there more parcels of secrets than in a building full of books? Davey's initial idea was to point to the shelves, but that felt incomplete, so he'd hidden a basket in the stacks with a symbol he hoped they would all find gratifying.

Satisfied he had all he needed, it was time to go to the basement and hide. Still, he lingered a little longer. It was unfathomable that Ronald wasn't coming to say goodbye, wasn't saying anything at all. He stood there in the empty workroom and waited, but Ronald's office door didn't budge.

Davey pocketed the last of his supplies and disappeared to the reference area, where the stairs to the basement were propped open and waiting for him. It was time to begin.

CHAPTER 11

MARY

"Ronald," Mary said, with a timid knock on his office door, and Ronald looked up from what he was reading. His glasses were sitting all the way on the very tip of his nose.

I'll tell him I'm leaving, and he won't suspect anything strange is going on, Mary told herself. She zipped the gold cross back and forth, the chain pulling at the tender skin of her neck. There was some political demonstration happening on the street outside Ronald's window, timed for the increased campus activity for convocation, no doubt. It had been unfolding behind Ronald the entire time he'd been sitting in his office alone, but just now he noticed it and instead of replying to Mary, he turned in his chair to watch the students and their neon placards.

Mary loved Ronald like no teacher she'd ever had. He was her boss, technically, but had always felt like more of a mentor. Three weeks into her employment at the library, she'd filmed Ronald opening a parcel that contained a recently acquired catalog from Roy Lichtenstein's 1963 exhibition at Galerie Ileana Sonnabend in Paris, the artist's first solo exhibition in Europe, and she posted the film on her own feeds. Whether it was the Lichtenstein catalog itself, Ronald's delight at the unboxing, or the gleeful Italian pop song Mary laid behind the video, something made it catch fire. When the

MLA asked Ronald to be the keynote at their annual conference, the video had been viewed 1.4 million times and a GIF of Ronald's delight became an international marker for joy. The whole thing was a happy accident.

Ronald was bemused at first but then he was proud. He told Mary over and over that she knew how to do something he'd never be able to and that her ability to shape images and connect with people was rare and valuable. She'd been hired to work with materials in Cantonese and Mandarin, and so she did, but Ronald always carved out time in her work week for her to practice the art of online communication. For the library's benefit, sure, but also for her own.

She stood in his doorway now, in front of this man who had been so good to her, determined to get through her script and get out of there.

"I'm leaving a couple of minutes early," she said, and Ronald, as if waking from a dream, finally looked at his watch and frowned when he saw how much the evening had escaped him.

"There are no readers," Mary said. "So Soraya's already gone."

It was unusual, the early departure. If Ronald was going to latch on to anything, it would be to this. They were paid until eight, he had every right to protest. Even if it was only five minutes, even if it was the night before graduation.

"Okay."

"Davey left at the same time, just now," Mary said.

"He won't ask any questions," Davey had assured her when he ran through the plan. "It'll be a one-way conversation."

"I see," Ronald said.

"I'm going to leave now, too. Everything is all settled up for the day."

"Okay."

"Do you need anything else from me?"

Zip, zip, zip, the cross against the chain, the chain against her throat.

"I suppose I don't," Ronald said. He looked again at the student protesters outside his window. "No reason for you to linger."

"Are you staying late tonight?"

"Not at all. The ITS shutdown. Can you read the signs?" He was talking about the protesters, and Mary squinted to try and see, but they were too far and the glare was too strong and she didn't want to talk about protesters; she wanted to get out of his office.

"So you're all set to lock up whenever you're ready," she said when Ronald had turned back around to face her. This was the important part, that Ronald not ask her to lock the cage in the basement. If she was asked to lock the door, then she'd be stuck on the outside.

"Mostly I wanted to come in and say thank you. Maybe I should have sent you a card, but it's been a wonderful experience. Working here." Mary laughed, though nothing was funny.

"I should be thanking you."

"There's nothing that special—"

"Online videos." Now he was the one who laughed. "Who would have guessed?"

"I'll see you at the ceremony then?" Mary said, taking a small step back, feeling the space to exit.

"The ceremony?" Ronald said.

"Graduation," Mary said, and for a moment, there was a flicker in his face. Did he know? He couldn't possibly.

"Of course." Just like that the flicker was gone. "I'll see you tomorrow," he said.

He stretched his arms over his head the way she knew he did when he was preparing to get up after a long time in his chair. Her grandpa did the same thing. It was time for Mary to go.

"Get some rest, Ronald. Tomorrow will be a long day."

When she had stepped backward all the way to the door, Ronald finally took off his glasses and, in a moment of feeling fatherly, or sentimental about the passing of time, about the departure of another group of students from his nest, he gave her his full attention.

"Goodbye, Mary," he said. "Good luck with all my heart. I can't wait to see what greatness comes next for you."

CHAPTER 12

FAYE

The elevator that brought Ronald downstairs dinged when it took him away. The bones of that machine were so old that it wasn't impossible to think it would break down right then and strand him there with the others, but no, Ronald locked the security gate and left them to their night.

He's going to find a reason to come look under this table, Faye thought, holding her breath the entire time he was downstairs, and when he left she released the breath in one long whoosh. There was only one room in the lock-up area, a small outcropping where materials for the upcoming exhibitions were taken for preparation, and she'd chosen it as her hiding place before realizing Umu and Ro were already there. They laughed when the elevator dinged with Ronald's departure, and Faye laughed, too. She was a new person.

Not too new a person because she stopped laughing when she heard a noise from somewhere else in the vast basement. She clutched her knees underneath that table, but no, it was one of the others, emerging from hiding, relieved as she had been that they'd made it down. In the exhibition room, Ro popped to his feet first and Faye followed, more slowly. I wonder if he's ever been afraid of anything, she thought.

Faye made eye contact with Umu and smiled at her, just as

WebMD advised. They'd met before, Umu and Faye, though she doubted if Umu remembered. Faye had been sitting at one of the picnic benches behind the administration building when Umu had approached her, big smile, familiar wave, talking about something to do with roller skates. When had that been—at the beginning of this school year or the last? Faye couldn't remember.

She'd walked right up to the table and rested her hand on it like she owned the whole campus, speaking quickly and confidently about the political science course they were both taking to fulfill a requirement and the longtime role of roller skating in Black social movements. "It's demonstrative, and political," Umu had said, tapping her red-tipped fingernails on the table. "But it's also just a roller skating party, you know?"

Umu kept talking while she took Faye's number and sent her a message with the whens and wheres, and then she'd turned and waved and yelled over her shoulder how excited she was to see Faye there, but her attention was already on the next picnic bench, the next set of students she wasn't at all afraid to speak to. Faye couldn't be sure, but she suspected that the message with the details was still unread, buried deep below the two-factor authentication texts that had rolled in during the intervening months. What did someone wear to a roller skating party? How did they behave? Were you supposed to show up right at the start time or filter in later? Did you arrive in your roller skates? And more than that, was this even a real invitation? Was it pity? Was she being mistaken for someone else? Or worst of all, was this some joke that she was to be the butt of? The number of variables had made Faye's head spin. Not for a second had she considered attending.

Without instruction, Faye and Umu and Ro and then the others gathered toward the back of the basement, where the books marked "B" were shelved. Books with no connection to one another besides the fact that they were between 10 and 12 inches tall. Like this strange scattering of people, together down in the library by chance more than anything else. They formed a sort of armor on the shelves, the books in the B section. Shelved precisely so there wasn't any shelf space wasted, every single one of the rolling shelves held thousands of pounds of books.

Mary was one of the first to get to the stacks, and she began turning the crank to move the first of the shelves on its set of rails so that the space between B2 and B3 disappeared.

They needed some floor space for the ritual, and where better than here among the books? Needing to feel useful, Faye took herself to the other end of the bay of shelves to turn that big metal crank. It wasn't easy work. This area of the stacks was at least sixty years old and whatever the weight limit of the shelves was, they were over it. If she turned the crank too quickly, the shelf swayed, threatened to tip, so they were slow and methodical and quiet, but eventually they parted the sea of ten- to twelve-inch books so to the right and to the left, the shelves were collapsed against each other and there was a big open space in the center that would be their arena.

Only Ro didn't offer any help. He didn't work there, and as far as Faye knew, he didn't go to school there, had no attachment to the place. As soon as the first bit of floor space opened up, he sat on the concrete and watched the others work. Soraya was the next one to sit down, on the floor near Ro, but not too near him. He was leaning back on his hands like he was getting some sun, taking up space the way men do, but her posture was more cautious, cross-legged and precise.

"It's not contagious," Ro said. There was at least a yardstick between them. Faye kept at the work of moving the stacks—she liked to feel useful—but she listened as Ro spoke.

"What isn't contagious?" Soraya said.

"I'm Ro," he said. "I brought the drugs you'll be enjoying. And you can sit closer. You can't catch poor from me; my rash is all cleared up."

"Ro's going to get ahead in life based on his charm," Umu said.

She came over and sat on the floor in the space between them. "Soraya, this is my friend Ro; he's a bit of a dick. Ro, this is Soraya; she's Kip's girlfriend."

"But not a human being in her own right?" Ro said.

"See?" Umu said to Soraya. "Charming."

Faye had been reading the story on which tonight's ritual was based. In it, Demeter causes a plague of sterility that would have starved the whole world until she got her way. Only once she was satisfied did she make the world heavy with fruit and leaves and flowers.

Demeter, Faye would have bet, would have sat on the floor and made someone move those rolling shelves for her.

"What is this backpack?" Davey said, holding a green canvas thing by the strap. To Faye's eye, he was delighting in a sense of authority, like he'd been waiting all day to begin giving directions.

Kip had been leaning against the nearest stack. There was no risk of moving it or toppling it since it was pushed back as far as it would go. Faye didn't know him well, but even to her, he seemed quiet during the setup. Only now, he made himself heard.

"Poppies," he said.

Umu and Ro and Soraya and Faye and Mary and Davey stopped what they were doing, stopped their side conversations, to look at him. There was a peculiar nature to his voice. Like the gods were already speaking through him. A blankness to his eyes, too, as he snatched the backpack from Davey, his movements graceless, and lifted the flap to reveal not a poppy, but an ear of corn.

"For the goddess," he said.

Complaining that someone else had brought supplies, that someone else was trying to help, that wasn't the move, that wasn't the way to court influence over the others. But Davey had a more basic argument.

"When did you bring that backpack down here?"

Those vacant eyes, that leathery voice. If there was a god speaking through Kip, it made a quick exit and he was just Kip again.

"When I came in to start working this morning. Before I went to the reading room."

"Did Soraya let you down?"

Soraya and her crossed legs and perfect posture said nothing. She hadn't let him down. Readers weren't allowed backpacks in the library, and even if he spent a lot of time in the place, Kip was just a reader. It was her last day, and she was about to do drugs and hang out in the library all night, but on the clock, Soraya respected rules.

"My family pays to repair the elevator I rode to come down here this morning," Kip said. He let his backpack fall to the floor but the ear of corn, he held on to. "I think it's safe to say I'm not going to walk out with a backpack full of books." Then he took the ear of corn and tossed it into the center of their makeshift arena, where it landed very nearly at Soraya's feet.

Seeing art where the others saw conflict, Mary pulled out her phone to take a picture of the ear of corn on the cement floor.

"No pictures!" Davey yelled. A new rule that allowed him to take back control of the room.

"Listen," Mary said, looking at the way the light fell across the ear of corn in her photo and adjusting the saturation. "I'm not about to post stuff through the library's official feeds, but a few artsy shots on my finsta? That shit builds mystery."

Davey held out his hand for her phone.

"In the ancient world, anyone who revealed the secrets of the ritual would be killed by the other participants," Davey said. "I'm not even suggesting murder. I'm suggesting you hand over your fucking phones."

"Do you know how to have an experience and not post about it, Mary?" Kip said, handing Davey his phone.

Davey didn't like the idea of Kip taking his side. He reached over to where Kip had let his bag fall and tossed his own phone, and Kip's, into it.

"Not just Mary. I need everyone's," Davey said. "They'll all be kept together so we have the same rules for everyone, and they're in the bag, so no one is going to scroll through your dick pics."

Faye had a six-year-old iPhone that used a plastic case to hold together its cracked screen. She put it in the bag gently to keep it in one piece.

"I don't even know any of you," Ro said. He had his phone in his hand. The background image was of a giant white dog of indeterminate breed, all shaggy hair and goofy smiles. "I don't exactly think we have mutuals."

"You're here, you have the same rules as everyone else. I promise it'll be worth it." Davey plucked the phone from Ro's hand and dropped it into the bag.

"Does anyone have a second device?" Kip said, once they had all dropped their phones. He was looking at Mary, and Faye couldn't help but think, too, that Mary had a backup somewhere. "A standalone camera?" Kip said. "A BlackBerry you only use for messaging?"

"A BlackBerry?" Mary said. Ro laughed openly. Umu, who had once relied on Kip for grading, was a bit more subtle. Davey fumed that Kip was giving instructions at all. But Mary cackled louder than any of them. The hunger was making her punchy. "Sit down, Dad. I'm pretty sure no one snuck in a BlackBerry."

Davey threw Kip's backpack, now full of phones, off to the side. "Enough. We have everything."

"Some of us have better things to think about than which phone camera makes our eyes look the least slanted," Kip said, under his breath, slurred even, but still audible.

The laughter stopped.

The smirk that lingered on Mary's face after the BlackBerry joke stayed put. She didn't flinch, didn't so much as blush, didn't give any indication of Kip having landed a blow. Faye figured it had taken a lot of practice, this impermeability.

Faye was from the prairies, farm country, where demographics dictated that racism was more in theory than in practice. As a consequence, it was the most hateful thing she'd ever heard one person say to another. What happened now, after Mary's failure to flinch, Faye thought. A takedown? A physical confrontation? But when the laughter stopped, there was nothing that came after. Finally it was Ro, Ro who didn't know them at all, who got to his feet.

"He's with you, right?" he said to Soraya, as if Kip and his hatefulness were somehow her responsibility. "It's going to be a long night if you can't keep your man in check."

"All right, all right," Davey said, once Ro's threat had cleared the air and allowed them to look at one another again. "Ronald's locked up, so we know he won't be back down tonight, but he's still in the building. We'll hear a beep once he sets the alarm. But we can't start, or we shouldn't, until he's all the way out of here."

Seven faces turned upward. To the concrete ceiling above them, through it another layer of basement, another set of stacks, then another concrete ceiling, and only then the fine Persian rug that warmed the oak floor in Ronald's office. Ronald, who was at work later than he'd said he'd be.

"If there's an alarm, won't it go off the minute he sets it?" Ro said.

Those of them who knew the library best—Davey, Mary, Soraya—shook their heads in unison, but even Faye could have guessed the answer.

"Entry and exit alarms only," Soraya said, testing her voice after remaining silent about Kip's ugliness. "The space is way too big for motion detectors."

Faye was the only one still looking up at the ceiling.

"What about lights?" she said. "Won't he turn off the lights?" She hadn't been in the dark, the real dark, since leaving home. The campus was always lit up with security lights.

"If he was going to, he'd have done that when he was down here, locking up," Davey said. "There's no switch upstairs."

All around her were relieved faces. Faye wouldn't have been bothered either way. She rather missed the dark.

"We should dose now," Ro said. "It takes a while before it all happens." He was wearing dove-gray sweats. Faye hadn't noticed them before. Kip and Davey were both wearing chinos, they'd never have worn sweats to the library, but Faye thought they were beautiful. Not shapeless at all, they grew tighter around Ro's calves and ankles and the fabric looked soft enough to wrap a baby in. Faye didn't know anything about clothing, but she suspected that Ro thought quite a bit about how he presented himself.

"Who has the party favors?" Ro looked at Umu, who pointed at Davey.

Relishing the theatrical, Davey went to the shelf. He ran his finger across the books, one item at a time, before stopping at a slim, beige volume. He pulled it out with the tip of one finger and then held it aloft for the approval of the others. A collection of poetry, of course. A limited edition run of *The Hill of Dionysus* from the private press of Roy A. Squires. A bit on the nose. He handed the volume to Ro, who let it fall open and reveal seven tiny baggies, each containing a small white square with a little picture printed on it. Their guide to the underworld, wrapped in miniature Ziploc.

"Won't we be licking each other's eyeballs in five minutes if we take those now?" Kip said. "We're here for a ritual, not a bacchanal."

Ro handed each of them a baggie, starting with Davey. One for Umu, one for Mary, one for Faye, one for Soraya.

"Oh sorry, mate," Kip said. "Bacchanal means an occasion of wild, drunken revelry."

"Thanks, *mate*," Ro said. He hung a baggie between his thumb and forefinger in front of Kip's face. "It'll be thirty minutes, maybe an hour, before you feel anything at all. So if you want to stay on earth once the rest of us go airborne, by all means, wait."

Kip snatched the baggie, opened it up, put the tiny paper square on his tongue, and swallowed.

"You're not supposed to swallow it, asshole," Mary said. She grabbed the backpack of phones from where Davey had dumped them. "I'm going to go put these by the door so we don't lose track of them. We can grab them on the way out tomorrow." She flapped her little baggie in the air and disappeared around the corner with the backpack.

"Under your tongue and leave it there," Ro said. "You won't even feel it and it'll dissolve nice and slow."

"So, what the fuck, am I not going to feel anything at all?" Kip said.

"So, what the fuck, next time wait for instructions if you don't know what you're doing," Ro said. "You'll feel something, it'll just take longer."

Faye fiddled with the plastic between her thumb and forefinger. The tab was tiny. It had a blue star printed on it. Such a little thing, such a big decision.

Now, for Ro, taking a tab of acid in front of a group of strangers may well have been a regular Thursday evening activity, and in her heart she was sure that he gave it scarcely more thought than he would have given an invitation to join a pickup basketball game. Though if Faye was being honest with herself, wouldn't she be just as terrified of subjecting herself to the ridicule of sport?

She turned to her grounding of science, data always having been more palatable to her than intuition, but even that didn't help. The tab would loosen her inhibitions, certainly, but would it remove them altogether? What would she do? What would she say? Like with the roller skating all those months earlier, there were too many unknown variables. In a study she'd read in the journal *Psychological Medicine*, almost as many study participants had experienced anxiety after taking LSD as had experienced a blissful state.

She didn't even know any of these people. If she refused the drug, she'd look stupid; she knew that. But if she took it, she could look worse than stupid. She could experience a prolonged psychosis. She could be the butt of their jokes for years after. They're all going to talk about you, she thought. They're going to wish you hadn't come at all. Soraya put her tab under her tongue. Umu and Ro *cheers*ed with theirs like they were glasses of champagne. Optimism was significantly increased in study participants for the two weeks after taking the dose. That sounded nice. That feeling of optimism wasn't felt by all the study participants, though, and the researchers hadn't been able to find any sort of correlation with other behavioral traits that might predict who would have a positive outcome and who wouldn't. There were too many unknown variables.

"I'm good," said Faye. She held the baggie back out to Ro. "High on life, you know."

Ro took the baggie from her and slipped it into his pocket. No one mocked Faye. No one said anything at all. That was almost worse. She knew they were saving it all to say behind her back.

"I don't feel anything yet," Kip said.

"We know," Soraya said. She wasn't inclined to be patient with him given how he'd just treated Mary. She stayed on the floor near Umu, making it clear she wasn't with him. "The kid just told you it'll take a while to kick in." She laid herself flat on her back on the cold concrete, looking at the ceiling like it was a sky full of stars. "What's the rush anyway? We haven't heard the alarm; Ronald's still here."

"You going to be able to get it up for my girlfriend after your dose?" Kip turned his attention to Davey. He snickered, actually snickered, at his own question. "It's just a shame we couldn't get a virgin. Or is that why she's here?" He pointed at Faye.

Faye, who already wanted to melt and turn invisible, felt her blush creep from her neck onto her cheeks with such ferocity, she was sure she was glowing.

"No," Kip continued. "It was always about Soraya, wasn't it? But you've gotta please the girl if you're going to please the gods, so make sure you can perform, Davey. Or you're going to need me, or god forbid, the kid, to step in."

Ro hadn't sat back down after handing out the drugs. He didn't know the others well enough to be offended for them, so until now, Kip's display had been mildly irritating but mostly funny.

"Problem though." Kip had come over to put his arm around Ro. "Look at the kid's pants. Do these look like the pants of someone who can please a woman? I'd bet a buffalo nickel that if Ro here is getting it up for anyone, it's for me or you." He patted Ro on the chest and then stepped away before Ro could push him. "You heard 'Greek' and you came running, huh, kid?"

Kip slurred and swayed like he was already intoxicated. Faye didn't know well enough to know if that could be true, but she'd met men before who used a drink or two to cover for a meanness that was always in their blood.

"Maybe you should go for a walk?" Umu said. Umu, the only one who'd been spared his wrath so far, put her neck on the block.

"A walk?" Kip said. "Sure. I'll go for a walk. I'm going to go find a bucket to take a piss in."

He turned and left them. He even began to whistle as he walked away, as though to prove he didn't care what they thought of him at all.

In the bookstack behind her, Faye caught sight of a couple of names she recognized. Copernicus. Swift. The ornate quality of the books—their gilt spines and leather bindings—was something Faye could never wrap her head around. So much decoration and all she'd ever cared about were the contents. Copernicus's model of the universe was no less valuable without marbled end papers.

She kept her eye on the books until she was sure Kip was good and gone. Perhaps the basement had a secret passageway that opened after hours and he'd stumble into it and disappear. In her eyes, a party with the six of them was no worse than a party with seven. Maybe even better.

Umu had wrapped her arms around Ro, the comfort of an old friendship, and now neither of them looked fussed at all. Soraya was still on the floor, but Soraya walked out hand in hand with Kip every day, even when his behavior was barbaric. Davey was busy pulling supplies out from behind books where he'd hidden them throughout the week, and Mary—Mary who should be furious!—was braiding a section of her own hair.

Kip is disgusting, she thought. Every one of Faye's muscles was tense. She couldn't believe how much she hated him all of a sudden. How much she hated him and how certain she was that he didn't deserve to be down in that basement with the rest of them.

CHAPTER 13

STILL FAYE

I

No one can pinpoint the exact moment sobriety leaves their body. Faye learned that in a first-year chemistry elective, when the professor began to expound on blood alcohol level and she'd been interested enough to look up a couple of papers after the class. There are moments before and after sobriety when the subject is aware of their state, but the precise crossing of the line remains one of life's mysteries. Maybe Ro, who had been back and forth more times than most of them, could come closest to finding the border, but the others were kept guessing as the minutes ticked by. It was nine o'clock.

Soraya hadn't left the floor. Faye didn't blame her. The concrete was cool, nice. There were dust bunnies—not in Soraya's direct vicinity, tangled around the base of the rolling shelves—but Soraya didn't look like she minded them. Once or twice, in the early minutes of their wait for Kip to return, of their wait for something to happen, she called out that she could see the dust bunnies moving, and the others laughed because, yes, the dust bunnies had moved, but only because something nearby disturbed them. She didn't say as much, but Faye suspected that Soraya would prefer to be very high by the

time Kip returned and that she hoped he'd be the same. Everything
is more forgivable when you can't see straight.

Faye hadn't considered the need for a bathroom until Kip left,
and now it was all she could think about. She didn't have to go—
she hadn't eaten anything in twenty-four hours—but not having
access to a bathroom had always accelerated her bladder. It was like
the game where you're not supposed to think about elephants. She
supposed that, once Ronald left, they could go upstairs and use the
regular staff bathroom, but then again, she had no idea whether
the alarms were on the entrances and exits to the outside world or
whether the interior doors were alarmed, too. Davey would know,
Soraya would know, Mary would know, but Faye could think of little
that was more horrifying than having to ask someone for details
about the bathroom.

She imagined Kip, detestable Kip, wandering around the stacks
looking for somewhere to relieve himself. "What if he shat his
pants?" She contemplated saying that aloud, wondered if it would get
a laugh, but decided it was too crass. But isn't that how friendships
are made? Over lewd jokes and hatred of a shared villain?

Trying not to think about the bathroom—what if she suddenly
found she was menstruating, what if she broke her fast and then
immediately felt sick—she focused on the others. It was Umu who
she saw the change in first. She began to open and close her mouth,
slowly. First she parted her lips and then her teeth and then allowed
her tongue to separate from her palate making a noise that was either
very rude or very pleasing, depending on one's culture. And she did
it over and over again.

The corn, tender yellow kernels carried safely in its leaves, was
still on the floor by Soraya's feet, and as the minutes stretched Faye
found herself fixated on it, and on the idea that once they started she
could break her fast, once the ritual had begun she wouldn't need to
purify herself with hunger anymore and she could just eat. She was
scared of eating the corn, scared it would make her ill, scared it would

make her need a bathroom (don't think about elephants!), but she wanted to devour it all the same.

Not long after Umu began making her noise, Soraya finally sat up. She said nothing, looked at no one, and moved so slowly it was hard to notice her at all, but in the space of what felt like fifteen minutes, she went from flat on her back to sitting with her arms wrapped around her knees.

"The long day wanes: the slow moon climbs: the deep moans round with many voices. Come, my friends, 'tis not too late to seek a newer world," Soraya whispered, breaking up the rhythm of Umu's mouth sounds. Then she climbed to her feet so quickly it startled all of them, even Faye, who had no cause to be startled. Soraya sprang over to the bookshelf and pulled a volume down and now Faye could see it: a slim volume bound in red leather with POEMS stamped on its spine. Soraya wasn't making a declaration. She was reciting a line that Faye knew too little to recognize.

It was a quarter past nine. Still an hour before the drugs would peak, but long past time to get started, and Faye, for whom time wasn't bent or stretched, for whom time was just time, was impatient for the sound of Ronald departing or Kip returning. Whatever tonight would be, she wanted it to begin.

"So what's the bet?" Davey said, getting shoulder to shoulder with Soraya by the bookshelf. "Is he off somewhere crafting an apology?"

Soraya slid the book and its unknown poems back with the others. Her dark hair had fallen right back into its neat bob when she got up off the floor. By some miracle her clothes were free from dust and she looked as clean and in control as she'd ever been, and yet to Faye, she was changed. It could have been the sight of her, an exemplary student, the shining employee, taking the drugs, but no. Fairly or not, to Faye she was stained by proximity, by association, because of Kip's repulsive rhetoric.

One of the items Davey had retrieved from his basement hiding place was a small wicker basket with a fitted lid, like something a teenaged girl might keep her private keepsakes in under her bed. When he'd first invited Faye to participate in this party, this ritual, whatever this was, he'd described very little, but the next time he'd spoken to her, when he told her she'd have to fast, there were more details. She wanted to get at the "why." It must have been so obvious to him that he spent the whole time talking about the "how"—that there would be a sequence of "things done," then "things shown," and then "things said" until finally they conjured Persephone and that was all well and good, but *why*? She looked for the same answer in the book about the rites, and the closest she got was that they would emerge unafraid of the horror of death. Faye was afraid of lots of things, but death wasn't something she often thought about.

"So you figure he's off drawing us all a card?" Davey said again, gesturing to the space beyond the makeshift arena where, somewhere, Kip was all alone.

"It's easier for us than it is for him," Soraya said at last. She had the tip of her finger extended to the shelf and was running it up the spine of one book and down the other, delighting when she hit a bump or indentation. "We graduate tomorrow. Stressful, sure, but then the rebirth happens right after. By, what, September at the latest, we'll know who we're going to be. Some of us will know by tomorrow. Maybe we'll all emerge from here so confident in our blessed postgraduation life that we'll all know by tomorrow. But Kip isn't dying yet."

Faye wouldn't have said this aloud, but wasn't she in the same camp as Kip? Graduating but coming right back to graduate school. Staying in the same apartment, working in the same lab, nowhere nearer to real life than she'd been last week or last year.

Soraya lifted her finger from the books and finally looked at Davey.

"He isn't graduating, I mean. It's harder. That sort of life in limbo."

The cold crept up Faye's back as she listened to Soraya and Davey talk about Kip. Again, she wished she hadn't come. Soraya's voice was so lyrical, so even, like she was reciting a poem in iambic pentameter.

Obviously no one dies in the ritual, Faye thought. Soraya had resumed her work tracing book spines, and Davey leaned himself against the stack. Not soon, but eventually, he'd be in the path of Soraya's finger and she'd have to decide whether to abandon her project or whether she should run her hand up and down his waiting body.

At the far side of the basement, they all heard a sound, probably coming from near the exit. The alarm wasn't on yet. Ronald hadn't left, so despite the layers and layers of concrete, they wouldn't call out and tell Kip he was being ridiculous.

Things done, things shown, things said. Didn't these rituals always have a sacrifice as one of their components? She'd half expected Davey to pull a cage with a mouse out from behind a volume of Jane Austen. Faye wasn't squeamish about the idea of cutting an animal open; she'd taken biology courses, she'd seen her share of tiny pink lungs drawing their last breath, though she might feel different if the purpose of the death wasn't science. It was the lack of a mouse that was more worrying. If it wasn't an animal who would die, then who would it be?

"Maybe he fainted from hunger," Faye said. From his perch against the shelf, Davey looked at her like he was just noticing for the first time she was there, she who he had invited himself and even spoken to, more than once, about what she should expect. "Maybe that was the noise," she said. "The sound of Kip hitting the ground."

Now everyone was looking at her, but no one was jumping up to see if she was right. If Kip was crumpled somewhere, his large body overwhelmed by its emptiness. It wasn't a mystery worth investigating for this group.

"Unlikely," Soraya said, freeing Faye from the burden of having been the last one to speak. If there was supposed to be a follow-up to her single word of denial, Soraya forgot it. She went right back to tracing the spines of those 10- to 12-inch books on the shelf.

They'd been waiting for it for over an hour, but every one of them was surprised when it came. The beep signaling that the alarm had been set.

In the seconds after the noise, no one moved: Soraya's finger on a leather-bound volume, Davey against the bookshelf, the others spread out across the ground. Davey had promised them that there were no motion detectors. Soraya, Mary, and Faye had never seen motion detectors, and yet they dared not move.

Ro broke the spell. He reached forward with his right hand, flexed the fingers, which by then must have been dancing before his eyes. And nothing happened.

"I told you guys there were no motion detectors," Davey said. "I don't know what you're so freaked out about."

No motion detectors, no Ronald; the strings that had been holding them in place, the strings they hadn't even seen, were broken. They moved their limbs, they spun around, they laughed as loud as they wanted. They were alone, really alone. The library was theirs to do with as they pleased.

"Death is the end of life; ah why, should life all labor be? Death is the end of life; ah why, should life all labor be?" Mary began to bellow at the top of her lungs. Umu laughed and joined in. "Death is the end of life; ah why, should life all labor be? Death is the end of life; ah why, should life all labor be?" They put their faces almost right against one another, these girls who had just met, and turned the chant into a kind of song.

"You guys are cheesy as shit," Ro said, but it was infectious. His shoulders had started bouncing to it.

"Is this part of the Greek ritual?" Faye asked. Davey wasn't joining in, but maybe that was the point: that they should start and he would join in later.

"This is a Tennyson poem," he said.

Again, her face got hot. They were people who went to parties, people who could add a beat to any collection of words to make it something you could dance to, and people who walked around with the full text of Tennyson poems in their heads.

"I knew that," Faye said.

"They're being idiots," Davey said. He wasn't bouncing his shoulders to the rhythm of Umu and Mary's chant at all. "But let them. We'll get serious when Kip gets back."

Faye almost smiled. She didn't fit in with Umu and Mary, but at least she wasn't the only one immune to the charms of Tennyson. She almost made a joke about it—she was just putting the words in the right order, but she never got them out because everything around her went black.

II

By instinct, Faye put her hands to her face first; the terrifying prospect of being without her glasses was always the first fear that came to mind. She'd worn them since childhood, and since she'd become dependent on them for vision, there was always a violent flinch when something came too near her face. She wasn't afraid of being hurt. She was afraid of the disorienting blur. Tonight, the glasses were where they should be, but still, she couldn't see. Somewhere very near her, she could feel the movement of another person—Mary, she realized quickly it was Mary, not because the energy of this other person was familiar but because she began to scream.

We're going to die down here, Faye thought, not moving, not breathing, certain that if she didn't move the air near her at all she could disappear and change her past decision to have come here in the first place. It must have been a full minute that she stood that way, holding her breath while Mary screamed, while the rest scrambled, while she waited for some unseen arm to come and cut her throat until slowly the realization about what was happening dawned on her and she knew there was no reason to be afraid. She let her breath out and reached her hands out to find Mary, to find some way to stop that terrible screaming.

"He said he thought of everything, but no one thinks of everything," she said under her breath, though she counted herself as brave for saying it aloud at all. The depth of the darkness was absolute. It was perfect. They were so deep under the earth that there was no chance of a sliver of sunlight creeping in, and they'd rolled so many bookshelves against each other to create their arena that they'd barricaded themselves from even the light of an exit sign. Surely there must be an exit sign, Faye thought, but there was only black.

"Didn't he say the lights would stay on?"

It was Ro's voice somewhere in the darkness. The sound of it was one of the most soothing Faye had ever heard—a person, there was a person, one who wasn't screaming, one who wasn't out of their mind, one who had come to the same realization she had.

Maybe it was because it was a male voice, maybe because it was because Ro had spoken at his full volume, but as soon as he said it, Mary stopped screaming.

"The lights are just Ronald leaving?" Mary said. "I can't see my nose because Ronald turned off the lights?"

"What the fuck happened to 'there's not even a switch?'" Ro said.

Faye listened for Davey's reply, but there was none. In the dark, in the screaming, in the confusion, she had lost him in space. He'd been leaning against the bookshelves, she knew that. Was he behind her now? Or could she reach her hands forward and touch him?

Davey might have stayed silent forever, might have let them grope in the dark for him forever, but he wasn't offered that comfort, wasn't allowed to stay hidden. There was a flick and a click and a flame and then Ro's face came into sight and the weak light given off by his lighter was enough to illuminate them all.

"It's not as though I've spent a lot of nights down here," Davey said. He was still leaning against the bookshelf, which was indeed still behind Faye, and if she thought he'd apologize for his error, she found she was wrong. "I've never seen a switch. Turns out there is one. The dark's not the end of the world. I'm pretty sure we'll live."

There was a rustle from over by the bookshelf. There wasn't enough light to see what he was doing, but in a moment there was another flick, another click, another flame. Davey had had a lighter with him all this time.

They should be furious, Faye thought. He'd misled them and he wasn't even sorry. He could have been wrong about the alarm, too, he could have had the police down here and the rest of them

hauled away and he wasn't even sorry. They should be furious, but
they weren't because the light from that second flame, the weak light
that doubled what had been available to them the moment before,
was a great relief.

Now Davey was illuminated in a way the rest of them weren't.
It was only Ro they could see as well, though Ro was in the same
place he'd been before the lights went off. Ro wasn't moving, whereas
Davey had dropped to a crouch on the floor and was sweeping his
hands, was hunting for something with only the meager flame from
a ninety-nine-cent lighter to guide him.

Faye discovered she was holding her breath again, watching this
quest or whatever it was. The lighter had to be growing hotter and
hotter against Davey's fingers, and every few seconds he had to flick
it again to relight it. And soon, sooner than they needed, certainly
sooner than the morning, the gas in that lighter, in that lighter and
in Ro's lighter, would go out and they'd be cast into darkness again.

"Are you looking for some paper to burn?" she asked. They were
surrounded by the stuff. Just one volume under that flame would give
them a thousand times as much light as they had right now.

"No," he said, so loud the sound echoed off the concrete ceiling.
She went red again, flushed with the stupidity of her suggestion. Of
course Davey wasn't looking for a book to burn, certainly not one of
these books that were only down in this collection because of how
precious they were. "'Tis not too late to seek a newer world." Was
that the line Soraya had said before? She was down here with these
people and it hadn't begun as she had hoped. She'd been afraid, she'd
felt herself in danger, but it didn't have to be that way. It wasn't too
late for Faye to make herself the person she wanted to become.

"Got them!" Davey said, and by that weak, flickering light he
showed them the big box of taper candles he'd found. Of course
a ritual would have candles, of course they weren't going to burn a
book.

Davey let his lighter go dark, and he tore open the plastic on the box of candles. Ro, finally motivated to move, came over to help, and between the two of them, they lit six candles in a blink, and even a couple of extras that they placed on the floor, far from the shelves where they might do damage, and then as quickly as they'd fallen into it, they weren't in the dark anymore.

III

"Something done, something seen, something told," Umu said, running her fingers back and forth through the flame of her candle. "That's how it's supposed to go, isn't it?"

She was speaking to all of them and none of them at once. Her trip, too, had started, but she was a more experienced traveler than Soraya. She wasn't afraid, she wasn't in awe, but she didn't want to waste the feeling.

"There's still Kip," Davey said. "Or there isn't Kip. Wherever he's hiding he's probably trapped in the dark now. Serves him right, but it all works better with seven of us." He was speaking slowly, fighting against what the chemicals were doing to him, working to stay in control of himself and the group.

"Forget him," Soraya said. "I want to start."

"I was going to say the same thing," Davey said. "Forget him. It works better with seven, but forget him."

"There's light now," Umu said. "There's light and there'll be noise and it'll lead him back to us. We've left him a trail of bread crumbs."

It was ten o'clock. The library had only been closed a moment, but somehow it had been closed two hours and Faye, like Umu and Soraya, was eager for them to start. All that had happened so far was that she'd felt embarrassed and then afraid of the dark and there wasn't much in those feelings, embarrassed and afraid, that she didn't feel regularly anyway. She wanted to start so she could feel something different.

"The ear of corn is a symbol of Demeter." Davey picked it up from the ground, and Faye salivated when he touched it. "There are other symbols, mysteries, things that are hidden, but the corn is a good way to invoke her."

"I thought you were mad Kip brought the produce," Ro said. "It's giving a bit of inconsistency, my dude."

"So we're doing it?" Mary said, like she hadn't just heard them speaking, like she hadn't just heard them decide to go ahead without Kip. There was something about Mary's energy that was different from the others, at least in Faye's viewing. A sharpness in her movements, but then Mary always did a thousand things at once, spoke a mile a minute in two, four, six languages, recorded her videos for social media that hundreds, thousands of people fawned over, dazzled her professors, dazzled library donors. Perhaps even LSD couldn't quiet all that energy.

"What's in the basket?" Ro said. "Is that where you keep the bodies?"

"So we're just going to go ahead without Kip after all that?" Mary said. No one was listening to her. They were all excited now at the prospect of beginning. "Won't he be mad? If it were me and I had fasted and done all that and then you started without me, it might hurt my feelings. Do you think we'll hurt his feelings?"

"Don't touch the basket!" Davey said, rushing over to it so that Ro couldn't open it.

"We can't see the secrets yet," Soraya said. She had wandered over from the bookshelf and sat herself on the floor. Her candle had most of her attention, but she explained to Ro what Davey wouldn't. "It's the wrong order. The secrets come second."

"It's a basket full of secrets?" Ro said.

"So like, is Kip just gone? Should we go tell him we're starting?" Mary said.

"He'll hear us," Umu said. She led Mary by the shoulder and they sat on the floor, too, in the arena next to Soraya. "He'll hear us and he'll come."

"Why did you even come if you weren't going to take it seriously?" Davey said to Ro.

"I'm just asking questions, my dude." He motioned to Davey to put the basket back on the ground, and then Ro took a seat on the floor, too, a show of good faith that he was prepared to be serious, that he was as eager to be free from fear as the rest of them. It was just Davey and Faye who were standing now.

"The Eleusinian Mysteries were a secret aspect of Greek life," Davey said.

"Sort of like the orgies," Ro said. "And all the sodomy."

"We know there was ritual sacrifice, but we don't know what form it took," Davey continued.

"When we cut you open down here, no one will be able to hear you scream," Umu said to Ro. He threw a hand in front of his face, miming fear, and then they both descended into giggles. It was infectious. Even Faye laughed.

"We know there was a ritual washing after the sacrifice," Davey said.

"What about the ritual ordering of six pizzas to break the fast?" Mary said. "At what point in the festivities did the Greeks do that?"

"Hear, hear," Faye said. She was hungrier than she was shy. Was no one else hungry?

"What's amazing is that a huge number of people partook in this ritual," Davey said. "Women, slaves, everyone was allowed, but so little is known about how it played out. A perfect secret."

"Women *and* slaves," Ro said. He mimed a shocked gesture. "*And* slaves," he mouthed to Umu.

Without drawing too much attention to herself, Faye took a seat on the floor next to Soraya, so now Davey alone had the floor.

"They drank kykeon," Davey said. He held his candle below his chin like the best storyteller around a campfire knows to do with their flashlight. He'd been scratching at his eye all night and his eyelid had begun to swell. The flicker from the candle made it look like it was pulsating. "It wasn't until recently that historians understood kykeon had psychoactive properties. It unlocked the whole thing for researchers."

"Bring on the kykeon!" Umu said, thrusting her candle up in the air. The movement of doing so reminded her how high she was. She brought her arm down slowly, fascinated by the bones in her hand.

"I think the kykeon's already here," Mary said.

"Chanting's an important part of the ritual," Davey said. "So we know it must have occurred, but there's no way to know what they recited and when. It might have changed from year to year or there might have been a sacred text that was whispered between participants. Maybe it'll reveal itself to us before we leave here tomorrow morning."

In a quick motion, Ro was on his feet. Crouched, poised to jump like some sort of hunter.

Or a dancer.

"It has already revealed itself," he said.

He grabbed Umu by the arm and pulled her up, though she needed little goading.

"Death is the end of life, ah why, should life all labor be? Death is the end of life, ah why, should life all labor be?" They chanted in low, deep whispers. The beat hadn't dropped yet. Umu took Soraya's hand, poor stoned Soraya, but she rose without protest. The chanting felt good.

"Death is the end of life, ah why, should life all labor be?" The three of them sang it.

If what came next surprised the group, it surprised Faye more. She didn't wait to be asked, didn't wait to be invited; she got to her feet and even pulled Mary up behind her. Now the five of them were chanting it.

"Death is the end of life, ah why, should life all labor be? Death is the end of life, ah why, should life all labor be?"

She wasn't sure who started the circle. Maybe no one did. Maybe once you're chanting, physical movement happens spontaneously. However it happened, whoever initiated it, they surrounded Davey. They crouched and stomped and held their candles and walked clockwise around the ritual's leader, chanting it over and over and over.

"Death is the end of life, ah why, should life all labor be?"

Maybe they would have stayed that way forever, chanting and laughing until morning, if Davey didn't finally interrupt them.

"Where the hell have you been?" Davey said. It was nearing eleven o'clock. "We thought you settled in with the Cyrillic backlog and fell asleep."

The outline of Kip appeared in the distance by the end of the shelving bay, about as far as the light from their candles would reach.

"I was worried, babe," Soraya said. Her sleek hair was mussed from the movement, stuck sweaty to her head in places. "You should have called out; we would have come to find you."

Kip said nothing.

"We waited for you," Umu said. "We waited for, like, a real long time."

Kip took two steps toward them, but they weren't steps at all. He staggered.

"Are you okay?" Faye asked.

He wasn't okay.

He made a sound. It wasn't speech and it wasn't a scream. It was lower than that. A low, wet gurgle that was more terrifying than any scream could have been. Then he staggered forward two more steps and fell fully into their light.

His face, his button-down shirt, his trousers, were covered in blood. He made the wet noise again.

"Kip!" Soraya yelled when she saw it.

He staggered again, but the effort of it was too much and fresh blood oozed from his mouth. He threw himself at the closest comfort he saw, at Soraya, but she wasn't strong enough to hold him and he collapsed to the ground with a terrifying thud.

IV

Soraya looked down at the front of her, at the short-sleeved green silk shirt with delicate little buttons, at the black pencil skirt she'd tucked it into, even at her oxfords, all covered in Kip's blood. When she screamed, Faye didn't hear it as a scream for Kip. Soraya screamed for herself. For the horror of being soaked in blood. That it was someone else's blood and not her own was somehow worse, or it would have been for Faye. Kip was in a heap at her feet, unmoving, and Soraya didn't care, how could she care when she was covered in blood?

"Please get it off," she said. "Please, please, please get it off."

She was swiping at herself, trying to shake off the blood like it were so many ants crawling on her, but she was succeeding only in making it worse. Smearing it on her stomach when she tried to get it off her shirt, covering her arms in it while trying to clean off her legs. At some point her candle had hit the ground and Ro had moved quickly to stomp on its flame but now he could only stare. The problem wasn't only that she was so high, it was that they all were. If she'd been hallucinating it, someone could have talked her town, assured her it wasn't real. But it was real. Wet and sticky and real and she was soaked in it.

Faye, the only one of them who had full control over herself, would have liked to have helped Soraya, but there was a man in a heap on the floor and no one had moved to do anything about it.

"Someone needs to help him," Faye said.

Ro reached down and picked up Soraya's extinguished candle. "I'll hold this for you."

"Is this part of the ritual?" Mary said. "I don't like it if it is. Some people faint when they see blood. Not me, but some people."

"It's not part of the ritual," Davey said slowly. "Unless Kip planned this. Do you think Kip planned this? Kip, did you plan this? It's not funny, man. None of us are laughing."

"Please get it off me," Soraya said. Umu stepped forward to try and help but there was so much of it and she was so high and the slick red of it looked like it was dancing in the light of the flame from her candle so then she didn't help. She just watched Soraya.

"Someone has to help him," Faye said.

"No one has to do anything; he's pretending," Davey said. "He couldn't stand the idea that this wasn't his thing, so now he's staging whatever this is." He pointed his toe in the direction of the heap like he might kick at Kip. "Get up, asshole."

"I don't think he's pretending," Faye said.

"Whichever of you planned it, do you know that some people faint when they see blood?" Mary asked.

"I don't want to be high anymore," Umu whispered to Ro, though of course they were all so close to each other, Faye couldn't help but hear it.

She was suddenly so cold. Every inch of her skin was covered in goosebumps, the flame of her candle quivering as the hand that held it shook. She was so hungry and so tired and so cold and she had no choice but to do what she did next.

"Can you please hold my candle?" And she handed it to Davey without waiting for his answer.

"He's pretending," Davey said. "The moment you touch him, he's going to yell 'boo.'"

She lowered herself to a crouch. Slowly. If her instincts were right, then there was no rush about it. Davey, out of generosity or curiosity or the creeping realization of what was happening, lowered the candles so Faye could see.

When Kip had fallen, he'd crumpled with this face to the floor. He hadn't hit his head; that was such a particular sound, a head hitting concrete, that Faye would have recognized it. It was the only thing that gave credence to Davey's argument. If Kip was pretending, if this was all some elaborate ruse, he'd have been careful to make sure he didn't hit his head.

She had to take him by the shoulder to turn him. There wasn't blood on the shoulder of his shirt, mercifully. She couldn't see the source of the bleeding at all.

"Help me move him?" she said to Davey, who lost that generosity or curiosity or whatever it had been and took a step backward.

Kip had at least fifty pounds on Faye and she was trying to be gentle, because what if he was hurt, what if he needed help, so it took time and sweat to move him. She pulled at his shoulder and nothing happened, and she had to grasp the fabric of his shirt in her fists and pull with all her might before she finally did it. It took a grunt from Faye, but then Kip was on his back.

"Turn him back," said Ro, burying his face in Umu's neck. "Turn him back so we don't have to see."

There was so much blood. The front of his shirt was soaked in it, his chin was soaked in it, his hands; it was everywhere. Faye held her breath, the way she'd learned to hold her breath when she did anything distasteful—taking horrible cough medicine, listening to her parents fight.

"He might have a pulse," she said, but the only way to know was to touch him again and to stain herself with his blood. It was fresh, he was slick with it, but she reached out and put two fingers on his Adam's apple.

No one breathed. There could only be one answer, but they needed her to say it aloud, to confirm what they could see plainly in front of them.

"He's dead," Faye finally said. "Kip is dead."

V

Faye scrambled to her feet to get away from the body. There was blood on her hands.

"We have to get help," she said.

No one moved.

"We have to get help! He's dead!" she said.

"Please, please, get it off me," Soraya whimpered.

They were still in the middle of their arena; Davey's little wicker basket with the fitted lid had been left abandoned; so, too, had the ear of corn. The books watched them, wise and silent, but they were alone, now just six of them in the basement, and they had to decide what to do.

From the ground floor reference area, there was an elevator that went to the first basement, then the second basement, where they were now. Next to the elevator was a flight of emergency stairs—the stairs most of them had taken to get down. The door to those stairs was always kept locked, unless someone was scheming to hold a ritual in the sleeping library.

The stairs were locked now. It was on the checklist Ronald would have completed before leaving for the night.

The elevator required a tap from a staff pass card to bring a rider down to the basement. A necessary precaution. They couldn't have readers wandering through the reference area and helping themselves in the stacks. It wouldn't have been a problem, they had plenty of pass cards between them, but there was a gate between the group and the elevator.

Faye started toward the exit and was relieved to find the others were following her. Running was the thing to do. Running for help but also running from that horrible body. He was dead, Kip was dead, a person was dead. And Faye had no idea why or how.

Soraya was bringing up the rear. She'd taken off her right shoe for reasons Faye didn't understand, so she was limping along, but she was coming. It was in everyone's best interest to do so. Faye didn't want to be alone, and no one wanted to be left with the body.

"We'll get someone," Davey said from behind Faye, like it was his idea. "Campus security. Campus security will know what to do."

Faye would have loved to run, but she had only the light from the candle to guide her, and if she even walked too quickly, the flame wobbled and shrank. You're brave enough for this, she thought, and then she turned and saw the faces of the others, her own terror reflected in them, and she didn't feel brave at all.

The gate was really more of a fence. Someone in the decades since the library had opened had campaigned for the fence to be installed, likely after some library or another nearby reported the theft of a rare book. There was a lot of construction in the basement that was amateurish—those wobbly rolling shelves squeezed in at strange angles, the haphazard stacks of packing skids—but the security gate was a professional job. Two-inch metal squares, poles that stood so steady they must have been sunk three feet into the concrete floor. In some places it reached the ceiling, in others it left room for plumbing or wiring, but everywhere it stood guard against the possibility of theft. It surrounded the bookstacks all the way through the basement, and it separated the six from the elevator.

Like someone had pulled an emergency brake, the six of them stopped when they got to the exit gate. Umu and Ro gripped each other, but they stood closest to Faye, quivering with anticipation at the idea of being sprung free. Mary and Soraya walked together. Not arm in arm, Mary wouldn't have risked touching Soraya, but supporting each other anyway. Davey, who knew the library better than any of them, would have come to the realization first. He slowed down before the rest of them did. He was the last to arrive at the gate.

"Open it, open it," Ro said, when Faye paused at the gate. She reached forward, pulled at it, but she knew right away it was no use.

She didn't have to say it to Ro; he understood immediately.

"No, no," he said. He gave his candle to Umu and then grabbed the door himself. He yanked at it, pushed at it, swore at it, and it barely trembled.

"Where the fuck is the key?" he screamed at Davey, when the last of their party finally came to the gate.

"It wouldn't be very secure if we kept the key down here, would it?"

Faye was having trouble taking a full breath. Kip was dead. A man was dead. She'd been in and out of this gate a million times. During the day it was swung all the way open so there was just a doorway through the grate; you scarcely thought about it as a gate at all. It was the first thing the opening librarian did when they arrived and the last thing the closing librarian did when they left was to secure the gate. She'd never seen it closed, so she'd never, for a second, considered the fact that it didn't open from the inside.

"This is a fire hazard!" Ro said. He had his fingers laced through the grating and was yanking it with all his might.

"There aren't supposed to be people down here," Davey said. "It's not like the books could walk themselves out in case of fire."

Mary left Soraya, shivering and scratching at her skin, and came to the gate with Faye and Ro. She gave a half-hearted tug. There wasn't even anywhere to insert a key on their side of the fence. The door was designed to be unlocked from the outside, and the outside only.

"Did you know?" Mary said. She turned to Davey. "You must have known we'd be locked in here."

"I left stuff at my desk I was hoping you'd use later," he said. Behind his eyes, the gears were turning. "But nothing so important. So sure, I guess on some level I knew."

"What's your damage?" Umu said.

"It wasn't supposed to matter. We were supposed to be down here all night and then leave the same way we came in. If Kip hadn't fucked it up—"

"Kip is dead!" Soraya yelled, the first sign she could still hear them since Kip had collapsed on her.

"Obviously I'm not blaming Kip," Davey said, though he very much had been. "Though we wouldn't care about the gate if things were going to plan."

"Paramedics," Faye said. "You guys all took drugs. You have no idea what's in them. There are a million reasons we might have needed the gate. What if we needed to call for help?"

If they really were trapped in here, didn't that mean that whatever had killed Kip was down there with them?

Mary, the least able to extricate herself from her phone in daily life, thought of it first. Everyone but Faye was high, processing at a different speed than they were used to, and Faye didn't use her phone very much at all, but Mary was rarely parted from hers, and she'd been the one to bring the backpack over in the first place.

"We can call Ronald!" she said.

"Or, like, 9-1-1." Umu didn't work at the library, had no relationship with Ronald, and very much wanted to see someone in a uniform, even if she was chemically altered at the moment. "We could call for help to the people who are supposed to help."

Nothing had felt strange about dropping their phones into Kip's backpack, but now that he was dead, it felt terribly wrong to reach in and pull them out. Like defiling a tomb. They had only the light from their candles and the faint glow of the exit sign on the other side of the gate. Had Soraya been in better control of herself, they'd have asked her to dig through Kip's bag for them, but she was in no state, so Mary, who was the most eager to be reunited with her phone, did it instead.

"Mine has a case," Faye said. "It's sort of…rubbery?" Why did she say rubbery? What a disgusting word.

"I don't care whose is whose; just take them," Mary said. She had a fistful of them held out, waiting for someone to grab them. The candlelight flickered against the glass screens.

Ro recognized his and Umu's, and he took them from Mary. She held another but, having lost her patience, she let it clatter to the floor and she went in for another handful.

"Here." She shoved Faye's phone, in its rubbery case, at her. The cracked screen, the cheap old phone, she was so happy to see it.

In a moment they were all bent over like that—candle in one hand, phone in the other, soothed by the familiar motion of scrolling up with their thumbs to bring the thing to life. There was one phone left on the ground untouched—Kip's. No one dared pick it up.

They wrote their messages or dialed their numbers. To who? 9-1-1, Ronald, their mothers, whoever they felt was best equipped to help. Soraya didn't type, she only stared at the picture of her and Kip on her home screen, but it hardly mattered if everyone else was calling for help all at the same time.

If not for the level of panic, Faye would have known. Before she dialed the phone, before Mary handed it to her, before they tried and failed to open the gate, as soon as she'd held two fingers to Kip's throat and felt no pulse.

The call didn't connect.

She dialed 9-1-1 and hit the happy green icon and waited, but nothing happened.

"My texts won't send," Ro said. "Umes, what's the Wi-Fi password?"

"It's not ringing," Faye said, at nearly the same moment.

"The ITS work is happening tonight," Mary said, talking over both of them.

Umu and Davey stood there, too, phones in hand. They didn't say it. They didn't have to. No one's call was going to go through.

Above their heads was a thick concrete ceiling, above that, another layer of basement, tens of thousands of books crammed onto shelves that could scarcely support them, and then another concrete slab before there was the ground level and access to a cell signal. The whole idea of a place like this was for it to be secure. It was built to keep water, pests, thieves, out. And now, those same protections would trap them inside.

CHAPTER 14

FAYE, AGAIN

I

Their phones came down, one by one. They weren't useless: they were repurposed as flashlights, their white beams replacing the flickering white candles. Poof. Poof. Poof. The candles were extinguished and allowed to fall to the floor, and in the bright new light, they could see the full spectrum of fear on one another's faces.

"Do you think Kip fell and cut himself?" Soraya asked Faye. She must have known that was impossible; there was so much blood.

"You don't need a phone signal to call 9-1-1," Ro said. He alone hadn't switched on his flashlight. He alone was holding his phone high above his head. "Someone stabbed that guy. I have to be able to call 9-1-1."

'Tis not too late to seek a newer world, Faye thought. She was beginning to believe it less. What new person could she make herself, trapped down here with a killer?

"It's not connecting, but you're not supposed to need phone service for 9-1-1." He walked away from them, screen lit up with the unfulfilled promise of that 9-1-1 call.

"You don't need a phone service provider." Ro was almost out of earshot when Faye spoke up. She didn't know if it was true about the phone service provider, had never had occasion to try it, but she thought she'd heard some fact like that, once upon a time. That a cell phone right out of its box would always be able to dial 9-1-1. "But you still need to be able to connect to a cell tower," she said.

"If I could do that, I could just FaceTime to make a call!" Ro's phone was still high overhead, his face grotesque in its green light.

"I work down here all the time," Faye said. She tried to be kind. The best thing you could be with a desperate person is kind. "My phone never works. It's too far down. The concrete's too thick."

"It's impossible," Ro said. "Everywhere has cell service. The New York City subway has cell service. There's a spot, a transponder or a modem or antenna or whatever."

"Whoever stabbed Kip, they've gotta still be down here, right?" Mary said.

The question made Faye touch her back pocket, a reflex. She hadn't forgotten about the scalpel in there, not exactly. She was aware of it when she sat down. She'd meant to put it back with her things on her worktable. The end of the day had been so rushed that from the moment she'd cut open the mascara until now, her need to sterilize the thing and put it away hadn't come to mind. There was supposed to be so much time tonight that it shouldn't have mattered. No one had stabbed Kip. But if someone had, it would have been Faye who had the weapon to do it.

"This isn't New York City," Umu said. It was her job to calm her friend, but she could hardly calm herself. She wanted her mother. "You'll drain your battery if you keep trying and you need the flashlight, Ro."

"Everywhere has cell service," he repeated.

Faye and Umu and Mary and Davey, all had their flashlights pointed right at him. He walked backward. Because the light from their phones was hurting his eyes, because he didn't want to be near them, because he was certain that somewhere in that basement there was a spot where his phone would break through.

"I don't think he was stabbed," Faye said. "There wasn't any cut…" She wanted to reassure them somehow, but how could she? Kip was dead. A man was dead.

"There's so much blood," Soraya said. She looked down at her clothes, a reminder that she was covered with it. "Someone cut him right open."

"He wasn't stabbed," Faye said. "The blood was his vomit, I think. I saw the body, Soraya. No one hurt him. He ingested something and it made him sick. It's terrible, but no one hurt him."

She was lying. Not about Kip having been stabbed—that was true—but someone or something had brought on all that blood.

"Babe, stay with me," Umu said to Ro. There was a pleading quality to her voice. A pitch to it that Faye was hearing for the first time that night. What must it be like, Faye thought, to have a friend like that, who spoke in tones that only you could understand?

Alas, Ro's hearing wasn't working as it should have been. He held his phone up, up, as if the extra two feet lent by the length of his outstretched arm would make the difference against all that concrete.

"Somewhere has cell service," he said, and then he and the glow of his phone disappeared around the corner of a bookstack and into the dark.

II

The five of them remained at the gate, in the not-insignificant light cast by four of their flashlights. Soraya was in the most obvious distress. The background on her phone had gone dark, but she was still looking at it, and she stood there shivering, her teeth actually chattering, as things became worse and worse and worse.

She wore her fear the most, but she wasn't alone in it. If they weren't high, it might have been clearer, if they knew each other better it might have felt safer, if the lights weren't moving, if time wasn't going in the wrong direction, if they could know for absolute certain that whatever was out there, and had hurt Kip, wasn't also here with them.

It was supposed to be spiritual, it was supposed to be ecstatic, but then the fear got in and now it covered them like bugs.

"What do you think happened to him?" Davey said. He went to Faye and took her hand, actually grasped her hand the way a little boy would grasp his mother's hand before crossing a busy street. She didn't know you could do that. Just take someone's hand without asking them if it was okay first. "I don't really know you, but you didn't take anything, right? So maybe you see something we don't. You didn't take anything?"

But he did know her. He'd spoken to her at least nine times before that night. It made her want to yank her hand away. His hand in hers, his eyes on her, it felt so hopeful. Mary and Soraya and Umu didn't share his look of hopefulness. They didn't know her. They scarcely knew each other.

"You didn't take anything," he said again, gripping her hand so tight it felt like a threat. "You didn't take anything so you have to help us."

III

Davey loosened his grip on Faye but he didn't let go. His hand was warm. When was the last time someone had touched her before tonight? Her mother, hugging her goodbye at the end of the summer before she got on the plane back to Vermont? The occasional hand on her arm or shoulder? Nothing as thrilling as this. He said he hardly knew her, but how could that be true when his hand was so warm against hers? When he needed her so badly.

"I can help," she said. "I'll figure something out. I can help."

"Is she going to turn herself into a key and get us out of here?" Mary asked.

Davey squeezed Faye's hand. Reassured her.

"She's smart. Physics, right?"

Faye nodded a little.

"Do you understand physics, Mary?" he said. "That's the whole universe. She understands the whole universe. If she understands the whole universe, then I think she can figure out basement level two."

"I'm sober," she said. It was thrilling to hear Davey tell the others she was smart. He did know her. He had been paying attention. "We're all smart. We wouldn't be here if we weren't smart, but my head's clearer than everyone else's, that's all. I can't open the gate—"

"Told you," Mary said.

"I can't open the gate, but I can make sure everyone's safe."

"She'll fix it," Davey said. "She's here because she's good and she's smart and she knows about the universe."

They were still by the gate, a conspicuous reminder that they were trapped inside that didn't seem to be doing much good for anyone's mental state. Davey, who'd been holding on to his faculties so tight, was finally beginning to slip in a way that worried Faye. He was her friend, after all, her closest ally, and as much as he was relying on her to know what to do, she relied on him for their basic needs. What other supplies he had hidden in the basement, who would be at the library to unlock the gates in the morning, these were details she would need to extract from Davey.

Mary seemed clearer than the others, her trip was going the most smoothly, but she radiated fury. If she had the mental capacity to be helpful, she didn't have the desire. Still, Faye was grateful to see that Mary would mostly be able to take care of herself.

The overwhelming sense from Umu was that she wanted her friend to come back. Umu was the youngest of them, younger than Faye even, and she looked especially babyish at the moment. Her pretty face was scrunched, she was chewing her lower lip, and while the others were pointing the lights from their phones at their feet, she was still pointing hers off in the distance toward the stacks, as though to beckon Ro back with it. She'd worn a silk skirt with flowers on it that day, and while her right hand held her phone aloft, her left was busy with the skirt. She held the fabric between her thumb and forefinger and rubbed it back and forth and back and forth and back and forth. She'd been doing it since Ro disappeared—it made a faint whooshing that was deafening in the silence of their vast cavern. If she kept it up, she'd wear the fabric out by midnight. It felt like they had been down there forever, but it was just after eleven o'clock.

Faye's real fear was how to bring Soraya through the night. Soraya and her single shoe. She wanted Soraya's second shoe to restore a sense of order. Before the lights had gone out, when Soraya was tracing the spines of the books with her fingertip, the pleasure had radiated from her, and now that body emitted only terror. At some point, while Davey had been complimenting Faye, Soraya had taken her shivering to the floor. She sat with her arms wrapped around her knees, her phone placed on the concrete in front of her, still dark, like she was waiting for a call that would never come. The blood down the front of her, Kip's blood, had begun to dry to a rusty brown, which had the effect of making Soraya appear dirty. Dirty was better than bloody. An improvement.

Her teeth weren't chattering anymore, but her whole body was shaking. She was clenching her jaw so tight that the muscles in her cheeks were flexed, and Faye worried that along with all their other problems, Soraya would shatter her back teeth and require a dentist.

Umu was the youngest and Faye was the least confident and Ro was a stranger to the place but it was still undeniably Soraya who was most in need of help. It was such an unpleasant choice to make, but Faye shook her hand free from Davey's. If he was right, and she could help them, if he was right, and she was smart and capable, then the first thing she needed to do was to attend to Soraya. Faye knew that to approach children and dogs, you were supposed to get down to their level, and as little as she knew about children and dogs, she knew less about people who had taken psychotropic drugs directly before experiencing a traumatic event. But she figured a cautious approach was likely the right one, so to start her approach to Soraya, she got down on the floor with her. If Soraya had been Beans, she'd have calmed down immediately. Beans was afraid of fireworks and on the Fourth of July, he always found somewhere to hide and shiver, but as soon as Faye got down on the floor with him, his heart rate settled.

"Tell me how I can help you," Faye said, as gently as she could but still making Soraya flinch when she came close. She didn't touch Soraya, she didn't dare, only waited next to her on the floor until she was ready to speak. There was blood clumped in her eyelashes.

"Open the gate," Soraya said. "And let me go home and wash off the blood."

"We're safe if we stay together," Faye said. She didn't say what they were safe from. Wasn't she the one who'd said that whatever had happened to Kip was just a matter of something he ingested? "We'll take you somewhere that you can go and rest."

Getting away from the gate, she told herself, would be the beginning of the end of their troubles. It was a reminder, taunting them, of how trapped they were. If there was no getting out, then there was no use sitting by it.

"You hid some supplies, didn't you?" she asked Davey. When she'd let go of his hand, he'd laced his fingers through the grating that trapped them.

"I prepared a basket of secrets," he said, and he looked like he knew how stupid it sounded. He'd wanted this night so badly.

"Let's go back," she said. "Would you like that, Soraya? To go back to where we were sitting before? Surrounded by books? That's not so scary." Faye looked to Davey for his support. "We can see what else there is, in terms of supplies. Maybe if Soraya ate something?" Her own stomach burned.

"What about the body?" Umu asked. "You don't think sitting by Kip's body might be scary?"

"Davey and I will move it," Faye said. She didn't know if Davey had it in him, but Ro was nowhere to be seen and if nothing else, Davey was strong enough to do it. She turned back to Soraya, her voice gentle. "I'm going, but only for a minute. Stay here with Umu and Mary and they'll take care of you, okay?"

Davey unlatched his fingers from the grate. She expected him to protest, but he didn't. "Yes!" he said. "I knew you were going to help us."

"It'll be a minute," Faye said, though no one was looking at her. "Stay here and we'll come right back for all of you."

Umu kept rubbing her skirt back and forth and Soraya kept staring at her dark phone and Mary kept seething with anger, so it was silent when Faye and Davey took themselves back to the arena.

"Was there anything to eat that you hid down here?" Faye asked. She'd give Soraya the corn if it came to it, though she hoped for something better. If there was food, she never learned of it. They arrived at the body so quickly—it felt like it had taken an age to get to the gate in the first place, and now they were back in just a moment.

"Do you want the feet or the head?" Davey asked. Kip looked just as horrible when they stood over him this time. On Soraya the blood had dried to look like dirt, but on Kip it was so clearly blood. Something he ingested, Faye told herself. Nothing scary about that.

"You take his feet," Faye said. "Keep your eyes closed if you need to and I'll tell you where to step." She laid her phone on the ground with the flashlight pointing up, and Davey did the same.

"I don't mind keeping them open," Davey said.

She was meant to be the one in control, but she would have liked very much to be able to keep her eyes closed. She took Kip under his arms and Davey took him by his feet and even still they couldn't lift him, only drag him—as respectfully as possible and as little distance as they could get away with. They'd left no space between the shelves in the B section when they made their arena, but just around the corner were the E stacks. Larger format books, those tomes over sixteen inches in height, lined up and whispering to one another. The first of the E shelves was up against the grating, but there was just enough space there to lay Kip flat. Respectfully, Faye thought, but out of the eyeline of anyone who might be disturbed by the sight of him.

"A scientist and a philosopher. A CEO and an influencer. And whatever it is Umu wants to be. Strange group we are," Davey said. Faye brought Kip's shoulders, his head, to rest gently. Davey let his feet clatter to the ground. He was moving slowly now, occupied by the goings-on inside his head.

"You forgot Ro," Faye said. Davey followed her back out of the arena, where the lights on their phones were still pointing up at the ceiling, illuminating a tiny sliver of the vast space.

"Did I?" Davey said. "Does he want to be anything that he isn't already?"

Faye looked over her shoulder. There was no bobbing light, no sound of footsteps, to signal that Ro was anywhere nearby. He could be on the opposite end of the endless basement, his phone still held high in the air searching for a signal. Or he could be just behind the next bookshelf. Watching them. Listening.

"We're on our way back," Faye said into the dark. Gently. She didn't want to startle anyone.

"Corduroy." It was Mary's voice she heard first when she approached the gate. "Do you feel the velvet? Do you feel the bumps?"

"I liked the silk better," Soraya said. An improvement. At least she was engaging.

Umu dropped her hand from the pretend corduroy when Faye and Davey came into view.

"Did you find Ro?" she asked.

"We're touching fabrics," Soraya said, her hand outstretched and stroking Mary's arm.

"We weren't really looking for him." Faye dropped to a crouch to pick up the scattering of candles that had been abandoned in favor of the phones. Their batteries wouldn't last forever.

"I went to a fabric store on acid once," Mary said, though no one had asked. "I was there for seven hours. It was soothing."

"We'll go back to where it's comfortable," Faye said, stretching her hand out to help Umu up. "With the noise and the light, he can find us whenever he's ready, even if his phone dies."

Once Umu was up, she offered her hand to Soraya. Soraya took it, got to her feet. Another good sign. But when she came close to Faye, she reared back.

"You smell like him," Soraya said. "Like his blood."

It was true that Faye's hands and forearms and shirtfront had the telltale rust stains of dried blood, but she couldn't smell anything.

"We had to move his body," Davey said, like he was describing the completion of a household chore.

"I don't like it," Soraya said, and Faye sniffed at herself self-consciously, but all she could smell was the familiar smell of her own sweat.

Their four lights—Soraya's phone stayed dark—led them through the stacks and away from the gate. They had to pass the E stack, where Kip's body was hidden, and Faye tried to shield the spot with her body, but Soraya stopped walking while everyone else passed.

"He's there, isn't he?" If she'd had her light on, she'd have seen him, his unmoving flesh. "I can smell it."

Faye, her own light pointed at the floor, reached to take Soraya's arm, to guide her to the B shelving, where she wouldn't see anything she wasn't supposed to. Her fingertip was almost at Soraya's elbow when a deep, frustrated scream from across the basement stopped all of them. It was Ro.

"I know how he feels," Soraya said. Ro's anger, his exasperation, had broken her concentration. She kept walking toward the arena, guided by the light of Davey's flashlight.

"Ro!" Umu called into the dark, but no one answered. "Why won't he come back here?" Umu asked. "Ro!" she called again.

"He's frustrated," Faye said to Umu. "Let him have his space. He'll come find us when he's ready."

Back in the arena, Mary and Davey put their phones on the floor with the lights facing up, and Faye followed suit. They could hear rattling as Ro took his frustration out on the security grating.

In the center of the arena, not far from their phones, was that ear of corn. Were none of them hungry? She'd intended to offer Soraya the corn, the pop of delicious, sweet kernels being the most soothing thing she could think of, but no one else seemed bothered by the lack of food in nearly twenty-four hours. She might have considered the drugs a moment longer if she'd known they would keep her from feeling the intensity of her hunger.

"You're wrong," Umu said.

Davey and Faye and Mary all turned to her, to see who she was talking to, what she was talking about. Only Soraya was uninterested.

"About Ro?" Faye asked.

There was a new kind of color in Umu's eyes. They reflected the flashlights more sharply. Or maybe it was that her eyes were darting back and forth between them all. She'd been languid before, playing with the fabric of her skirt, but now she was clenched, taut.

"About Kip," Umu said. "It couldn't have been something he ingested. He didn't ingest anything. He fasted. We all did."

It was a puzzle she'd been putting together since the idea of Kip being stabbed had been taken off the table, and she'd finally slotted the last puzzle piece into its place. But Umu didn't make her announcement with any sort of pride. She spat it like an accusation.

"I saw him," Faye said. Eyes to Soraya, eyes to Umu. The two girls and their two different ways of being afraid. "I saw him and the blood was in his vomit. That's awful, I know." Eyes to Soraya. How much detail was too much detail? "There wasn't a cut on him. I promise no one hurt him."

"It was the gods who hurt him."

Davey. She'd lost her focus on Davey.

He picked his light up off the floor and swung it over to where Kip lay. It was too far to illuminate anything, Kip was too well hidden, but it was still a threat.

"He ate a pomegranate seed, and he was punished," Davey said. "It's just like the story of Persephone. It's perfect, really. We purified ourselves for the ritual by fasting. Everyone did, right? Look at the way Faye has been eye fucking that corn. You can tell she kept her fast. If you eat or drink anything in the underworld, you have to stay there forever."

Faye approached Davey with caution. The girls were afraid, but he was in a different sort of headspace that was just as dangerous. She touched his shoulder to swing him and his beam of light back toward the girls. She didn't want anyone's attention on Kip's body.

"We don't have a lot of answers right now, Davey, but I think we can rule out Hades."

"The ritual has to be underground. That's why we came into the basement. It symbolizes the underworld. Kip broke his fast so—"

"He didn't break his fast," Umu said. All the eyes, all the attention, turned to her. If there'd been a spotlight, she'd have been standing under it. "Persephone had to stay in the underworld because she ate the pomegranate—"

Faye would have killed for some pomegranate.

"—but Kip didn't eat anything. He texted me this afternoon about how hungry he was. He texted me about Persephone."

"We're a group of intelligent adults, and blaming whatever is going on here"—Mary waved her hand in the general direction of the E stacks—"on Hades would make us insane. Do you hear yourselves?"

"Why was Kip texting you?" Soraya said.

"It was definitely Hades."

If Davey heard any of the rest of the conversation, he didn't show it.

"To remind me to fast," Umu said. She took the fabric of her skirt between her fingers again and resumed her swishing, though now the sound of the fabric was more frantic, almost threatening.

"Did you need reminding?" All of Soraya's dark energy, the barbs that hung in the air around her, were now focused on Umu. "He was your teacher, right? You do a lot of texting back and forth with your teachers? Checking in on their weekend plans?"

"Maybe he's trapped in the underworld for wanting to add a student to his body count," Davey said.

"Enough about the underworld!" Mary piled her hair on either side of her head like earmuffs. "She's not his student anymore, is she? He can, or could, get it in with anyone he wants."

"Is that true, Soraya?" Davey said, not willing to leave it alone. "Can Kip smush whoever he wants?"

There was no getting the situation under control anymore, but Faye wanted Davey to pull back on the meanness, if nothing else. "You've got to stop it, Davey."

"This is enough," Soraya said. Maybe it was the dark, maybe it was the drugs, maybe it was her anger, but there was nothing left of her honey-brown irises. Her eyes were all pupil. "Whatever else is going on here, the kid is right about one thing." Umu, the kid, didn't look up. She kept to her swishing. "Kip didn't break his fast. He wouldn't have."

They all knew she was right when she said it. No matter how much or how little they each knew Kip, they understood that he was the type of guy who loved to do something hard, then lord over everyone around him how easy it had been.

Soraya continued.

"If Kip ingested something that killed him, it's because he was poisoned."

IV

"Who would do something like that?" Davey said, and despite themselves, everyone laughed. It wasn't funny, not really. Kip was dead, a man was dead. It was that the man who was dead had been so repulsive to so many people that was the morbid humor in the thing.

There was something soothing about the realization. Kip had been poisoned. Terrible, but soothing. Getting bad news is never as hard as waiting for bad news and, if nothing else, they weren't talking about Hades any longer. It was half past eleven. Two hours ago they'd chanted and stomped in a circle, reciting Tennyson. When Mary sat down, then Soraya, then Umu, and Faye and Davey, they were in that same circle. Not surrounding anyone now, certainly not chanting and laughing, but there was something soothing about being mostly together, back where they'd begun. Faye still had those candles. She signaled to Davey for the lighter. If they weren't going to move around for a while, then she'd prefer the candles to the phones. The light wasn't as bright, but she wouldn't mind something that kept them stationary.

"The culprit poisoned the toilet paper," Umu said. "Then Kip wiped his ass with it, and hours later he met his untimely end."

Mary gave a half-hearted laugh. Faye lit the first of the candles. She didn't want to talk about how Kip had been poisoned. Or by who. Thinking about it was scary enough. Saying it aloud was worse.

"The murderer dipped Kip's pencil in poison," Davey said. "And when Kip came to a difficult passage in his text and began to chew his eraser, he sealed his fate."

"Mine was better," Umu said.

Faye dripped wax from the newly hot candle onto the cement floor, a trick her father had taught her. Once she had a good-sized pool of it, she turned the candle upright and stuck its base into the hardening pool of wax.

"It was his phone," Mary said. "The killer painted his screen with poison, knowing that Kip would get it all over his hands as he sat there, flipping through the Instagram stories of undergraduate snacks." An uncomfortable pause as everyone looked at Umu. "When he'd exhausted his eyes with all that beauty, he reached up to rub them to clear his vision, activating the poison that covered his fingers."

Faye held the candle in place while the wax at the base rehardened. She released it, pleased with the result. The candle held firm, the warmth of its light flickering across their faces in the circle. The candles gave her something to do, something to think about besides food and murder.

"The candle," Soraya said. "Someone poisoned the candle, and when the wax dripped on his fingers, it killed him just like that. Poof."

Of all the theories, outlandish or banal, Soraya's was the only one that was impossible. Kip hadn't lived long enough to pick up one of the candles. None of the theories were funny, but all of them laughed. The longer they made jokes, the longer until they confronted the obvious. Kip had been poisoned by something, or someone, that was down in the basement with them.

"It's not the first time someone's died at the library, you know," Davey said. Storytelling was one way to keep them from asking questions about one another.

Faye did know. She researched the place when she'd applied for the job, as if they would ask her questions about its history in the interview, as if they had so many candidates who could prepare X-ray fluorescence samples for rare books. Still, if Davey wanted to tell the familiar tale, she was happy to listen. Anything was better than the morbid show-and-tell of possible causes of death.

"Ronald told me about it," Davey began. "It was the eighties, right after he started here, and he said the place was a bacchanal back then. You've all heard the stories…" Though of course Umu and Faye hadn't. "Cocktail hour would start at three o'clock every day and they'd sit in the workroom and smoke and take turns having their corn ground in the bathrooms or the stacks or on the reference desk."

"Truly, the most shocking part of all that is the smoking near the books," Umu said. She kept looking over her shoulder. She was listening to Davey but hadn't stopped checking for Ro, or for someone else who might be out there.

"So they have this 'anything goes' attitude and everyone's trading off partners and there's this librarian, new guy, who gets hired away from the British Library, and they weren't angels there either but we're talking about the woods of Vermont here, people get crazy when there's nothing else to do."

"So, what, he overdid it with the Jim Beam one night?" Mary asked. "Drifted off in a snowbank on the way home?"

"How unimaginative," Davey said. He scratched at the bulge by his eye. "His first month here he stays late in the basement with one of the library assistants, this lady who's married to a history professor. They mash the fat, and his tender British heart can't take it. He tells her he loves her, tells her she needs to leave her husband for him, the poor guy was probably just homesick and pouring it all on her, but that's hindsight."

"He killed her husband?" Umu said.

"Let me tell the story." By now, Davey had accepted one of the candles from Faye and he leaned down toward the flame. "He tells her that if she won't be with him, that he can't be there at all, that to be near her is driving him mad."

"He killed the library assistant?" Soraya asked.

"So they close for Christmas, like always, and the library is empty for two weeks and when they come back there's a smell. Facilities thinks there's a rat or a raccoon in the walls and they begin to open things up and look, but someone finally does a walkthrough of the basement and they find the British dude, hanging from a rafter."

"That American pussy drove him out of his mind," Umu said.

"Or if we follow Davey's logic," Faye handed Umu her own candle. "He dared eat a couple of pomegranate seeds before coming down to the basement one night."

They might have laughed, if given the chance. At one of her jokes! It was in the air, that laugh, but then from across the basement, they heard Ro again. Another frustrated growl, another rattle of their cage. After that, they weren't around a campfire telling stories anymore. They were back in a hole with a body.

Now Umu had a candle, too. She hadn't dripped the wax on the floor to make a candleholder, not yet. She held it, savoring the warmth of it in her hands.

"I knew someone who died of poisoning once," Umu said. She looked over her shoulder again; it was a reflex now. "It was totally awful. I was only a kid but my mom ended up telling me, like, way more than she should have, because it was her friend and I guess she didn't want to talk to my dad about it. This lady was a chemist. She and my mom had been college roommates for a minute and then they stayed friends even though my mom didn't know anything about, like, beakers. This happened when I was seven or eight. The chemist lady is working away in her little lab at Harvard, measuring this, mixing that, firing up that Bunsen burner. She's working with some form of mercury but, like, a fancy kind."

"Dimethylmercury," Faye said. She knew this story. They told it in safety presentations in labs at the beginning of the semester. There was a sense of proximity to celebrity, knowing Umu was connected to the story.

"So the safety information on the fancy mercury says she has to wear gloves and, of course, sis is wearing gloves. A swanky lady chemist! She's no fool! She drops a little bit, one drop of the fancy mercury on the back of one hand, but it's okay because it lands on her latex gloves. Cleans herself up, washes her hands, grabs new gloves, thinks nothing of it. You know, you think of poisoning as something that happens right away, like in the movies, but it doesn't. She got a little sick pretty quick but she stayed sick for months. She's over at my house one day, and she's a skeleton because she can't eat anymore and she's all dizzy and shit, and my mom begs her to go see a doctor, and finally she does and like a week later, she's dead. Before she went into the coma, she was blind and deaf, and she couldn't speak."

"Holy shit," Mary said. "So did someone poison her with some of her chemicals?"

"Nah," Umu said. "For a long time my mom was sure it was on purpose. If I'm being honest I'm pretty sure she and the lady chemist were more than friends after a couple of glasses of wine, you know? When I was a kid, I was sure my dad did it."

"Your dad murdered your mom's lover?" Mary said.

"No. I *thought* my dad murdered my mom's lover. Turns out it was the fancy mercury that dripped onto her gloves. She was wearing latex gloves and they weren't strong enough, and the stuff got into her bloodstream and ate her brain. She wasn't murdered; she just wasn't careful."

"I think," Faye said, sprung into action by the repeated use of the word "murder" and her need to distract them from it, "that I'm going to steer us away from stories about terrible ways that people died."

"Are you jealous because people in whatever Mennonite community you're from only die in really prosaic ways?" Mary asked.

Faye lit a candle for Mary and passed it to her in the spirit of generosity. Mary was scared; they were all scared. "I'm not from a Mennonite community. It's going to be a long night, it's been really stressful, an awful thing has happened, it would be helpful if we could talk about things that aren't quite so ghastly."

"What are you all doing after graduation?" Umu said. She was looking at Soraya. "That's a happy thing, right? Your brand new lives."

"We're down here because that's a terrifying thing," Davey said. "Future plans are just as off-limits as gruesome murders."

Soraya nodded her agreement. She'd also recently received a candle, and the hand that held it shook, just a little. She was looking at the group of them the way Umu was looking over her shoulder. Like she knew there was something there about to come for her.

"He did break his fast." Soraya spoke quietly, her eyes moved from person to person. "Not with food, not with pomegranate seeds or whatever Davey's talking about, but Kip did ingest one thing."

Mary zipped her necklace back and forth, and Davey scratched at his eye as they waited for Soraya's proclamation.

"The acid. He ate the tab of acid. We all did."

Seven little tabs in seven little baggies.

"I really don't think we should talk about—"Faye tried to interject.

"He put it right into his mouth in front of us," Soraya said. "It's not food. Was everyone else trying to think of food? I was trying to think of food. But anyway. We all saw him swallow it."

"We'd all be sick, though, if that were it." Davey looked around the circle for agreement. "I mean, if we all took the same thing, we'd all be sick by now, or at least beginning to feel strange."

"I feel pretty fucking strange," Soraya said.

"That's because you're high on acid." Umu was the only one who didn't appear energized by this new theory.

"I mean, there's a pretty significant difference," Mary said. "Remember right when Ro was passing them out and Kip acted like he knew everything the way he always acts like he knows everything? He swallowed his, right? And then Ro gave him shit for it and then the rest of us put ours under our tongues so they would dissolve. Maybe his stomach acid made something activate more quickly? I don't know. But if the way you take it can change the high you get, then who knows what else it can change."

"I don't think that's what happened," Faye said.

"I don't know." Soraya was gazing in the direction of the body again. Like she really could smell it.

"If Mary's right, that means it's a matter of time for the rest of us, doesn't it?" Davey said. He was speaking slowly, deliberately, adding the figures up in his head. "Kip swallows his drugs so the stomach acid or whatever activates the poison and all of a sudden he's bleeding out of his eye sockets—"

"He did not bleed out of his eye sockets," Faye said, to reassure Soraya, to get control of the situation.

"It should follow that the rest of us will start bleeding out of our eye sockets any minute now. How long's he been dead? An hour? Longer? Mine mostly dissolved under my tongue, but I swallowed it eventually."

"Okay," Mary said, rolling Davey's argument around in her head. "What if Kip's tab was the only one poisoned?" Zip, zip, zip, that cross against her chain, the chain against her throat.

"I like that I'm not about to start bleeding out of my eyeballs," Davey said. "So you mean he lost some sort of weird game of Russian roulette he didn't know he was playing?"

"Kip is exactly the type of guy who would insist he could win at Russian roulette," Umu said. Faye laughed a little. No one else did.

"I guess it could be that," Mary said. "Russian roulette is random. Could have been any of us. But like, the drugs weren't random at all."

"What are you saying?" Now Davey laughed a little. A nervous laugh.

"When you play Russian roulette, you spin the chamber or whatever it's called and then you pull the trigger, and if you get shot in the head, you get shot in the head. Shitty luck." Mary mimed a gun against her temple with her thumb and forefinger. "But the drugs weren't random. The tabs had those little pictures on them."

Faye had been enjoying the bit where they sat and told stories. Too morbid to ever say it out loud, but this is the sort of thing people did, wasn't it? Told each other tall tales, exaggerated a bit, made each other laugh, made each other a bit sad. Did Umu really think her father murdered a noted chemist? Unlikely. Made for a good story though, didn't it?

"Let's not speculate," Faye said. "We're only going to drive ourselves crazy or make ourselves terrified. The thing of it is to stay calm." But she wasn't calm. Because Soraya was right.

Soraya didn't look as though she had good control over the flickering flame of her candle. Any modern library wouldn't allow for candles at all. Strictly speaking, they weren't allowed in this library, but there were none of the complicated technological systems to dissuade them. Faye was sure that just thinking about a flame at Yale would set off all manner of alarms, but the William E. Woodend Rare Books Library was a different sort of animal. It was in financial trouble almost from the day it opened, so there was never any sort of question of upgrades or improvements, save for the security fence and the air-conditioning system (donated by an alumnus who insisted on refitting the whole campus because he thought it indecent to sweat). There were materials donated, sure, but no one with money wanted to use it on something so unglamorous as a fire suppression system.

Dr. William E. Woodend (the doctorate was honorary, awarded after he donated the funds for the library) made his fortune as a broker of some sort in the latter part of the nineteenth century. A Princeton man, he chose not to give his money to that institution, with which he mostly lost touch after graduation. That, or his sources of income were too questionable for the Ivy League. He liked Vermont. People weren't fussy about where money came from; they were only glad when you had it.

He donated the money for the library to the university in 1903. That same year, he summered on Long Island and was sued by his neighbors when he used a shared roadway for the purposes of exercising his show horses and used a rented cottage as a stable for those same horses.

He was an asshole, was the thing about William E. Woodend.

By 1904 he was bankrupt. The Princeton alumni magazine detailed the smashup of his brokerage firm and listed his residence as "address unknown." In fact, he was in Vermont. Rents were easier in the Green Mountain State, and he'd found himself embroiled in a further legal matter as he tried to get the university to give back the money he'd gifted for the library.

Having made no effort to maintain positive relations with his fellow Princetonians, he didn't have a network of fellow captains of industry that he could run to when he found himself in dire financial straits. The $400,000 that he'd donated for the construction of a grand campus library was a drop in the proverbial bucket when he promised the funds and signed them over in 1903, but by 1904 it was a fortune to him, a fortune that could have kept him clothed and housed for a good, long time.

Donations generally have a "no take-backsies" policy. Even a hundred years ago, cultural institutions didn't deal in promises; they dealt in legal agreements, and Mr. Woodend had signed documents promising the money, had instructed his bankers to forward the money, had posed in the newspapers announcing the donation. As the university's lawyers and his own told him, as much as he wanted it back, the money was no longer his.

It being America, he sued anyway, despite being told by anyone with a legal opinion that he had no legal claim on the funds. The lawsuit was unsuccessful, but it dragged on for years and proved an expensive proposition for both Woodend and the university. It branded the library as persona non grata (instituta non grata?) when it came to donations and other sources of funding. The matter wasn't settled until after the First World War, at which point most of the great American industrialists either lost their fortunes or committed them to other causes. There was nothing left in the pot for fire exits, backup generators, or extravagances of the like.

When development officers from the university tried to court new donors, and brought up the possibility of the library as a cause, they were immediately rebuffed. Despite his empty coffers, Woodend did a remarkably good job of making his case in the press, and donors lost all faith in the library's ability to steward their resources.

Woodend and his wife, an equestrian who never forgave him for the sale of her prized horses after the change in the family's financial circumstances, spent years settled in the very same Vermont town where the university stood. The case was being heard in Montpelier, but also Woodend liked to hang around the campus during the construction of the library building, watching his dimes and nickels be spent. Surely, it was never their plan to stay so long, but Woodend was a difficult plaintiff who fired lawyers at a whim and dragged the case out in every manner. Eventually the Woodends had children in Vermont, which complicated things further because Vermont, as it turns out, is a lovely place to rear children, and having become accustomed to it, Mrs. Woodend found herself quite unwilling to leave.

The whole sorry chapter in the library's history was finally settled in 1919, when William Woodend was imprisoned for the murder of his equestrian wife. He'd taken a $400,000 life insurance policy out on her, desperate to recover his funds by any means available to him, and she was found at the bottom of the stairs in their family home with a broken neck only days after the policy went into effect.

—

"Kip really liked you when you were his student, huh?" Mary turned her attention to Umu. It was phrased as a question, but spoken as a statement. An accusation.

"He was nice to all his students," Umu said.

"Kip? Kip was equally nice to all his students?" Mary laughed. Kip was a lot of things, but he wasn't nice. Everyone knew that. "Okay. I'm sure he was equally nice to every student so long as they're beautiful and thin and brilliant and read Greek. That's why he invited all his other students tonight, right? Because he was equally nice to all of them. I'll bet your bestie loved that. How *nice* Kip was to you. I'll bet your lifelong bestie who's so impressed with his darling Umu he can barely stand it thought there was nothing weird, nothing shady about your teacher and the special attention he was giving you."

"Did you tell Ro that Kip was hitting on you?" Soraya asked. Faye was still holding out that candle, trying to distract Soraya with the flame, trying to soothe her with it, but there was no distracting anyone from this thread. It was unspooling.

"He's the one who brought the drugs," Davey said.

"Where's Ro now?" Mary said. "Still looking for phone service? It's been an hour. I think it's safe to say at this point that he's not going to connect. Why's he still gone? Why isn't he here with his bestie who he loves so much, who he came here to watch out for? Kip is gone and all of a sudden, Ro doesn't feel like he has anything to protect Umu from."

"Where did Ro go?" Soraya said. "Did he get out? Did he find a way out?"

"No one got out," Davey said. "The gates are still locked. He did what he came here to do and then he disappeared—he's hardly going to stay around and make eye contact."

Their circle of five, lit by candles, lit by their flashlights, settled around the lights like a campfire, had begun to cast more frantic shadows.

"What if he can hear us?" Soraya leaned forward and whispered. "What if he's just around the corner, listening?"

"If he hurt Kip, he could hurt any of us," Davey said. "What was his problem with Kip, that he hit on Umu? That he violated some sort of ethic of the teaching assistant? If he's willing to kill Kip over that, you don't think he's willing to hurt the group of people who know what he did?"

Soraya wasn't seated any longer. She was crouched like a runner at a starting line, slightly off-balance on account of the missing right shoe. Was she preparing to run from something or toward something? Impossible to know.

"He hates people like us, doesn't he?" Soraya said. "People like him, all blue-collar and bad opinions, they always hate people like us."

Was she a person like Ro, or a person like Soraya? Faye wasn't sure which group she belonged to.

Davey had a foot up too now. With him Faye didn't question it. He was preparing to run at something.

"Where is Ro right now?" Davey said. He was whispering now, too. "I'm not going to wait here to be hunted."

"You're being insane," Umu said, but her tone was so much less convinced than Soraya's and Davey's.

"He was on the other side of the floor." Davey put a finger up to his lips to quiet them all. Was that the sound of the cage rattling? Was that a footstep? It was hard to hear anything over the sound of all their hearts pounding.

"I'm not waiting," Soraya said, now fully on her feet. "I'm not sitting here and waiting to be hunted because, what, because my parents have a summer home?"

Davey was on his feet now, too. Mary and Umu and Faye rose, too. Because they agreed it was time to run? Or because it's a human impulse to jump up when the person next to you does? She was meant to retain order. Faye was meant to keep them calm until morning, but now Davey and Soraya were moving, were running, toward the other end of the cage and Faye found herself running right behind them.

V

Faye hadn't considered that Ro could be anything but a friend of Umu, anything but a kid who had been invited along with his friend and found himself trapped in something terrible, until she found herself running toward him. What an insane idea this was, running toward the danger. She followed Davey and Soraya, Soraya with her one bare foot. They navigated the rows and rows of shelving with only the meager lights from their phones to guide them. What did she know about Ro? That he sold drugs. That he had kind eyes. That he wore soft, dove-gray pants. What else? Had he ever committed a crime? Selling drugs was a crime. Was he violent? Was he quick to anger? He sounded angry when he shook the grating. Every instinct told her not to run toward him but to run away. I'm running because I'm the only one who can keep everyone safe, she told herself. But that brought the obvious follow-up question—who would keep *her* safe?

"Ro, where are you?" Umu called into the dark. The volume was startling after so much whispering. "Ro, yell out and let me know where you are so I can find you!"

Davey kept moving forward, even if he didn't know exactly where his end point was. "You're warning him we're coming?" He hissed back at Umu. "If you were so sure he hadn't done anything, why would you be warning him we're coming?"

"I'm trying to find him," Umu said, raising her own light high in hopes that Ro would see it, a beacon through the dark. "I'll find him and he'll explain you're crazy."

"Umes?" A voice out of that darkness. Ro's voice.

"He's over here," Davey whispered, and then began to lead the others, his flashlight first and Soraya's—Soraya had finally turned on the light on her phone—behind him.

"If he'd done something, he wouldn't want to be found," Umu said. "If your crazy theory was right, wouldn't he be hiding from us?" Davey and Soraya didn't answer her. Her point was undercut by the fact that they had to seek him out in the dark at all.

"We should leave him alone," Faye said, unhelpfully. "We can stay where we were and he can stay where he was and it'll all get sorted out in the morning." She was scared of what Ro might do to them. She was scared of what they might do to him. In any case, it didn't matter because she turned a last corner, rounded a last shelf behind Davey, and there was the man they were all seeking.

"Did you get it open?" Ro said. His question was for Umu, he cared only about Umu, he must have long decided he was done with the rest of them. "Umes? Did you find a way to get the gate open?"

Impossible, the position Umu was in. The beautiful girl, all long limbs and silk skirt, shrank in on herself. She pointed her light at the floor and Faye could smell the regret oozing from her pores. She wished she hadn't brought the others to find him, she wished she hadn't brought him to the library in the first place. There were only bad outcomes left.

When they came across him, Ro was standing on a shelving stool. A knee-high round thing made of plastic and metal with a corrugated nonslip coating on its step. Standard in any library, there are usually dozens of them scattered about so the library assistants can have a seat while working with volumes on low shelves.

"Anything you want to tell us, pal?" Davey crossed his arms and shone his light in Ro's eyes.

"I'm not your pal." Ro stepped off the stool, was right in front of Davey now. "Umes, did someone get their phone working? Did you guys figure out how to call out?"

"Not yet," Umu said.

Ro turned his back to Davey and got back on the stool.

"This thing gives me another foot and a half. That's not nothing."

"Get down here," Davey said.

"I'm talking to Umu." Ro held his phone in the air.

"There's not even remorse," Davey said. He and Soraya were shoulder to shoulder, a little audience for Ro on his stool.

"Stay with me, Umes," Ro said from his stool. "It's faster if there's two of us, and the sooner we can find the spot with the phone service, the sooner we can be out of here."

"He wants to keep her with him?" Soraya whispered to Davey. "Imagine what he has planned for the rest of us if he's insisting on keeping his friend close by?"

"He wants to keep her safe," Davey said. "That's what he keeps saying."

In the glow from the flashlights, everyone's features were harsher, meaner. From behind Soraya and Davey, Faye watched it all unfold like she was the audience and they were players on a stage. In this production, there were only bad guys. Frustrated that he was being ignored, Davey stepped past Umu and tugged Ro's sleeve to get him off the stool, to get him down to eye level. Ro flicked him away.

"Who are you trying to call?" Davey said. "The police? Seems like a strange choice considering what they'll find when they get here."

"They think the drugs were what killed Kip," Umu said, her tone somewhere between apologetic and searching. "We all fasted, so it would have been the only thing he ingested in close to twenty-four hours." She was close enough to touch Ro. To reach out and take his hand and pull him down from the stool herself. She didn't. She stayed back from him, both hands clutching her phone. She looked afraid. Afraid of her own best friend. Umu's fear crept into Faye. It rose from the floor like an electrical current and soon tore through Faye's whole body. Is this what a murderer looked like? Shaggy-haired, in gray sweats?

"You take a risk every time you ingest a street drug." Ro stepped off his stool, but only so he could move it over by a foot and a half, and stepped back on, still seeking a signal for his phone. "Don't you remember those informational videos they made us watch in grade school? Or do they not show those in private schools? They don't want you feeling limited? Even in your ability to buy cocaine from strangers in public restrooms?"

"Babe, was there something wrong with the drugs?" Umu asked.

"Does it feel like there was something wrong with the drugs?" Ro said. "Don't you feel high, just like you wanted to? Don't you feel on top of the fucking world for the amazing ritual, or party, or whatever the fuck you wanted to have in this basement? There's something wrong, but it's not the drugs."

"Get down and talk to us," Soraya said. "My boyfriend is dead. My boyfriend who you're not even treating like a real person is dead, and you're up there trying to get phone signal? Get down!" This time she pulled on him. Harder than Davey had. Hard enough that he stumbled, though he kept his footing atop the stool.

"Are you insane?"

"She's trying to talk to you, pal," Davey said.

"Soraya's not being careful," Mary whispered. She was pulling her necklace so hard that the chain disappeared into the flesh of her neck. "She doesn't know what he's capable of, and she's not being careful."

"Why do you hate us all so much?" Soraya had her hand on Ro's wrist. "Because you have to wash dishes or sell drugs or do whatever it is you have to do? Is that Kip's fault somehow?"

"I thought he was the worst of you," Ro said. "I thought he deserved to go, but it could have been any of you, huh? You motherfuckers are all exactly the same. A different haircut on the same set of ideas."

What a funny thing words are. There's a giver and a receiver and words are shared. But it's not like a gift or a parcel. If a giver wraps a toy elephant in a box, the receiver will open a toy elephant. Did Ro gift wrap an admission of guilt? An accusation?

"You know what I'm going to do when I get out of here?" Soraya said. "I'm going to pour a giant glass of expensive scotch into an expensive tumbler, just like I'm sure you imagine rich assholes do. And I'm going to toast to the memory of my boyfriend and toast to the piece of garbage who thought he could get away with hurting him, who I made sure will never hurt anyone ever again."

Soraya took her hand off Ro's wrist. She let her phone clatter to the floor and she reached up at Ro's hips, because Ro's hips were what was at eye level, and she pushed.

If she hadn't been so little, or so malnourished, she could have done a lot of damage. As it was, she succeeded in getting Ro off the stool, but he landed on his feet.

"Are you out of your mind?" he said. "Umu, talk to your insane friends and tell them to get away from me."

"We're not her friends!" Davey said. Davey and Soraya had advanced toward Ro, to where he now stood behind the stool. There was quite a bit of floor space between them and the other three. "We don't even know her, remember? Her friend was Kip, but you've killed him. Or did you forget that part, too?"

"Umu, are they being serious?"

Faye took a tentative step forward. It meant releasing Mary's arm, which she hated to do, but she was too far from the others. She picked Soraya's phone up off the floor. The screen had cracked; it now looked like her own. She was responsible for keeping things safe, for keeping everyone calm. She was responsible for intervening.

"Maybe we can go back to the arena and talk about this?" Faye said. She held out Soraya's phone to try to return it. But Soraya only had attention for Ro. "We can try to get some sleep and sort out the rest in the morning. Everything always feels better in the morning."

"I'm not going anywhere with you all," Ro said. He was in a slight crouch with arms out in front of him like a lion tamer in the ring. "You needed a sacrifice for your janky ritual; you got your human blood. I don't want anything else to do with you."

Soraya lunged first. Soraya, who had been so lethargic. Soraya, who had scarcely spoken all night, who was newly energized by this proximity to the man she believed had killed Kip. If she hadn't had the smell of Kip's blood still flooding her nostrils, she might not have been so quick to violence, but she pounced on Ro, throwing her arms around his waist and succeeding this time in throwing him to the ground.

His phone skidded across the floor when she did that. There was already so little light, and now there was less. Ro sprang up quickly, walking backward to get his phone so he could keep his eyes on Soraya as he went. It had landed face up, the beam of light totally covered, but when he retrieved it he didn't shine it again. Faye saw the quick calculation that he would need his hands. He stashed it in his pocket.

"You're high and you're scared, and you're not thinking," Ro said. "I can chalk it up to that. But if you dare touch me one more time, I'll be less forgiving."

"Come with us so we can talk about this," Faye said. With all her bravery, she advanced. It was only Umu and Mary who hung back now.

"I'm not going anywhere with him; he's a murderer," Soraya yelled. Her pitch was so high and she kept moving forward toward him. Why wouldn't she just back off?

Ro put his hand out again, his lion tamer's arm. "Get a hold of your bitch," he said to Davey. "If she comes at me again, I won't be responsible for what happens."

The next part happened so quickly. Soraya made another lunge for Ro. Whether she was trying to hurt him or incapacitate him was never clear, but once she had lunged the first time, she couldn't stop attacking. True to his word, Ro knocked her aside like a gnat when she came at him. Her body hadn't yet hit the floor when Davey made his own attack. His chivalry or his adrenaline demanded it of him. He was a less easy bug for Ro to shoo away. Davey was a head

taller than their guest at the library, though a lot less experienced at
conducting himself under the influence of chemical substances. He
lunged at Ro the same way Soraya had, throwing his arms around
Ro's waist to try and bring him to the floor.

"I'll kill all of you."

They all heard Ro say it, and as Faye took another step toward
them, another step toward fulfilling her promise of maintaining the
sanity of the group until morning came and help arrived, she put
her fingers on the steel scalpel in her back pocket. She had changed
the blade just that afternoon. Strange how much courage steel could
lend, how much it could soothe her, as she moved toward and not
away from the violence playing out in front of her. The blood rushed
to her ears; that was her body putting up armor for her. If she couldn't
hear the grunts and screams and squeals of pain as Ro and Davey and
Soraya writhed on the floor, if all sounds except for the sounds of her
own body were blocked out, she could be so much braver.

Ro was on the floor with Davey and Soraya over him; then, before
any of them could breathe, he was on his feet again. Faye moved
ever closer, the situation slipping into and out of control with every
breath. The flashlights on their phones were their only source of
light. They'd left the candles burning on the floor in the arena and
that felt out of control, too, like if she moved wrong the whole place
would go up in flames.

If only Umu or Mary had moved to help.

If only Ro had walked back willingly to talk things through with
them.

If only Soraya and Davey hadn't cornered him.

If only he hadn't brandished the shelving stool as a weapon.

If only she hadn't been carrying the scalpel.

Ro hadn't dared blink since Soraya and Davey had descended
upon him. Then, his eyes burning and his heart pounding, he was
no longer able to keep them off. Soraya was screaming that he had
to pay for what he'd done and most of the light had vanished as

phones had been dropped, pocketed, or turned away. He picked up the shelving stool because it was there and he held it out because it created some distance between himself and Soraya and Davey and then he swung it because Davey was lunging at him.

Faye wished he hadn't swung that stool at Davey's head. If he'd swung it low, at his legs, at his stomach, then it wouldn't have threatened Davey's life. If Ro swung that stool with all his might and connected with Davey's legs, he could have caused a lot of damage. He might even have broken a bone, but it wouldn't have been life threatening, so she could have let it happen.

The shelving stool was heavy, made of metal, made to bear the weight of an adult and to last a library's lifetime. The corrugated plastic that formed the nonslip coating on the steps ensured that Ro had a strong grip. If he connected with Davey's head, he'd make ground beef out of it.

'Tis not too late to seek a newer world, Faye thought, she hoped. A world in which she was a hero. She'd promised that she'd keep everyone safe. So when Ro swung that shelving stool, when Ro threatened to make contact with Davey's head, he wasn't the only one moving, he wasn't the only one with a weapon. Faye pulled out that scalpel and Faye lunged and, before any of them could breathe, she was upon him and she did the only thing her panicked body could think to do to keep Davey and Soraya safe: plunge the blade of her scalpel into Ro's neck and spill blood all over his dove-gray sweats.

———

Ronald, who hadn't thought of the library since he locked it up earlier that night, contemplated a second glass of wine but thought the better of it when he saw the time. Professor Kopp was already sleeping. Every one of the graduate students who had come on Davey's tour was out at a bar and had been overserved. The ITS group working on the scheduled network maintenance was taking a break for some pizza. Across campus, a crew put the finishing touches on the tent they had erected for the graduation ceremony. On the other side of the country, Faye's mother turned off the episode of *Downton Abbey* she was rewatching and hoped her daughter was having a nice time at the party before taking herself to bed. It was midnight.

CHAPTER 15

RO

In the telling of the story of this awful night, Ro would have said very little about the mousy, quiet girl with the glasses. She made very little impression right up to the moment when she plunged a steel implement into his throat.

When he'd been passing out the tabs and she'd refused hers, he had a brief welling of affection for Faye. Not that he cared one way or another who did the drugs—they were paid for—but he appreciated people who knew their own minds and didn't bore everyone around them with a lot of explanation.

Three weeks earlier, when he'd been standing in line to apply for his first-ever passport, he'd thought a lot about being that very sort of person. Decisive. He'd gone online and bought a one-way plane ticket to London that very morning, and the strength of his decisiveness propelled him to the passport office immediately after.

It was strange. Waiting in line and not texting Umu to pass the time. But decisive people didn't explain.

"Good morning," he said to the tired-looking civil servant when at last his name was called. "I've come to—"

"Renewal or new application?" The gray-eyed woman with droopy undereyes cut him off.

"New," he said.

"Speak up, son." Her voice came through a crackling speaker, a layer of plexiglass separating them.

"A new application." Ro found a stronger voice. "I've never had a passport before."

"Do you have proof of intent to travel?" she asked, without looking at him. The skin under her eyes was hypnotizing. Like deep pools. "A plane ticket? Otherwise, the wait time is twelve to fifteen weeks."

Ro went into his backpack. He'd read this part online and he'd printed his flight confirmation. He slid the printout through a slit at the bottom of the plexiglass.

The gray-haired woman smiled.

"London's a great first trip," she said.

He could have hugged her. She was the only person in the world who knew he was going to London. After he'd bought the ticket, he'd spent a little time looking at job boards for restaurant staff in London. Plenty of cool-looking places in Soho were hiring.

The gray-haired lady clattered away at her keyboard, working on his application.

"It'll arrive before August first but probably *just* before," she said.

He'd read that part online, too, but he appreciated the warning.

"So many people," she'd said, staring off into the distance as she waited for his credit card to go through for the application fee, "so many people wait their whole lives for a passport and then when they get one, they drive across the border to Montreal or Tijuana. Good for you, son, for swinging bigger."

He knew it wouldn't arrive until late July, but he still checked the mailbox like it was Christmas morning every day. That old lady at the passport office was still the only one who knew his plan.

Umu was thinking about grad schools and considering staying in Vermont, and he hated that idea, that he'd hold her back from going somewhere more exciting. In a sense, she was holding him back, too. Being held up against Umu and her achievements, or holding himself up against them, was exhausting. He'd always feel like nothing, because she was everything.

On its own merits he was excited about, proud of, the London idea. But as soon as he told Umu, it would be a little worse. She would say he was going off to London *just* to be a bartender when he could be so much more. Ro didn't need anything more than bartending; he just wanted to live an interesting life. It was only in light of Umu's expectations for him that his confidence in his plan waned.

He would tell her the day the passport arrived so he could show her it was a real thing. That was what he was thinking of when the hot blood began to bubble and choke him. When he tried to cough the iron tusk out of his throat and found himself unable to draw a breath, he thought about the passport and how he'd be dead before he ever got the chance to hold it in his hands.

CHAPTER 16

FAYE

I

Mary stepped forward as Faye stumbled back. Faye's hands were empty; she had left the scalpel plunged into Ro's neck and she had lost her phone at some moment in the commotion—where was her phone? Mary had her light and she brought it to fall upon Ro's quiet body as though he were some strange object of fascination. Sweeping her light from his feet up to his head, she said nothing.

Davey was on the floor. He'd either been knocked down or he'd thrown himself there to avoid being struck in the head with the shelving stool; no one could quite remember the order of things. In the meager light from Mary's phone, he found his own and picked up Faye's for good measure. He handed her device back to her and then, like Mary, he went to stand over the body, sweeping light back and forth at the horrid, bloody thing on the floor.

Faye, crouched there with the phone Davey had returned, didn't dare approach the body, but she was brave enough to cast her light on it. Why did you do that, Faye, she asked herself, the way she often did when she said something embarrassing in front of someone she'd like to befriend. In what little light they had, the blood that soaked Ro's lovely gray sweats looked black, not red.

"He might be alive," Faye said. Her voice sounded alien to her.

"There's an awful lot of blood," Mary said. She swung back to look at Faye, but she kept her light trained on Ro.

"Well, the human body has an awful lot of blood!" Faye said. Someone should help him, she thought. Someone should check to see if he's alive. Someone should do something.

Faye was so ashamed that she couldn't move. I came here to be friends with these people. I promised to keep them safe, and now look what I've done. She moved to get up, but her head spun and she thought she might throw up. She stayed on the ground. Back at the arena, their candles were still arranged in a lovely circle and somewhere there was an ear of corn, and maybe Davey had even hidden some bottles of beer in the stacks somewhere and it all had the makings of the night she'd imagined for herself.

What an awful place the library was, Faye thought. The endless rows of gleaming spines, the pages pressed together, keeping their secrets from the outside world. In the orderly lab where every action was noted, where everything was in its place, this couldn't have happened. If she'd never come to the library, if she'd only stayed where she was comfortable, she'd never have hurt someone as she had here tonight.

"Why isn't anyone helping him?" Umu fell to her knees in front of her friend, though she'd been just as frozen as the rest of them until that very moment.

"He's beyond help." Davey kept his light trained on Ro's neck. "Unless you'd like us to try a reanimation ritual, but I don't think I'm into that in this case."

You should go and help to prove you're still good, Faye told herself, but then she didn't move because she couldn't.

"Should I pull it out?" Umu had her hand on the blade, the blade that was the best-lit thing in the whole damn basement. "Do you think it's hurting him? If it's hurting him I want to pull it out?"

In perfect darkness they wouldn't have seen she was crying. It was a quiet sort of crying, no gasping hysterics, only silent tears that slid down her cheeks and onto Ro's face, onto Ro's neck, reflected in the beams of those flashlights.

"Check for a heartbeat, if you can." Faye surprised herself by speaking up. I'm helping, she thought. I'm good and I'm helping. "If his heart is still beating, you can't pull out the...you can't pull it out."

"Now you have advice?" Umu said. She leaned over him to put her ear to Ro's chest. To check for life in a stranger, you put your fingertips to a pulse point. To check for life in a best friend, you lay your whole body on top of theirs.

"She's a scientist; you should listen to her," Davey said.

"It's physics," Faye whispered, but no one heard.

Umu did it. She pulled the blade out of his neck, and they all thought there had been a lot of blood before but they were wrong: the blood only came now.

"Yikes, you totally shouldn't have done that," Mary said, and she took a step back to protect her shoes, but she didn't move to help.

Umu pulled her body off Ro's and reached for the nearest thing that might stop the bleeding. An 1873 typography manual with marbled endpapers off the bottom shelf. She chose well, the fine cotton paper could hold more than its weight, and it quickly turned crimson as she pressed it down on Ro's throat.

"Maybe he was alive after all?" Davey said. "Weird. Wouldn't have guessed that."

The next volume Umu grabbed was a personal account of the First World War. The paper wasn't as fine as the first book, but at 298 pages, it was beefier and could hold more of Ro's blood. She tossed the typography manual aside.

"Here," Davey said, having gone to the shelf. He held a volume out to Umu. He's helping! Faye thought. Davey is helping! All of us are good, all of us are trying.

"The one you're holding is a presentation copy from the author,"

Davey said. "Can I trade you? This is the exact same text but it doesn't have the personalized inscription."

"You're a monster," Umu said. She took the new book from him, but she didn't give the inscribed copy back. Now both were being used to try and stem the bleeding.

"I think it's pretty clear that we've slayed the monster," Davey said. "The monster is bleeding out all over the words of Terence MacDermot as we speak."

"He's not dead," Umu said. "He couldn't be bleeding like this if he were dead." The presentation copy was bled all the way through. She tossed it aside. The next volume in arm's reach was a first edition of Ayn Rand's *Atlas Shrugged* with its dust jacket intact. No one objected.

"Well, he will be unless you plan on cutting your wrist to give him an infusion," Davey said.

"Can I do that?" Umu asked. "Is that a thing?"

"So dramatic," Davey said.

"You absolutely should not do that," Faye interjected.

"We're safe now," Davey said. "Umu, you can stop. Your friend was the danger but now the danger's gone. You can stop."

She didn't stop. She wept and applied pressure and wept and applied pressure. The quality of paper that Random House was using in 1957 was quite poor compared with the older volumes Umu had tried first, so the Rand was having little effect at stopping the river of blood that kept coming from Ro's neck.

"I pity you," Umu said, though she was the one most deserving of their pity. "If you think Ro could have done this, if you think Ro could have poisoned the drugs, then I pity you."

"He brought the drugs, Kip ate the drugs, the drugs killed Kip," Davey said. "Case closed."

"I ate the drugs, too!" Umu said. "He handed out the tabs and he watched me eat one! Have you never had a friend in your whole, sad life?" She tossed the Rand aside and now just used her hands, nothing but her fingers to try to get the blood to stop. "I loved him and he loved me. If the drugs had been poisoned, he'd never have let me near them."

That original slipcover on the Rand, the thing that had lent it most of its value, was torn and stained. The picture was of a train's light in the distance, cutting through a green mist. But the light flashed red instead of yellow, a sinister warning. The red now bled all over, absorbing much of the green in the cover image. It wasn't a warning any longer: it had been fulfilled.

"I saw Kip's body," Soraya said. Suddenly unfrozen, she came to stand over Ro and Umu.

"We all saw Kip's body," Umu said.

"No, but I touched it; it was on me." Soraya ran her hands down her face, her throat, her breasts, her ribs, her hips. "You don't understand because it wasn't on you. We're safer now that what happened to Kip can't happen to anyone else."

The fear, or the drugs, or the dark, were making Soraya blind. However much blood had been on Kip, there was more on Ro. However much of that blood had soaked her, there was more dripping from Umu.

"You're disgusting," Umu said. Her fingers were so slick with blood it was hard to keep them laced over Ro's wound. "You did this."

"I mean"—Mary raised her hand—"I think we all saw pretty clearly that Faye did this." She turned to Faye. "No offense."

"She started it," Umu said. Her attention was still on Soraya. Ro's blood had plastered a curl to Umu's forehead and it was dangling into her eye but she didn't care. "You're like one of those chicks who spills her drink on a bodybuilder in a club and then leaves your boyfriend to get his ass kicked by him. *You* started in on Ro, *you* got physical…"

"Your metaphor doesn't work because I can't leave my boyfriend to fight my fight because your boyfriend killed him!" Soraya wailed.

"Babe?" Mary crouched down, found a clean spot on the floor, and put her phone flashlight side up. "Can I call you babe?" She put her hand on Umu's shoulder.

In the bickering, Faye had remained quiet. The full weight of the event landed on her only when Mary pointed out that she'd been the one responsible, that she was the one who had done it. Perhaps she could have done something more, perhaps she could have made herself useful, if not for the feeling that settled upon her. Another man, this one scarcely more than a boy, really, was dead, and her hand had delivered the blow. She put the fingers of her left hand to her lips to stop herself from screaming, and only in doing so did she see how violently she was trembling.

"Babe," Mary was saying to Umu, "he's not bleeding anymore. You can let go; there's no more bleeding."

"Did I stop it?" Umu said. She lifted her hands from Ro's throat and, indeed, the blood had stopped coming. She wasn't a stupid girl, but it was a stupid question.

"No, babe," Mary said, "it just...stopped."

II

Once the blood stopped, Umu let her hands fall to her lap and for a moment, they were all silent. Respect for the dead, or uncertainty about what came next.

"An eye for an eye, or whatever," Davey said, breaking the silence sooner than it needed to be broken. "It's all over now."

"That would be true," Umu said, "if Ro had done anything to hurt Kip, to hurt anyone. But he wouldn't, he didn't, he couldn't."

"It doesn't make a difference now," Davey said. He offered her his hand to help her up, but she didn't move.

"It does make a difference," Umu whispered. "Someone poisoned Kip, and it wasn't Ro."

"Come on!" Davey yelled. "This is enough. Everyone can see what was happening here. Kip has a hard-on for you—sorry, Soraya—he invites you along so he can get it on with you in the library basement, your in-love-with-you-since-childhood bestie tags along and takes out the creepy older guy who's trying to get it in. Tale as old as time."

"Great theory," Umu said, getting up without Davey's help. "Except Ro was gay."

"I've definitely told girls I was gay to get them to take their tops off in front of me," Davey said.

Umu went to the stacks and started to pull down armfuls of books. "Then you're a psychopath," she said. "Ro wasn't gay in theory; he was gay in practice. He loved dicks. Dicks, dicks, dicks, dicks, dicks. He didn't care that Kip wanted to fuck me—sorry, Soraya—and he didn't kill anyone."

Umu let a pile of books fall to the ground next to Ro with a deafening "thwap" and then went back to the shelf for more. In the best of circumstances, on the best of days, Faye wouldn't have had the courage to walk up to Umu and be the one to try and strike up a conversation. Yet here she was. With trembling hands and a head that was still swimming, Faye approached Umu.

"I'm so sorry about your friend," Faye said.

Nothing from Umu. She kept pulling down volumes. She had time now to be more selective than she'd been when trying to stem Ro's bleeding. Anything in an acid-free box stayed on the shelf—too much trouble to unpack it. Heavy leather-bound things, too: they were more weight than they were good. Not that the volumes she left behind were safe; the blood on her hands stained them as she flipped past, or they flopped over or onto the sticky ground. She didn't care.

"Did you mean what you said," Faye continued, "that it was impossible for Ro to have poisoned Kip?"

She needed to know. Had she killed a killer? Or just a boy?

"Are you really trying to talk to me right now?" Umu said. The stack of books she was holding reached her chin. "Your conscience is your problem. You need to take several seats and shut your mouth."

"What are you going to do with…" Davey began to ask and then trailed off as it became clear what Umu intended to do. She knelt back down in front of Ro and picked up the first of the volumes that had fallen on the floor. She opened it and tore out a fistful of pages.

"Let's get you clean," she said to her friend.

What was the book she was destroying? Was it something prosaic? Something that had wound up in the library because a pile of money in pinstripes had donated it along with the rest of their collection and the institution had been too polite to decline it? Or was it something truly scarce, perhaps the only copy in the whole country, in the whole world, that was being used now to sop up this young man's blood?

"Umu?" Mary tried again to take her turn at being the voice of reason. "It's beautiful what you're doing, what you're trying to do for your friend."

Umu continued, tearing pages out of the book, using the paper to clean Ro's blood off his body, then tossing the soaked paper to the side. Over and over—rip, wipe, crumple, discard, rip, wipe, crumple, discard—with no end in sight to the supply of blood that soaked Ro.

"What a way to honor your friend," Mary continued. "The trouble is, I'm almost certain the police will object to the body having been cleaned when they get here in the morning or whenever they get here. Strictly speaking, you're disturbing a crime scene."

It could have been all the blood; it was almost certainly all the blood, but Soraya retreated in on herself. The shelf where Umu had grabbed her books was largely empty now and Soraya crawled onto it; she crawled right on and curled into a fetal position in that little nook.

Umu finished with the book she was shredding. There were no more pages. There was plenty more blood. She tossed the empty cover aside and reached for the next. Faye could see from Davey's grimace that he recognized this one as soon as Umu took it in hand. The Latin text of Caesar's *Bellum civile*, his account of his civil war against Pompey. It had been printed in Venice in 1575. It had foldout maps and plates. Davey's face—he must have loved that book. It was beautiful.

"That's the *Commentarii*," he said.

Umu ripped.

"I can help you clean him, if you like," Faye said. If Umu heard her, she didn't show it. The pages of the *Commentarii* were vellum, it wasn't a particularly good material to sop up anything, and Umu struggled to separate the leaves from their binding. Books that old had been built to last forever. Umu didn't care; she kept at it. Faye crept forward. The next volume in Umu's pile had deckled edges, a sign it was printed on a high-quality paper and likely to be useful for Umu's purpose. With her hands still shaking, she picked it up and handed it to Umu.

"This one might be better," Faye said. "It might do a better job."

Umu slapped the book out of her hand. She'd grown frustrated with the *Commentarii*, and she tossed that one aside, too. She took the next book from her pile. The deckle-edged book, having been spared its fate, lay happily on the floor. She was determined to do her work alone, or at least without Faye's interference.

Now that the *Commentarii* was free from Umu's grasp, Davey came to inspect it. He crouched by where Faye had been when her offer of help had been rebuffed. Her hands were still shaking.

"You can hardly be surprised she doesn't want your help," he said, trying to pull apart the sticky pages of the centuries-old book.

"I did what anyone would have done," Faye said. A thank-you from Davey would have gone a long way toward assuaging Faye's guilt.

Davey had a pained expression. He held one of the leaves that had been removed and tried to slide it back into the volume. Finally, he looked up from the book and at the person and allowed himself a human impulse, or at least allowed himself to succumb to her human need.

"Thank you, by the way," he said, finally looking at her full in the face. "For intervening."

It helped. A little, but it did. Intervention was such a clever, delicate euphemism for what she'd actually done. She shouldn't have been surprised by his poeticism. Wasn't this a place devoted to language?

"I have a dog now. Isn't that ridiculous?" he said. "A Jack Russell. His name's Nero. I just got him."

Faye wanted to tell him about Beans and how much she missed him, but it felt too private for the moment.

"When I walk Nero," Davey continued, "he growls at any big dog that comes near us. He'd throw himself at them if there wasn't a leash."

Once Faye had been walking Beans out in a cornfield, the sun barely over the horizon, when a coyote had come upon them. The coyote raised its ears and bared its teeth and crouched so that it looked ready to pounce and Faye said a silent goodbye to Beans, but then he bared his teeth, too, and he barked and growled and held his ground until the coyote disappeared into the cornstalks. Beans and Faye ran all the way home.

"Nero leaves the little dogs alone, but he knows a threat when he sees one, and he always goes after the big dogs. You were… It was like Nero faced with a big dog," Davey said.

He gazed at her and she felt seen. There was an instant when she was sure he was going to reach out and stroke her cheek.

"You have blood on your face," he said. Then he turned back to the *Commentarii*.

It was only when he said it that she realized she'd been looking at him through blood-speckled glasses. She took them off to try and clean them, and the world in her vision, already dark and blood-soaked, turned even more terrifying when everything blurred. She put the glasses back on without cleaning them.

"You should clean his hands," Mary said. Umu was still working mostly at his face, but Ro's hands, which he had reached up with to stem the bleeding in his throat before he lost consciousness, were stained with blood, too. "I mean, you shouldn't really do anything until the body is cold if you're going to insist on doing it at all. But if you're going to clean him, you start with his hands. That's what they did with my grandpa."

Davey put down the *Commentarii* and came to stand next to Mary. In the near-perfect silence of the basement, he let out a tormented wail, then beat himself upon the chest with his fist.

Umu dropped the pages she was holding, Mary took two steps back from him, Faye wrapped her arms around herself, and Soraya didn't move from her place on the shelf.

"It's, like, respect for the dead," he said. "You have to mourn loud enough that they can hear you."

"His blood is on my shoes, so you're going to need a boom box, at the very least, to generate enough sound," Mary said. She turned back to Umu. "You're supposed to wait until the breath has left the body. He just died. I'll bet there's still breath in there."

Davey let out another pained yawp.

Having no talent for funerary custom, Faye again found herself at loose ends. The basement, which would have been large enough to host a regulation-sized soccer pitch had all the shelves been removed, felt tiny. She couldn't see any of the bars from where she was, but she felt the grating, was aware at every moment that she was in a cage. If Umu, Mary, and Davey found themselves contented and busy with the preparation of a body, or with arguing about the correct manner of preparation of a body, then there was at least one other occupant of the cage who was aware of being trapped.

Soraya lay trembling on her shelf.

"Whoever built this place really hated emergency exits, huh?" Faye said, kneeling on the floor next to Soraya. She could think of nothing better to say. She'd have commented on the weather if she had any view of the outdoors. "Do you think Woodend partnered with the architects to make this place a firetrap so he could use it to kill his wife if pushing her down the stairs didn't do the trick?"

"You have blood on your face," Soraya said, through her chattering teeth. There was so little light where they were, as the undertakers had commandeered most of the flashlights, that it was shocking Soraya could make out anything at all.

"I know," Faye said. She reached to push some of Soraya's hair out of her face. "Davey told me."

As much as she could in the tiny, cramped space on the bookshelf, Soraya reared back. She did so with so much violence that the metal shelves clattered and rattled. Had they been in the B ranges, where the old rolling shelves liked to wobble on their tracks, she might have sent a whole stack tumbling.

"I can smell it on you," Soraya said.

Faye put her hands to her face. There was blood on her hands, too, and Soraya buried her face in her arm to avoid the sight of it.

"I can't smell anything," Faye whispered. It wasn't unlike being a schoolchild on the verge of puberty and being told one stunk. She whispered it so the others wouldn't hear. So they wouldn't hear and come over and sniff and tell her they smelled it, too.

"You stink like his blood," Soraya said into her arm. She moaned like she was in pain, and indeed she must have been, bent into a new geometry, her teeth chattering, her joints crammed against the hard metal shelving.

Faye moved back a bit to give Soraya some space.

"I think it might be your imagination," Faye said.

"It's not."

"Or the drugs telling your body that there's a smell that isn't there. Your brain playing a trick on you." To give Soraya the benefit of the doubt, she stuck her nose in the air and took a big, loud, performative sniff to prove that there was no smell.

She found herself to be a liar. There was a smell. The faint hint of smoke.

———

They say you can't claim to be from somewhere until you've brought a baby into the world and put a body into the ground there. With the untimely end and subsequent burial of Mrs. Woodend, the Woodend family officially became Vermonters.

The librarians, university trustees, lawyers, none of them wished Mrs. Woodend any ill will, but they were all glad to be rid of her husband once he was finally incarcerated for what was very clearly a murder. It wasn't the way they would have chosen to end the story, but it was over, prison bars being the thing that finally prevented Mr. Woodend from pursuing his legal case to get his money back.

For the university's part, they launched a campaign to get the

Woodend name scrubbed from the library. It was an ugly episode, and they could hardly be blamed for not wanting to be reminded of it when they walked past the man's name carved into the stone facade every day.

It was on this matter that Mr. Woodend got his retribution. If the university lawyers had crafted an airtight contract that made it impossible for Mr. Woodend to get his money back once he had promised it to the library, then Woodend's lawyers had done the same to ensure that there was no circumstance in which his name could be removed from the building. There were years more in court fighting the matter. Woodend's guilt, his lack of character, that was never questioned, it was written into the court record, but it was found not to matter because the university had promised that in exchange for taking his money, his name would remain on the building in perpetuity.

In 1926 there was a judgment that the only way the university could proceed with the removal of Woodend's name from the building was by paying back his initial investment, adjusted for inflation. By that point they were willing to do so, but when Woodend was approached, via his lawyer, with the proposition, he refused to take his money back. Facing the rest of his life in prison, he had no need for $400,000.

The Woodend children, on the other hand, could have benefited from that money a great deal, though William Woodend made it clear that he didn't have a lot of concern for their needs the day he murdered their mother. Far from being resentful of their father and the stained legacy he left them, the Woodend heirs embraced the library—*their* library as they saw it. They were Vermonters, after all, tied to the land by the body of their mother. Over the decades the fortunes of the children improved, and rather than use this newfound financial freedom to leave the community that would always remember them as "those poor Woodend kids," they dug in further, involving themselves with the library, donating volumes to build the library's collection of books bound in emerald-green book cloth, attending every public reading, lecture, and symposium, and pointing to the Woodend name proudly. No matter their improved fortunes, no matter their involvement with the institution and their willingness to fill its stacks, no Woodend heir would ever donate a cent for the upkeep or improvement of the library building.

Faye was reminded of it all—the Woodends, their stance toward the improvement of the building, and the woefully inadequate fire suppression system—when she smelled that hint of smoke.

"We forgot the candles." Faye turned back to the others. One of them or all of them had begun to remove Ro's shirt but for some reason had stopped halfway through the process, and now he had one arm in a sleeve and one out of it while the three stood over him and discussed it. "Over in the arena. We forgot about the candles."

"Maybe you'll kill all of us with fire before the night is done," Umu said.

The candles couldn't be left there, they needed to be extinguished, but the truth was she was scared to walk through the dark alone. There wasn't a killer anymore, there wasn't any danger, there was only dark, and yet it was the most terrifying thing she could think of, being alone out there.

"Go put them out if you're worried," Mary said. "I don't know why you lit them in the first place; we have plenty of light from our phones."

Not true. And they'd have even less once the batteries started to go.

"They're probably fine, right?" Faye said. "We left them in the middle of a concrete floor. The worst that can happen is that they burn themselves out."

"They'll probably tip over and light us all on fire and destroy a significant portion of the world's knowledge while roasting us to death alongside these two corpses," Mary said. She had picked up one of the books from Umu's stack and was fanning herself with it. Was it hot? Faye didn't think it was hot.

Davey's full attention was on Ro's body. Faye was lurking now, over his shoulder, over Mary's. She was repulsed by them but she needed to be near them.

"Do you think I should go put out the candles?" she asked Davey.

"What candles?" In the light from her phone, she could see some fresh scratches on his cheeks. The scratches made his mosquito bite look worse, or his mosquito bite made the scratches look worse. He'd torn his cheek open with his own fingernails to demonstrate his grief or to demonstrate how one should demonstrate their grief.

"Is that how it is in the Greek ritual?" she asked, reaching partway for the scratches on his face.

"The Ethiopian," he said. He frowned at her like it was obvious. He wasn't making sense.

"You said we were reenacting the Eleusinian Mysteries."

He gestured at Ro's body in reply, as though she'd somehow missed seeing it.

"But now we have a death and that deserves a ritual, too." He didn't look sad about Ro, he looked sad about the idea of death itself, so much so that she again had the urge to reach out to him.

"Why an Ethiopian ritual?" she asked.

"A custom, really, not a ritual," he said. "It's the one I know best. The one I remember from my mother."

"Do you want to come with me to get those candles?" Faye asked again.

He shook his head.

"Faye, we're preparing the body."

She didn't want to go alone. She didn't want to stay here next to the grotesque evidence of what she'd done. She only wanted to be home.

"I thought it would be safer if someone went to get them," Faye said, but Davey was no longer listening.

She had a picture of it in her mind. One of the candles burnt down far enough that the heat from the wick warmed the pool of hardened wax that was keeping the candle upright. The thing tilting sideways, slowly at first and then toppling all the way over. Fine. No problem, not at first, but then a little tuft of that ever-present dust was stirred up and blew past the active flame. They'd be so happy to see one another, the flame and the dust. Fast friends. Maybe the tuft of dust would carry on blowing, alight with flame, or maybe it would just be an ember, but it would get to the stacks eventually. It wasn't the flames that would overpower them, Faye thought. It was the smoke that would kill them first.

"Soraya, I'm going to find a fire alarm!" Faye said, springing back over to Soraya with delight at her realization.

There was a flicker of lucidity in Soraya. She lifted her face a little, pulled it out of her shirt.

"I've never seen a fire alarm here," she said.

"No one sees fire alarms," Faye said. She wanted to stroke the hair out of Soraya's eyes, wanted to take her hand so they could both be touching someone. "They're ubiquitous. You don't notice they're there until you need one. We need one now. We'll pull it and help will come."

If she'd kept the light trained on the floor it might have been better or if she'd stayed a few steps back it might have been better, but there had been some real lucidity, she was sure there was progress for a minute there. The change came when Soraya looked her full in the face.

"Look at you," she moaned.

Faye looked down at her clothes, self-conscious, but this wasn't an older girl looking to tease her about her apparel.

"There's blood all over your face," Soraya said. "I can smell it, I can smell the blood on you." She buried her face back in her arm. Whatever lucidity had been there, it was gone.

"Can someone come with me?" Faye asked, looking back toward the others. "It'll be quicker with two people. We'll stay at the perimeter. If there's an alarm, it'll be along a wall somewhere. We pull the alarm and help will come and you won't have to do whatever it is you're doing right now."

Davey had a white sock, the last of Ro's clothing. He would have been a beautiful man if he'd lived long enough for real manhood. Nice calves, Faye thought. Perhaps because he had a job that kept him on his feet a lot.

"I'm going to find a fire alarm to pull," Faye said. "I'm going to get us out of here."

Despite only having access to paper and leather, Umu had done an effective job of cleaning Ro's face. In the dark, his eyelashes and eyebrows looked like they'd been darkened with makeup, not with blood, and the fine curve of his cheekbones was free from blemish.

"We should move to the anointing," Davey said.

"Where are you going to get oils for anointing?" Mary asked.

Here, finally, Faye could make herself useful. She went into her pocket, not for a weapon but for the rose-scented lip gloss. Without a word, she handed it to Davey.

"I have lip balm," Davey said. He held it like it had been his all along and showed the others. She didn't mind that he didn't credit her. She wasn't looking for plaudits; she was looking for peace with the dead. "Not exactly perfumed oil but pretty damn close for an improvisation." Davey held it to his nose and sniffed. "It's scented."

"Are you going to do the anointing, babe?" Mary asked Umu.

Standing to the side, her request for a partner for her fire alarm mission ignored, Faye waited for Umu to rage at the suggestion. Here was her friend, his youth radiating up at them now that his face was clean, who had been struck down by a group of strangers. How could she be anything but furious at this charade by the group who demonstrably had cared not at all about her friend in life, who had called him a murderer and celebrated his death?

Umu took one of her hands from the side of Ro's face. To shake a fist at Davey? To slap that lip gloss out of his hands? To tear her own hair out in grief?

No.

She took the makeup that Davey offered. Her own phone lay on the floor, face up by Ro's bare shoulder. It illuminated her face better than it did his, but the angle of the light cast strange shadows, made it impossible to clearly make out facial expressions because every feature was so exaggerated by the severe interplay of light and dark. Was she sneering? Weeping?

When she took the lip gloss, it was like the shadow disappeared and her features were just her features again. Soft and young and unbothered, like a twenty-two-year-old girl should be. Ro's lips were slightly parted, the skin at their bow slightly cracked. She took the cap off the gloss and applied it to those unmoving lips, first to the bottom, then to the top. In her own small way, she anointed him, laying the scented oil upon his skin so he would feel no pain when he crossed over to the other side.

"I'm going," Faye said. She was embarrassed by the intimacy of Umu's gesture. "You'll know I've found a way out when you hear the fire alarm ringing."

Umu put the cap back on the little plastic tube, and the moment was over. The shadows found her features again and formed a disgusting display. You could only think, when looking at her, that she'd swallowed something repulsive.

"This was yours?" Umu held the little pot toward Faye without looking at her. She kept her eyes on Ro.

The idea that Umu would thank her made it all so much more bearable, made her think that the door to forgiveness had been opened. She reached to take the pot back from Umu, knowing that for a moment they would graze fingertips and she'd feel that electrical shock of redemption.

Umu let the pot fall to the floor. The plastic lid snapped in two when it made impact.

"When we had that poli-sci class together, I remember you from that," Umu said. "I even told Ro about you. How I was impressed that you didn't wear any makeup, especially since there were so many lip-filler Barbies in that class. But I guess I was wrong about that, huh?" Umu did take her eyes off Ro, finally, but it wasn't to look at Faye, it was to look at the broken pot of lip gloss. "Guess nothing about you is quite what it seems though, is it?"

She didn't want to go alone, Faye didn't want to go out into the dark alone, but she owed it to them. They weren't in their right minds, they were grieving, they were terrified, and she, with her prefrontal cortex in order, with her reasonable serotonin levels, had promised to protect them. She owed it to Umu. She needed Faye to find their way out.

"You'll keep an eye on Soraya?" she said. To none of them, to all of them. And she walked away, out into the dark to do the thing she had promised.

III

"You're not even chanting!" Mary said. Faye could hear them until she couldn't. She went back to the arena first. The way back was familiar; there would be light when she got there; it wasn't so bad, going there alone.

The Persephone myth, the one they were meant to be reenacting in the ritual, started a little like this, with a maiden who wanders off alone. When she read the story in one of those library books, Faye was surprised that she didn't already know it. If Demeter was the goddess of agriculture, shouldn't Faye have grown up with the story? She thought that may have been why Davey invited her. It was all wrong though. Real farm people were too practical for stories and prayers. They knew that the thing that made the corn grow year after year was work.

The story didn't start with Demeter, but with her daughter. Persephone was abducted by Hades, god of the dead, as she gathered flowers. As far as Faye could tell, the Greeks were always writing about maidens being abducted as they gathered flowers. It was like they thought the trope lent a little romance to their rape stories.

Demeter searched the world, or Greece at least, for her daughter, and then finally in her grief, she wandered to Eleusis, where she disguised herself as a mortal. When the Eleusinians learned there was a god among them, they were filled with awe. They built her a temple to honor her, but she didn't want honor; she wanted her daughter. She was too aggrieved to move from Eleusis, to rejoin the rest of the gods in the heavenly realm, and in her grief, she caused a year-long period of sterility in the harvest that threatened to starve the mortals throughout the world.

Zeus tried to bribe Demeter into returning to her place among the gods, but his gifts were as little use to her as the honors of the

Eleusinian people were. She wanted none of it; she only wanted Persephone. So Zeus went to Hades instead. Not with gifts but with threats. And it was those threats that finally freed Persephone. Hades said that he'd let her leave the underworld to go see her mother, but before she left, he tricked her into swallowing a pomegranate seed, and that morsel of food tied Persephone to the underworld forever.

Faye was starving. Her eyes watered at the idea of a mouthful of pomegranate seeds.

Demeter was devastated that she'd found her daughter only to lose her again, so Zeus and Hades struck a deal. Persephone would be tied to Hades forever, as he intended. She'd spend part of the year in the underworld with him and part of the year with her mother.

Faye had made a choice to move across the country from her mother. No one tricked her, no one forced her. But she was still devastated by the distance every single day. She'd arrived in Vermont with a bout of homesickness so intense she thought it might swallow her whole. And then time passed and what was left wasn't homesickness; instead, she walked around a dark blue sort of lonesome all the time.

"Introduce yourself to some people," her mother, who had lived in the same town all her life, would say on the phone. She was a great mom, but it was terrible advice.

When Faye had been sitting at the picnic bench the day Umu invited her to the roller skating party, it was the type of interaction her mother thought happened all the time. She never even told her mom about it because she would have been so disappointed that Faye refused to lace up her skates and go.

What if she'd gone roller skating? What if she hadn't been afraid for once in her life? How different would everything be?

Faye opened the messages in her phone and scrolled all the way back until she found it. She hadn't even bothered to save Umu as a contact because she knew the girl would never talk to her again after the declined invitation, but the text with the party details was still there. It was right below another message, from a classmate named Frankie inviting her to a study group. Frankie had likely sent that invitation to every person in the class, just to be polite. She'd declined that one, too.

She knew it wouldn't send until the morning, but she started to write a message, belatedly replying to Umu. Should she apologize about Ro? Suggest they go out for a coffee and talk about everything that happened? Offer to take Umu roller skating? She hovered in the light of the message screen for a long time, but she never could figure out what to say.

In the story of Persephone, after the bargain was struck, Demeter returned to live among the gods, and the world bore fruit and grain again, but every year when Demeter was separated from her daughter anew, the fields were once again barren. It was a story about an imperfect outcome.

When Faye arrived at the arena, she saw that one of the candles had gone out. It hadn't tipped over, it hadn't taken anything with it. The flame disappeared as though helped by a puff of air from a ghost. That would have been the little bit of smoke Faye smelled, when the flame went out. Around the corner, Kip's body was laid out flat, but she didn't go check on it. She could only hope the others had exhausted all the grief in their bodies on their treatment of Ro.

Faye went to the remaining candles and blew, puff, puff, puff. It was only in the light of the very last one that she caught sight of her hands. She'd been holding her phone, casting light with it all this time. She'd looked right at them when she'd been looking at her messages, but somehow the sight had escaped her. Her hands were stiff with blood. Blood in the dry beds of her fingernails and staining the lines in her palms. She scratched at it to try and flake it off, wiped it on her jeans, spit on the backs of her hands to try and get them clean, but she couldn't. The blood stuck like a tattoo so she couldn't forget what she'd done.

CHAPTER 17

SORAYA

I

Soraya lifted her head out of her shirt a bit. She didn't want to; she didn't want to see anything or smell anything or hear anything more. As it was, the noises were too loud, and the colors were too bright, and the smells—it was the smells she worried might kill her. She'd have stayed curled in on herself, but no matter the terror, it was a human reaction to raise one's head when one's name is called.

"You'll keep an eye on Soraya?" the new girl said, and then she disappeared around a corner. Faye, her name was Faye. Soraya's memory wasn't impacted, just her sense of what was happening. Faye had worked at the library for how long now, a month? Two? She crept around like a little mouse and kept to the basement, but Davey had reminded Soraya over and over to stop calling her the "new girl" and to use her name on the night in the library.

"We need a seventh and she's harmless," Davey had said, as though harm had crossed their minds at all. She wasn't a crocodile, the new girl, just wallpaper. "She's helping us by being there, and you'll scare her off by being unkind."

How would they categorize her now that she had stabbed

Umu's friend in the throat? Still harmless? Soraya wasn't upset Faye had done it. Whatever the boy had or hadn't done to Kip, she didn't like being down there with strangers, not feeling the way she was feeling right now, and he had been a stranger. Soraya reached down and pressed the blister on her bare right foot. It hurt, but that was what she was looking for—a sensation she recognized.

She was happy the new girl had run off to wherever she'd gone. Soraya didn't think she'd ever heard her speak, not before tonight, and she was startled every time the new girl opened her mouth. Davey and Mary were bickering about chanting at the moment, but Davey and Mary were familiar. There was nothing terrifying about the familiar.

"You've set yourself back three years." That's what her father had said to her when she'd come home and told him she'd be working at the library during grad school, instead of interning with a management consultancy or tech company. She read Greek and Latin because her father insisted she study them in high school when he still thought she was going to medical school, but she still felt like an outsider those first months at the library. Because her father told her she didn't belong there, because she had no illusions about making a career in rare books, because she took the job for the impressive hourly rate rather than what it could promise for her future. An internship at a management consultancy would pay nothing, and the library paid enough for her to get her own apartment, and if she wasn't enamored of the idea of the world of books and libraries the same way the others were in those first weeks and months, she made up for it fast. It's what the new girl didn't understand. You couldn't just work at this place. You had to give yourself to it.

II

Soraya met Kip after she'd been working at the library for two weeks. She was good at it—working at the library, that is—as she'd known she would be. The bibliographical functions of her job were precise and exacting, just like she was. Once Ronald had patiently run through something with her—how to measure a book's height to determine its shelf placement, the necessity to go through every single page of a book so she could describe if there were any plates or maps missing—she didn't have to be told twice. She liked to watch the minutes tick by while she worked and calculate how much money she'd made: $100 by lunch. Ten more times that and she'd have a month's rent that she hadn't taken from her father. It was a whole new world.

Her second week, she was assigned to work in the reading room on a day Kip came in as a reader. He was tall. She liked tall men. Soraya's father was short, and she liked to imagine bringing a tall man home and her father being the one who was made to feel inadequate.

"I have some materials that should be waiting for me," Kip said. "At least I think I do." He nodded at the shelving behind her where reader requests waited to be taken to one of the oak tables that lined the room. It was concerningly bare.

"I'm sure I can help," she'd said, with the bright positivity of someone who'd been on the job for less than a month. "You have to fill out one of these little slips, and we go up to the stacks and get what you've requested." She helpfully produced one of the printed slips. "Use one slip per book, if you're requesting more than one. Now, in the future, you can do this online and the books will be waiting for you when you arrive. There's a two-hour turnaround on book pickup, so you might have to wait a little bit today," she said. "Unfortunately."

He was smirking. She could feel her dress sticking to the sweat on her lower back, though she hadn't done anything wrong. The library was well air-conditioned, but Soraya was prone to sweat when she was anxious. They were alone in the reading room until that moment when Davey wheeled a groaning book truck through the creaky door.

"I should have known it was you," Davey said, and he abandoned the truck to come around and shake Kip's hand.

"You know each other?" Soraya said.

Kip was still smirking. "Yeah. I've been here once or twice before. But thanks for the run-through on the workings of the library. It was…" He cast his eyes down her from top to toe. "Educational."

"Kip is Kip Pickens," Davey said. "Like the Pickens collection?" Soraya braced when he said "Pickens" for him to say the next bit, but he didn't. Her well-paying job was the Pickens Fellowship. She was relieved that Davey had the tact to avoid saying that this man or some relative of his was paying for her to be there, was paying her rent. She fought back for some composure.

"So, this is all to say you know your way around a request slip?" she said.

"No, you were right that he doesn't," Davey said. He was piling the books from the truck onto one of the reading tables. Not exactly protocol. They were meant to sit on the shelf behind her and be doled out to the reader one book at a time so she could keep count of them. "Kip called in his list half an hour ago. Being the library's most important family has to have some perks, right, Kip?"

"For you, I can start using request slips," Kip said with a wink, and then he sat at his desk, surrounded by his pile of books.

They didn't say anything else to one another until Kip was ready to leave that day. Over the next couple of hours, as he sat reading and making notes on a yellow legal pad with an expensive-looking mechanical pencil and she helped readers claim their books, she caught him looking at her a few times, but she always averted her eyes. Holding his gaze would be too forward.

When he was ready to leave that day, he was again the only reader

in the room. Maybe he'd timed it out that way, waited for everyone
to leave so he could get her alone or maybe he didn't care, maybe
one didn't care at all about being overheard when they had the type
of cachet he did.

The reading room got its best light in the morning, and in late
afternoon it had a gloomy grayness, like it was lit as the setting for
a horror movie. Kip and Soraya dated for two years after that day,
after he came and sat on her desk and told her he was taking her for
a drink, and she'd always associate him with that grayness. She was
surprised when he asked her out, but she could hardly refuse. "The
library's most important family." It had to come with some perks.

He left the library with a promise to pick her up a couple of hours
later when she had finished her shift. The pile of books he'd been
using was still stacked up on his reading table.

———

"If you're going to let Davey fuck you, you should probably move
down to the floor," Kip said. Soraya opened her eyes and there
he was, sitting cross-legged on the concrete in front of her, the
crimson blood that stained his chin, his neck, his shirt, shining in
the meager light of someone's flashlight. It hurt her neck to crane
and look at him. Even sitting, he was so tall.

"You woke up?" Soraya said, trying to lift her head and see. Her
hand was still by her foot, so she pressed harder on the blister. Not
ten feet away from her, Davey and Mary and Umu were bent over
Ro's body, talking about wreaths or coffins or something. Strange
that they wouldn't have told her that Kip woke up.

"Stand up so I can look at you," he said.

She swung one leg off the shelf, and then the other. She had to
bend her neck at an unnatural angle to keep from bashing her head
on the shelf above. Kip's breath came out in cold weather clouds
when he spoke, though she didn't feel cold in the basement at all.

"Are you mad at me?" she said. She reached to touch his arm, but he pulled back from her.

"I told you why he invited you, but then you knew better. You always know better, huh?" Kip said. "Who's going to bring you flowers at graduation now?"

This Kip-like thing in front of her was tall like Kip, wore the button-down shirt she'd ironed for Kip that morning, sounded like Kip, was even mean like Kip, but she understood that it couldn't be Kip.

"If you weren't such a little slut, you'd still have someone to bring you flowers at graduation," Kip said.

It was her imagination, it was the drugs, it was her imagination and the drugs in concert with each other. Soraya was a smart girl, she knew that. Even if this figment of her imagination bore an uncanny resemblance to the real thing, it was her own invention. If it was her own mind that made him, then her mind should be able to make him go away, but no matter how hard she willed it, this eerie vision of Kip blocked her path to the others.

III

"You guys," Soraya called, trying to see around Kip to the others. "Can you come help me?"

When she was little, really through to when she was a teenager, Soraya would have terrible, violent nightmares. In movies when children had nightmares, they called out for their parents, and then someone always came running to soothe them and smooth their blankets and help them fall asleep. No one ever came to Soraya's room. For a long time she resented her mother for that, but in her late teens she learned that she suffered from sleep paralysis and that all those times, through her whole childhood, when she thought she was calling for someone to come and help, her body wasn't doing the thing she asked it to do. Her mother didn't come to Soraya's bedside because when Soraya screamed, it didn't make any noise.

Now, trying to see around Kip, trying to get attention from Davey or Mary, she felt paralyzed again.

"You want me to leave so you can be alone with him?" Kip said, blocking Soraya's path to the others. "You slut, my blood hasn't even dried."

"Soraya!" It was Mary who was calling her name. Mary could see her, Mary would help her. "Welcome back to the land of the living! Did you enjoy your little snooze?"

"You should lie back down," Kip said. "Right here on the floor with your legs spread until he notices you. That's what you want, isn't it?"

"No." Soraya managed to take a few steps toward the others. Kip stepped back as she moved forward, but he didn't step out of the way to clear her path. "Can you help me?" she said again. She hovered over their scene, over Ro's body. They had taken his clothes off. He had a tattoo that had been hidden beneath his shirt or that they'd just given him. Impossible to know.

"You coming to chant, babe?" Mary asked. "It'll make you feel better. It's catharsis." The lights from their upturned flashlights were bright and brought spots to Soraya's eyes.

Umu was seated with Ro's head in her lap and she was saying nothing. In her, Soraya could see the same type of unsteadiness she felt in herself. Mary was working through her trip more easily, it seemed. But then, things always seemed to come easily to Mary.

Soraya was so afraid. Why weren't the others more afraid? She thought of what they might have whispered while she was out of earshot. She'd seen that at work, too, Davey and Mary whispering sometimes. Soraya didn't look at Davey to see how he was coping. She didn't want Kip to see her look.

"A funerary ritual can get us back on the right path." Davey came right up to Soraya and whispered it in her ear. His right eye was swollen, and she could swear it was pulsing in time with her own heartbeat. "If we start here it means the night won't be wasted. There's still hours to do away with our fear."

His breath was hot against her neck. She didn't move toward him or away from him. She was too frozen in fear. Kip glared at him, at how close he was standing.

"I'm having a bad trip," Soraya said. "I can't tell what's real and what isn't, and I need to get out of the library." This time she said it out loud. She was certain she did.

"Come here," Davey said. He put his hands on her wrist. Kip wouldn't like that. "You're only frightened because you're over there alone."

"He can see you," Soraya said, but Davey had already turned his attention back to the body. His hand on her wrist, he pulled her over to Ro, and while he succeeded in getting her past Kip, his specter stayed behind her. Not gone, but out of her immediate field of vision.

Ro had a tattoo, and Soraya would have asked Umu about it if not for the smell. From somewhere down in their cage, there was a faint waft of smoke.

"Do you smell that?" she asked.

"If you start on about the smell of blood again, I'll have you tied up," Umu said.

Soraya looked behind her, to where she thought the smell was coming from. Kip was still there, looking at her in the disapproving way he had when she used the wrong tense of a Greek verb. She couldn't see any smoke, but then, she couldn't see much of anything. Was it real?

"It's really faint," Soraya said. "But it's smoke. Can you smell it?"

Then it wasn't faint. Almost as soon as she smelled the smoke, it was all she could smell, and while it was a relief to be spared the metallic and meaty odor of blood, the smoke quickly overtook her. When she looked back at Kip, he was bathed in a gray cloud.

"You're all crazy. We're going to burn," she said. When she ran past Kip, she was scared he would grab her arm and stop her, but he let her go.

It was the running that finally got them paying attention to her, but by then it was too late. She wasn't going to stop for anyone.

"Soraya! Stop running and I'll come get you!" Davey's voice cut through the dark. There was murmuring, too. They were murmuring about her. They'd all talked about it like it was so tidy. Ro killed Kip and then Faye killed Ro so there was no more danger, but now she could smell the smoke and they pretended they couldn't and she knew for certain there was someone down there who was trying to kill her.

"I'm not going to burn down here!" she yelled to Davey, and she kept going forward. It was so dark, almost fully black. She touched her pockets but came back empty. Where was her phone? Had someone taken her phone?

"She's not being a baby; she's having a bad trip," she heard Umu say. "Go talk to her about clouds or whatever until she's seeing straight and can sit here without whining about what she smells."

That they wanted her to come there, there where she had smelled the smoke, was proof that they didn't care about her safety. Maybe they weren't trapped down there with her. Maybe they were in on it.

Without her light she couldn't run, but if she wasn't running she could move quietly and keep them from finding her. She ran her hands along the edge of a shelf until she hit the wood and then she wound her way around and continued that way in the dark— fingertips against book spines until she felt resistance. Could she smell the smoke anymore? It didn't matter, it was there, somewhere, and coming for her.

"Soraya, you're going to hurt yourself." Davey's voice was some-where in the distance. She moved more quickly, fingertips on book spines, waiting to meet resistance until she knew where to turn when she ran into the hard metal security grating with her whole body.

The force of it was enough to knock her off her feet, the sound of it, of her body hitting the metal, reverberated through the base-ment. She didn't know if she was hurt and she didn't care. If she was at the grating, then she was close to a way out. In some places, not everywhere, but in some places, the grate didn't go all the way up to the ceiling. There was plumbing and electrical wiring that prevented it. She couldn't see where she was, she couldn't know if it was worth climbing, but a failed attempt was better than dying in here without trying. She was little; she'd subsisted mostly on green juice since she was sixteen. She only needed a bit of space to pass through. Finally, her deprivation would pay off.

She tried to wedge her toe into the grating, but the weave was too narrow. She kicked off her left shoe. With her fingers laced through the metal, she stuck her bare toes into the grate, but her first attempt to hoist herself up failed. It wasn't enough to hold on to, she couldn't carry the weight of her whole body with her toes.

She rolled the shelving stack closer to her and tried it that way. Fingers laced through the grate, bare foot on the second shelf, and up she went. She was climbing!

"I'm going home, I'm going home, I'm going home," she whispered as she prepared to swing her right foot to a higher shelf. "I'm going home!"

She had to support the full weight of her body—a body made of green juice but still an adult body—with her fingers through the grate for a moment as she swung her leg out and she was doing it. She was going to reach the top, until she felt a strong pair of arms wrap around her waist and yank her down.

IV

"Soraya, what the hell are you doing?" Davey said, and as he pulled her, the incomplete grasp she'd had on the grating dissolved, and the upward progress she'd made disappeared.

"I'm getting out," she said. She tried to twist away, to kick, to pull, but his grasp was firm.

"Soraya?" He held her tight by the waist as she thrashed against him. Her right foot was still propped up on the third shelf of the bookstack, that last little bit of proof that she'd been on the way up when he'd pulled her. "You're going to hurt yourself. Do you understand that?"

She wasn't wearing any shoes, and now that she was no longer climbing, she wished that weren't the case. Shoes would make her steadier. She gave a last thrash but succeeded only in kicking the bookshelf into a threatening sway and knocking Davey off-balance while he continued to hold her. They both fell to the ground in a strange slow-motion tumble that ended with her on her back and his fleshy palm supporting her head so she wouldn't hit it on the concrete.

"Where were you going?" he whispered. The hand that wasn't holding her head held his phone, the flashlight shining. In a subtle show that he didn't trust her not to run off again, he kept that arm crossed over her chest. It was all terribly confusing. His hand on her head made her feel safer, like when someone strokes your hair, and when she tried to, she couldn't smell the smoke anymore.

"Come back with me. Back to the others. We should have listened when you said you were scared. We weren't doing a good job of taking care of each other."

Had she dreamed the smoke in the first place? Or was it only imagination that the smell was now gone? She didn't know what was real and what wasn't, didn't know who was a threat and who wasn't.

"What about the fire?" Soraya said.

"The fire?" He shifted his weight and she could feel his ribs against hers. "We can go get the candles from where we left them. It's still six hours at least before someone comes down here. We can do a little bit of the ritual or even the whole thing, and none of us will have to worry about being afraid anymore. No matter what we saw down here, we'll leave here without any of our fear. How does that sound?"

"What do you want me to do?"

He was shining his light at her so he could see her, but the side effect was that the brilliant white light shone right in her eyes. She tried, but she couldn't keep them open. It seemed, thought Soraya, that lying flat on the floor, with her head supported and her eyes closed, was just about as far from harm as she was going to feel until the gates opened and she could go home to her sage-green linen sheets. Davey had said something about candles, but she'd already forgotten it.

"Try not to fall asleep," his voice said through the dark, but she was heavy and tired and comfortable, and Soraya thought it rude that he wouldn't let her drift off, that he didn't want to drift off with her when they were both so comfortable.

"I don't smell smoke anymore," she said.

"There was never any," he said. There had been smoke, she'd smelled it, but she forgot all about it because when she blinked her sleepy eyes to correct him, it was Kip's face looking back at her, it was Kip's arms she was wrapped in, not Davey's.

She knew better than to ask where Davey had gone. Kip wouldn't like that. And besides, he was here now, the mechanics of how didn't matter.

"Are you going to keep me safe?" she asked. It was the right question. Kip could sometimes have angry eyes, but he didn't right then and he liked being reminded of his promises. The hand on the back of her head, Kip had never done that, but he had always said that it was his job to take care of her. When they ate at restaurants and she suggested splitting the bill, when she suggested spending a night out with just her girlfriends, he wouldn't hear of it. It was his job to take care of her. She hadn't believed him most of the time, but just now the hand on the back of her head made her feel taken care of, and she was overtaken by a wave of tenderness that she hadn't felt for Kip in a long, long time. If she was being honest, she wasn't sure she ever had.

"I'm so happy you're here," she said, and it was true. If nothing else, Kip was a devil she knew. She lifted her head and kissed him.

"Are you sure?" he started to say, but she wouldn't let him. She didn't want to talk. His hands weren't free but hers were and she held the back of his neck and pulled him to her. He pulled back at first. She wasn't surprised. She so rarely initiated that he had to be wondering what she was doing, but she was insistent, and it didn't take long for him to respond, to kiss back with the same desperate ravenousness she had.

"I don't want to talk. I want to feel better," she said.

It felt good, kissing him. Better than it usually did. When he bit at her lower lip, he didn't hurt her. She closed her eyes. Soraya wasn't tired anymore, the feeling of being kissed this way, on these drugs, was so overwhelming she didn't think she'd ever sleep again. She didn't often close her eyes when Kip was kissing her.

The first time she'd slept with Kip was at his off-campus apartment after their third date. They'd gone for drinks with a group of other graduate students. He drank too much, she sipped a single beer all night, but he'd driven them and didn't like anyone else driving his car, so they walked to his nearby apartment. He started taking her clothes off as soon as they got inside, and the whole time he talked about the way his high school girlfriend used to like it best when he was on top. It was never dangerous or scary and he fell asleep quickly after, but Soraya's body knew something she didn't, and she always kept her eyes open after that. For what, she didn't know, but her body did and it kept her eyes open.

Kip's phone clattered to the ground and the hand that held it was on her skin. She remembered being afraid. She remembered that she'd wanted out of the basement, but her head was flooded with too much of everything and she couldn't remember why.

Did he unbutton her shirt? Did she? She didn't remember that, either, but it was open and his lips moved down her neck, over her skin.

She gasped at how good it felt. Kip had always told her she was lucky to be with him, but she'd never felt that way until this very moment, when his lips reached her belly. In the bliss of the moment, she turned her head and moaned and opened her eyes. Davey's phone was on the floor beside them, the flashlight faced up and pointed at the ceiling.

She saw the curve of the nose first. That nose that was always pointed up in the air, she saw it in silhouette, at eye level with her, so on the floor. She saw the shoes, brown leather, that she'd helped to pick out. The trousers, the ones that had been hanging on the back of the chair in the bedroom that morning. The bloodstained shirtfront and the fullness of that familiar face. She saw the whole of him, of Kip, illuminated by the light of the phone, lying dead not ten feet from her. She began to tremble, and it wasn't from pleasure. Because if Kip was lying dead on the floor, then who was lying on top of her?

"Why are you touching me?" Soraya said, and she leaped to her feet, pushing the man, pushing Davey, all the way off her. She stood with her back against the grate, fingers laced through it, and Davey lay on the floor, bracing himself on his arms and trying to meet her eyes.

A little giggle came from the right of them. It was a reedy sound like a poorly tuned flute. Kip, who had been lying dead on the floor a moment ago, was now standing to the right of them, giggling at her in his strange pitch.

"I thought we were on the same page," Davey said. His phone was still on the ground, between them and Kip, its light faced up to

illuminate the strange interaction. "I'm so sorry. I know Kip just…"
He looked to the right to where Kip was standing. "It's on me; I
should have known better."

"I can see your tits; cover yourself up," Kip said, and Soraya was
horrified that he was right, that her shirt was hanging open. She
pulled it closed, crossed her arms over herself.

"Here, let me help you," Davey said. He got to his feet and reached
toward her to help with her buttons.

"Was I right or was I right?" Kip said, and then there was that
sickening giggle again. "The only reason he wanted you here was to
fuck you."

Weeks ago, when he'd begun to plan the event, Davey told Soraya
that she was the first person he invited.

"Am I flattered, or do I take this to mean that you don't have
enough friends?" she asked.

"Neither, not exactly," he'd said. They'd been in the basement
together, this very basement, where he was helping her unpack a
recent donation. Two hundred boxes of books from the personal
library of a prominent midcentury philosopher. "I'm determined to
convert you," he said.

"Convert me?" She put her hand to her mouth, feigning a gasp.
"It's just as my grandpa feared when my parents got on that plane
to America."

"We've worked here for two years together now," Davey said,
tearing into the next carton with a box cutter. "In a few weeks, you'll
be wearing a Patagonia vest and sipping a free cortado in the break
room of whatever giant tech conglomerate or mercenary management consultancy is lucky enough to land you. Give me one last
chance to get you hooked on the *stuff* we have down here."

She was elbow deep in the stuff, but she couldn't argue. She'd never been romantic about the place the way the rest of them were. Taking the job in the first place, that was her great act, the way she showcased her poetic soul. Beyond that, she'd been too immersed in trying to be effective and efficient to spend her time swooning over every decorative drop cap. It wasn't that she didn't love the *stuff* as much as the rest of them, but she was a serious person brought up to always appear serious, and all that seriousness had paid off.

One night, she'd told herself. Go and be a fool and give yourself over to Davey's little ritual. Do some drugs and stay up until dawn for one night and then you can be serious for the rest of your life. She'd been so excited about it until Kip announced he was coming, too.

———

"Think he'll still get it up for you once you tell him the news?" Kip said.

She slammed against the grating, pulling back from Davey and his offer of help. "What is happening?" she said. Kip was right there, talking to her, but he was also there, dead on the floor, and Davey kept trying to touch her, and none of it made any sense.

"The drugs, the stress of everything that's gone on," Davey put his hands up and backed away from her. "We were over our heads. I was over my head."

"He was seizing the moment; he's always wanted a chance at your body," Kip said.

Davey looked where Soraya was looking, over at Kip.

"We'll find a way to honor him, to remember him, that you can feel really good about. When our heads are clear I can help you do that. For tonight though, we have to focus on getting out of here safely."

"Why are you being so nice to me?" she asked.

"I'm the one who trapped you down here," Davey said. He took a cautious step toward her. "I was excited when you agreed to come. I never could have imagined…"

"Why were you excited?" she asked.

"Here we go!" Kip clapped his hands together triumphantly. "We get some honesty!"

"You know that I've always been crazy about you," Davey said.

"That he's always wanted to fuck you," Kip chimed in. "I'll bet he killed me to get at you."

Was Kip right? Had Davey been the one to poison him? How? When? She wished her head were clearer.

"I didn't know you felt that way," she said, wrapping her arms more tightly around her own body. Was that true? That she hadn't known? Down in the basement with the philosopher's boxes, breaking down cardboard for each other, reaching for the box cutter at the same time and touching hands, staying down there longer than was needed. Didn't she know?

"You weren't supposed to know," Davey said. "You've been with Kip almost the entire time I've known you. But we were going to have this great last night together, I was going to emerge free from fear, and I was finally going to have the nerve to tell you. And if you rejected me, it wouldn't matter because it would be morning and you wouldn't work here anymore."

Kip came right over to Soraya to whisper in her ear, hissing hot breath at her.

"Now it's your turn to tell him. Let's see what some honesty does for his feelings."

"I'm still going to work here in the morning," she said, feeling, as always, that she had to do as she was told. "I'm going to work here tomorrow and the next day and for the foreseeable future."

Davey didn't look upset yet. He didn't understand.

"You're the one who's not going to work here," Soraya said. "I got the job. Not you."

"What the hell are you talking about?" Davey said. His hands were clenched into fists.

"The permanent job here. Ronald made us all apply. He offered me the job last week. The reason he hasn't said anything to you was that I only signed to accept the position today. I only decided today."

"He gave you *my* job?" Davey said. Now he was the one trembling. Not with fear, but with rage.

"Happy now, slut?" Kip whispered in her ear. "Now you have neither of us."

She reared back to get away from Kip's hot breath, to get away from Davey's clenched fists, and she stumbled on her Bambi legs. It happened in slow motion—one missed step, a failed recovery, a hand on the bookshelf that swayed again, threatened to spill over, and then she slammed onto the ground. Right onto Kip's cold body. She looked behind her and Kip's specter was gone. There was only his corpse, frigid in death, and Davey standing behind her, hot with rage. She had to get out of there. So she did the only thing her body would let her do. She ran.

CHAPTER 18

UMU

I

Save for the tattoo, Ro's naked body looked to Umu exactly the way he used to when they were children and they used to swim together. She was the stronger swimmer, he was the fearless one. He would drag them over fences, through bushes, to wherever there was water, and she'd sometimes have to drag him home, his scrawny arms wrapped around her neck as she kicked with all her might to get them back to safety. Back on the shore, or the dock, or the pool deck, he'd laugh and laugh and then pull them on to their next adventure. 'Tis not too late to seek a newer world. It was always just the two of them, and now here they were again, Umu and Ro, all alone. Except she couldn't pull him back to safety. There were no new worlds for them to explore.

The rest had gone to chase a fire that wasn't burning. Faye first, determined to pull a fire alarm that the rest of them insisted she wouldn't find, had been gone for what felt like half an hour. Good riddance. Her sad eyes and whispered apologies, as if Ro's death was somehow hardest for her, a tragedy for her, were more than Umu could stand. Not while Ro lay here, his body barely cold. If she had a heavy conscience, then good. Umu hoped Faye carried Ro's death for the rest of her life.

Soraya had gone after, chasing smoke the rest of them didn't smell. Umu wasn't surprised at Soraya's bad trip. From everything Kip had said about his girlfriend, it would be shocking to learn she'd ever even smoked weed before. Why she'd been willing to jump right to acid was a Stonehenge-sized mystery, as was the question of why her supposed friends hadn't planned on guiding her through.

Davey chased after Soraya, of course. She'd known them all of five minutes when she clocked that he was gagging after Kip's girlfriend. The only mystery was why Soraya wouldn't have gone for him over Kip. Neither Kip nor Davey was especially pleasant to be around, but Davey at least had the advantage of a nice smile.

Mary said she was going after Davey not long after he said he was going after Soraya. That part hadn't made a lot of sense, but it didn't matter, not to Umu. It was a relief to be rid of them all. Sure as she was that Ro couldn't have killed Kip, it meant that one of them had. She'd been placating them, letting them play at their funerary rituals to avoid arousing anyone's anger, lest she become a target, but what she wanted was for them all to stay as far away from her as possible.

Ro had been so mad when she'd told him she was coming to this stupid ritual.

"Your professor wants you to buy drugs from me?" he'd asked. He'd been shutting down the bar at Applebee's. She sat on one of his barstools, eating maraschino cherries while he unpacked clean glassware.

"He's not my professor. He's a TA. It's a different thing."

He hoisted a tray of wineglasses onto the counter for her to unpack into the cabinet on the other side of the bar. She hopped down from her stool. They had this part well choreographed.

"Sorry I don't have my higher education labels all straight," he said. "Please, draw me an org chart on a cocktail napkin."

"What I'm saying is he's a student, too," Umu said. "He's a PhD student. The professor gives the lecture and Kip runs the tutorials, helps grade papers, that sort of thing. We don't call him Mr. Pickens or Professor Pickens or whatever. He's just Kip."

"But he stands at the front of the classroom and teaches you things?"

"Yeah," she said, sliding wineglasses onto their dusty shelves.

"And he assigns grades to your work?"

"Yeah." She passed the empty glass rack back over the bar to Ro.

"And he wants you to buy drugs for him?"

At the time, she'd thought Ro was being weird about it. Jealous, even.

"He wants me to come to a cool, all-night party where a bunch of us are going to get high, and since I'm an undergrad, he thought I was more likely to have a hookup."

Ro climbed onto the narrow counter of his backbar to clear the dust off a light fixture. He wobbled a bit when he got to his feet, and she flinched, imagining the moment he fell, his head hitting the hard tile floor. He'd always been the fearless one; she'd always been the one to worry.

"Tell me," Ro said, his back to her as he dusted. "Anyone else in your class that's Black, or is it just you?"

In the second grade, when they were already inseparable, Ro had been coming to a parent-teacher conference with his mother, just as Umu was leaving with hers. The teacher, Mrs. Rakhola, put a hand on each of the children's heads and mussed their hair as the quintet exchanged hellos and goodbyes.

"These two," Mrs. Rakhola said. "My smarty-pants and my troublemaker."

Their whole lives, every teacher, every parent called Umu the smart one. Ro did it, too. Umu was his smart best friend. Umu was the only one who knew better. She could always count on her friend to find the fact that she was too dumb to spot.

Ro and Umu grew up in town down the road from the college,

reading about the Woodend family in the paper and seeing the town population swell every September, then shrink back down in May when the students went back to their lives in real towns and cities all over America. Umu knew her whole life she'd go to school there— not because it was such a great institution and not because she didn't dream of somewhere better but because her mom was a member of the English faculty and a family tuition waiver meant Umu didn't have to take on any student debt. That she got to stay close to Ro was a bonus.

Or it was a bonus at first. Umu's mom had studied at Columbia, which meant she had these fabulous friends she'd met in New York who would occasionally swan up to Vermont for a weekend to be charmed by quaint, small-town life. They wore incredible colors and smoked impossibly skinny cigarettes and had always just been to Berlin or Tangier.

Umu had no illusions about growing up to be that fabulous, but she wanted people like that in her life. Friends who would arrive unannounced at her door when she was forty and tell a tale of a love affair they'd just had in Mongolia and make her cooler by association.

Soraya, Kip, Mary, Davey, even Faye, none of them were from Vermont. She felt guilty about it now, but the motivation for coming to the party was that it all sounded so kooky and mysterious and so unlike sitting in her basement smoking weed with Ro, which was the very unglamorous way she'd spent most of her evenings since starting college.

———

"I'm coming with you," Ro said, jumping down from the bar counter and tossing his dusty rag into the sink. "You want me to get you acid, I can get you acid, but the condition is that you let me come with you."

"It's not my event. I can't just invite you along."

"You're not going to Buckingham Palace," he said. "You said it's a few people who are getting together to party, or to chant, or whatever. I like to party. I can manage chanting. I'm coming with you."

She'd been so irritated about it. Mean to him, even.

"Why do you even want to come? Why do you suddenly care about college events? Aren't you too cool for all that? Isn't that your whole deal? You'd rather spend your time at Applebee's?"

"I have no doubt it'll be insufferable." He untucked his uniform shirt as he spoke. Unclipped his name tag and put it in his pocket. She had landed a blow. "But I'm not sending you there alone, all night, with a bunch of privileged white assholes who are dropping acid, probably for the first time in their lives."

"You're a white asshole," she said.

"Not a privileged one," he reminded her. "I leave you there alone, they're going to offer you as a human sacrifice, or roast you on a spit, or your creepy professor is going to try to..."

"Stop. I get it."

She'd been so mad at him. That he didn't understand she would seem less sophisticated if he was with her. That she couldn't form a lifelong friendship with a hopelessly fascinating scientist the way her mother had if she had a tagalong. The alternative was to tell Kip she couldn't get the drugs, and then maybe she wouldn't have been allowed to go at all. So she assented. And because of her awful selfishness, Ro lay here dead.

Her phone was face down so its light could illuminate the space. She flipped it over to check the time. It was a little past one in the morning. Hours to go until someone found them. She sat there, still, with her legs crossed and Ro's head in her lap. Her legs ached from the position, from the cold concrete floor, but she didn't dare move. She owed him this discomfort. It was the very least she could do.

"Just me and you now," she whispered down at the body. It wasn't her friend in there anymore. Mary with her insistence on cleaning him, and Davey with his instructions and his self-flagellation, she hated that she'd let them touch him. If they really believed Ro to be innocent, then they would have begun to tear each other apart. Except for the one of them who *knew* Ro was innocent, because they had their own secret.

The lines on the tattoo on Ro's chest seemed to rise and dance, to pulse in time with a heartbeat, and Umu squeezed her eyes closed to get them to stop. She wished she weren't high. She and Ro smoked weed all the time, they'd done acid once or twice when especially bored in the quiet Vermont summers, and not once before tonight had she considered the need to turn a trip off once it had started. She crammed her fists against her eyes, hoping pressure on her eyeballs would be enough to get control of her body back and she and Ro went quiet that way, alone in their mourning pose until Umu heard the metallic squeal and boom and crash of a violent act from across the basement.

She had to rise slowly—so she could respectfully place Ro's head on the ground and because her feet had fallen asleep against the concrete. Could she have hallucinated the sound? No. The concrete floor had shaken when she'd heard it. Whatever it was, it was real. And it meant the violence wasn't over.

"Hello?" she called into the dark. There was no reply. She dropped back to her knees for a moment and kissed Ro on the forehead. "I have to go for a minute," she said. "But I'll be back. Don't be scared."

She took her light. That was the worst part. That she was leaving him alone in the dark. She glanced back at his body one last time, and then she and her sleeping feet shuffled forward to find the source of that awful noise.

II

Faye, Davey, and Mary arrived before Umu did. Maybe they'd been closer to the source of the sound, maybe they weren't hampered by sleeping feet. She arrived on pins and needles, seeing the backs of their heads before there was enough light to see what the three of them were staring at.

Eerily, they weren't moving. When her light caught them, they were a strange tableau. Each more than an arm's length from the other, like strangers in a bank line. Not moving, not speaking, wholly overcome by their own guilt or their own fear or the awe at what they were observing.

"What was the sound?" Umu said, her attention mostly back on Ro, worried that he was frightened, alone in the dark. Faye and Davey and Mary. None of them spoke. They only stood and stared, and finally Umu fell into the light and saw the terrible and inevitable scene and the source of the horrible crash.

"Has it ever happened before?" she asked.

Davey, it was Davey who moved first, finally turned his head, making her flinch when he did, noticing for the first time that she'd arrived.

"Probably," he said. "Before our time though. We're always so careful now."

Though, strictly speaking, that wasn't true. Just that night, when they'd been arranging the arena, they hadn't been careful then. They'd been so haphazard about it all.

The scene would have appalled any bibliophile. Six stacks in total. Those rickety old stacks, arranged on tracks so they could be pushed together to preserve space. Each stack heavy with the weight of hundreds or thousands of volumes, overstuffed by any-one's count. The stacks that swayed and threatened no matter how slowly you moved them on their tracks. It was inevitable that one would come down eventually. But here were six in a sickening pile. Their contents torn and frayed and scattered about like someone had ripped open a vein.

It was horrible to see but also, the level of harm, of damage, wasn't it on par with the devastation they were already feeling? Umu found the dominos of shelves, the shredded mass of books, the splintered wood, almost satisfying. If they had bled, shouldn't the library bleed, too?

Faye and Davey and Mary, and now Umu, made up that tableau. Umu was so caught up in the horrible image that it took her a minute at least to realize what else was wrong.

"Where's Soraya?" Umu said, when at last the absence became clear.

No one said anything.

"Soraya!" she yelled into the dark. Soraya with the bad trip, Soraya who had been curled up and lying on a shelf since Ro was killed. Had she found herself another perch? Was she sleeping somewhere in the dark, oblivious to the crash?

"Soraya!" Umu called again, her voice breaking this time.

Faye and Davey and Mary, they said nothing, did nothing; they only stared at the collapsed stack. They'd all arrived at the scene first. Did they know something she didn't? Had they seen Soraya somewhere, sleeping safely? Or was there a truth even more terrifying than one of them being a killer? What if they were all in on it together?

"Davey," Umu shook him by the arm, willing herself past her paranoia. "You went looking for her after she ran off. Did you find her? Where's Soraya?"

Davey said nothing. Did nothing.

"Soraya!" Umu yelled again.

"Stop," Mary said. Like she was mad at Umu. Like Umu was the one who was acting crazy. "She's there." Mary pointed at the pile of books and steel and paper and cardboard. What did she mean Soraya was there?

⸻

She didn't know any of these people. She might die with them. And even if she didn't die here, she'd be tied to them, these killers or victims or whatever they were, forever, in a way she found disgusting. She'd read stories before about strangers who were united after some sort of shared trauma—because they'd been in the same movie theater during a mass shooting, or they were the scattering of survivors after a train derailed, or they were trapped in an elevator during a daylong power outage. Strangers who had nothing to unite them except for the fact that they'd chosen the same bad time and the same bad place to gather together and the power of the event they survived together bound them like handcuffs. People fall in love with one another or invite their partners in trauma to come to their children's weddings. They break bread and tell stories and continue to survive the horrible thing they survived in the first place with the help of these participants in their lives.

Umu didn't want to be bound to Faye and Davey and Mary forever. She had no idea how the night would end, but she knew that when she walked out of the basement, she didn't want to see any one of their faces ever again. Not in the least because there was a good chance one of them was a murderer. She knew Ro hadn't killed Kip, and that could only mean that one of them had.

Of the three of them, Davey seemed the most agitated about the disappearance of Soraya. The idea of him pushing one of the bookstacks with all his might and sending the shelf and its contents tumbling down on Soraya seemed unlikely. Not impossible, but unlikely. But of the three of them, there was no doubt that Davey hated Kip the most. To Umu, he'd seemed barely fussed when Kip

died his bloody death. He could be forgiven for his impassive attitude to Ro's death—Ro might have killed him in self-defense if
given the opportunity—but Kip's death was totally unprovoked and
Davey hadn't so much as wrinkled his forehead. He was weeping
now, though. Silent tears, pooling in his frown lines and reflecting
in the light of his iPhone flashlight.

Does a motive, or the lack of one, make a killer? In mystery
novels, on *CSI*, certainly, but in real life, wasn't murder more a matter
of opportunity? Did Mary hate Kip? Umu had no idea; Kip hadn't
ever mentioned her in class. Did she hate Soraya? It didn't look that
way from the outside. If anything made Mary look suspicious, it was
that Umu had no idea where she was before the crash. Faye went to
go look for a fire alarm. Soraya ran from the smell of smoke. Davey
followed Soraya to comfort her. Mary hadn't offered an explanation
and maybe she didn't need to, but her lack of a position during the
fracas had Umu picturing her with two hands pressed against the
old pine bookshelf, her leg planted behind her for stability, the veins
in her elegant neck popping from the effort of the push.

Faye had more sense than to disappear without explanation. Kip
hadn't ever talked about her in class either, and she hadn't crossed
paths with her since they'd had one class together, but Umu had the
sense that she hadn't been around the library for very long. If she
was looking for a killer, should she be looking any further than Faye?
Wasn't she the only one of them who had proven, right there in the
open, that she had it in her to end someone's life? There's something
about a person who wears glasses that makes them improbable as a
villain, and Umu had to restrain herself from running up to the girl
and tearing the silver frames off her face, unmasking the monster
that might hide behind them.

"You're not going to leave her there, are you?" Umu said. She
didn't know Soraya at all, but she felt like she did. Kip used to talk
about her all the time. His girlfriend who was going into tech, his
girlfriend with the overbearing Pakistani father, his girlfriend, his

girlfriend, his girlfriend, as though invoking her had the power to protect him from any accusation of impropriety if he sat too close or texted too late at night.

"There isn't anything we can do," Mary said. Wasn't that something a killer would say?

"I can't look," Davey said at the same time. Was that a murderer protesting too much?

Faye was silent. What was more damning than failing to find the words to say? The only thing the three of them had in common was that none of them moved.

There were six collapsed stacks in total. The first and the second were stacked up against each other—lips pressed tight to keep their secret. They hadn't even allowed enough space to spill their volumes out onto the floor. Could there be a body between those shelves? Not likely.

The latter four had fallen at an angle, right off their track. They were shingled like a hand of cards and had wrought most of the destruction. Umu approached them to peer under, but it was too dark to see, it was all too broken to see, so she found herself climbing, on and over and around.

"Soraya?" Umu called. She wasn't stupid, she knew it was no use, but she called anyway because it was easier to say something than nothing. "Soraya?" She called the name again, lifting a splintered piece of wood and peering under it with her light. There were only books, no Soraya.

"You're scaring me, Umu," Faye said. "Can you please get down?" Of course Faye's voice, Faye of all people, only emboldened her, and she kept digging. Leather-bound volumes, cardboard bound, in original dust jackets, in protective acid-free boxes, she tossed them all aside.

"Soraya?" There were so many books, there was so much wood. Soraya wasn't under the third stack, or under the fourth. The fifth and sixth had collapsed against the steel grating. The contractor who installed the grating was to be congratulated. How many thousands of pounds of books had stressed the perimeter when the shelf fell? The grating hadn't even flinched.

Umu's climb had her up against the grating now and she was beginning to doubt there was a body at all. "Soraya?" It was half-hearted this time. Was it a trick? Was Soraya somewhere safe, sitting quiet, enjoying their panic? Was Soraya the type who played tricks? The type who would play this type of trick when there were enough bodies scattered throughout the basement? Umu didn't know enough about her to be able to answer that question.

She was just about convinced—Soraya wasn't under this pile, Soraya was safe, when her light found it. A mass of hair, first. Soraya wore her hair short, but there was a lot of it. A bob, always shining, always flawless. You could tell if she wore it longer her hair might be unruly, but Soraya wouldn't ever allow for such a thing.

It was just a little bit of hair first, then Umu lifted a board and the question answered itself. A bit of hair and the rest of it, and then her head, or what was left of it, what hadn't been pulped by the impact of the collapse. Soraya wasn't safe somewhere. Soraya was right here, and she was dead and one of the three people standing and watching Umu had killed her.

III

She dug like a dog at the beach. Crouched on her knees, her hands working furiously to toss books, bits of wood, steel shelf brackets, behind her. The quiet basement had become quieter when Umu made her discovery, and every time she tossed something that hit the concrete floor, there was an ugly, reverberating echo. Still, she dug.

It was all so unstable that some of her digging made things worse. She would toss a book behind her, and two more would slide back down in its place but no matter, she kept at it. She exposed Soraya's face. The back of her head was crushed but her beautiful face was intact. Umu hadn't ever had any interest in Kip, except as a key to something, but she'd always been so fascinated by Soraya. When she pictured her future life, her fabulous friends who would pop in on her and make her glamorous by association, she always pictured someone like Soraya.

There was a twisted piece of metal, part of the mechanism for the crank that had moved the shelves, and Umu tossed it aside. This time it felt like the whole basement rumbled when it hit the ground. Had sounds become louder? She pulled a heavy volume off Soraya's shoulder, and now her whole right arm was freed. If she'd been alive, she could have reached that arm up into the dark, waved it for help like a drowning swimmer.

Soraya's shirt was unbuttoned. That flawless girl looked sloppy in death, and Umu was less concerned about why her shirt might be open than with resolving that indignity, so she paused her digging and took a moment to fasten the buttons. It was dark and her hands were shaking and there was blood again—still Ro's or newly Soraya's or perhaps even her own—but she buttoned Soraya's shirt to her chin.

She put her phone between her teeth. The light shone down on her hands, illuminating her work. She used a sort of rubbery case, meant to make the thing harder to drop off the side of a bridge or out a car window if she was trying to get a perfect photo, and it was helpful now in keeping the phone fixed between her teeth.

As she buttoned the shirt, she could see the blood that stained her hands sparkle. The sight of the sparkle was as intense as the sound of the reverb, so she knew neither thing was real. You have to calm down, she told herself. If your trip starts to go bad, you can't keep yourself sane, so you have to calm down and not feel your feelings. She'd been around enough bad trips to know what the worst looked like, so she paused when she finished with Soraya's shirt to blink over and over, sure the blinking would help her remember what was real.

When she resumed her work, she did so more slowly, doing what she could to avoid throwing something to the ground that might make that awful sound. It might have saved her life, this reduced pace. The next thing she pulled up was another long strip of wood. One of the sides of the bookshelf had broken in two as it fell and was now part of the litter that covered the left side of Soraya's body. Umu had to shift her own weight off it, and then she gave it a gentle tug, and when she did the whole ugly mess groaned and slid and pushed her against the grating and Soraya's lifeless body fell against her. Soraya's right foot, bloody with a freshly popped blister, pressed against Umu's cheek.

The sound or the sight or just a flicker of common sense finally broke Davey's trance, and he was quickly upon her, a hand under each of her armpits, yanking her off the wobbling pile.

"We are surrounded by bodies," he said. "Can you stop trying to create another one?"

She shook him off her as soon as she felt concrete against her feet. He'd pulled her free, but Soraya, poor Soraya, was still in the mess.

"I don't need your help," Umu said. Demonstrably untrue.

"Crush yourself to death the way she did, then," he said. "But we're running out of people to perform funerary rites."

During the fracas, Mary and Faye had begun to pick up fallen books from the perimeter of the scene of devastation and place them in tidy little piles. Having shaken Davey off, Umu was slow to climb back up on top of the heap. Up there it was blood and danger. Down here, there were neat stacks of books, lined up and waiting for some future when the library basement was just a library basement again, and someone picked up each of those stacks and placed them on a shelf.

"There's a body under there," Umu said. She was too overwhelmed, too angry to be afraid of him, of any of them. "She's mutilated. She didn't do that to herself. I didn't know her, but you all did. How can you stand here, how can you *tidy*, when there's a body under there?"

Mary put down her latest stack of books. It wasn't just any body under there; she and Soraya had been friends.

"She was tripping, and she wasn't careful, and she brought the stacks down on top of herself," Davey said.

Mary and Faye paused what they were doing, long enough that she knew they were calculating if what Davey was saying could be true. That Soraya knocked the stacks over onto herself in some sort of freak accident. But Soraya was so little and the destruction was so big.

"Climbing up there and getting hurt makes it harder for everybody," Mary said, moving past Davey's claim without addressing it. She pulled at the slender gold chain at her throat. "I'm not trying to tidy. I'm getting Soraya's body out. But I'm not trying to get myself hurt while doing it."

"Doesn't matter if you try to get hurt or not," Umu said. She kicked the stack Mary had just put down. "We're being hunted down here, and one of us is going to be the hunter's next prey."

Faye and Davey and Mary. Their motives, their opportunities, it was all making her dizzy, just when she most needed to keep control of herself.

"One of you did this to Soraya, just like you did it to Kip," Umu said. "You probably got a real laugh out of all of us, stalking after Ro, attacking him, doing the hunting on your behalf."

Mary placed a new stack of books down, and the sound was like an explosion. Umu wasn't in control of her faculties, she knew she wasn't, but the hunter was as real as the tiny hairs on her forearms that were standing up.

"Which of you decided we should go after Ro? Quite the sense of humor on you."

"There's no hunter, Umu," Davey said.

"You were so sure Ro killed Kip but now Ro is dead and someone's killed Soraya, and I'm supposed to believe that it's not one of you doing this?" Umu said. Her own voice echoed in her ears.

Faye's cell phone was their main source of light—face down on the floor by one of the book piles. Umu lunged at it. She flipped it over so its cracked screen was face up, and the space went that much darker. She poked at the screen, but there was only an exclamation point where there should be bars indicating cell service.

"I'll bet your phones are even working," she said, though she'd just been disproven. "Separating us from the outside world before picking us off. Stop with the books!" She kicked over another stack, and again the sound made the building shake. "Which of you is doing this?"

She moved quickly over to Mary's phone on the other side of the pile. Faye had picked hers back up and was shining the beam at the ground so it made only a meager light, as if to give Umu some privacy in her raving. Or to throw her even further off-balance in the dark.

Now that she'd begun to point fingers, now that she'd told them that she knew one of them was the killer, she couldn't stop. The three of them watched her in the half darkness, waiting to crush her skull or cut her throat.

"Don't touch my phone," Mary said when Umu approached. She snatched it up off the ground.

"You're going to regret doing this," Umu said, unsure if she meant committing the murders or failing to unmask the killer.

"There's plenty I already regret," Mary said. "I'll take my chances."

Umu's dread rose and with it her control over her own body. Were those Davey's eyes, lustrous in the light of Mary's phone, hungry for more blood? Was that the shuffle of Mary's foot against the dusty floor, flexing before she pounced on her next victim? Her whole body was braced, every muscle held taut, prepared for the feeling of being struck by the hunter's arrow, the hunter's blade.

The last time she'd done acid, she and Ro had prepared by purchasing three bags of chips. Plain salted, ruffled, and Doritos. There's nothing more powerful to an intoxicated mind than the Dorito. Her body remembered every corner of every chip. The way the cheese dusting coated the little air bubbles that sprang up in the deep-fried corn flour. The way the saliva filled her mouth when the powdered topping hit her tongue. It was bliss, eating those chips, until she took one at a wrong angle, and the sharp edge of a triangular chip pierced the chapped edge of her mouth and she'd been fleetingly certain that she'd accidentally eaten shards of glass. For a few terrifying minutes, she prepared to die, certain the glass would pierce her esophagus and then her intestines and she'd bleed to death from the inside.

Ro was high, too, that night, but he was straight enough to talk her down, to convince her that the Doritos were just Doritos and that if she died, it wouldn't be at the hands of Cool Ranch. The momentary terror stuck though. It was how she felt now, waiting to be hunted.

"It's Faye," said a voice over the sound of Umu's rapid breath. "You're panicking. I think—I'm in physics, not medicine, so I can't be sure—but I'm pretty sure you're having a panic attack."

Now the face fell into focus: Faye, Faye, who had killed Ro with her bare hands, all of a sudden wanted to be Umu's doctor. Faye had crept up to her like *she* was the wild thing, like *she* was the thing that should be feared down in the basement, and the sight of that flushed face, those smudged glasses, it would have made her laugh if she weren't so disgusted.

"Back up before I bite your nose off your face," Umu said. "One of you did this. *You* did this."

Faye glanced back at Davey, and Davey shook his head. Cahoots! They knew something she didn't. They knew that hers was the next neck on the chopping block.

Faye hadn't backed off the way Umu needed her to. She was standing within easy arm's reach in a way that felt like a taunt. Umu took the proximity to mean that Faye wanted her to know that she could reach her throat just as easily as she had reached Ro's. I'll be ready for her, Umu thought. Ready in a way that Ro wasn't.

"Ro didn't see you coming, but I do," Umu said to Faye. "I won't go down as easily as he did." His blood still clung to her clothes, was still buried under her fingernails, but she wasn't scared of it anymore. She was energized by it. She wore Ro's blood like a shield.

"There's no hunter," Faye said. "Ro killed Kip. Soraya's death was an accident. There's no more danger."

It was telling that none of the three of them was as frightened as they should be. It was telling how easily Faye swallowed Davey's lie about Soraya knocking the stack over herself. Faye was still too close to Umu's face, and she was mumbling something about corduroy, about visualization, and Umu tried to look past her so she could keep an eye on all three of them at once, when Faye stepped even closer and Umu had no choice but to strike her with all her might across her stupid face.

"I told you to get away from me. All of you get away!"

Open palm against hot cheek. Umu's hand was sweating a little, as was Faye's face, and the sweat held them together for a half second after the moment of connection. Umu had never hit anyone before. It rang in her ears. It made her palm ache.

She liked it.

Faye stepped back, finally, clutching the side of her face. "You hit me," she said, as though there could be any doubt about what happened. The sound of the strike got Davey and Mary moving; they approached Faye to perform concern as though she was the thing they needed to worry about, not the reality that one of their group was surely the next to die. The fools.

Faye brushed Davey aside. "Don't worry about me. I'm fine."

How big of her, Umu thought.

"It's Umu who needs you. She's freaking out. She was doing okay all night, but she must have started hallucinating."

It was a strange strategy, Umu thought, to call the danger a hallucination when they were all soaked in Kip's and Ro's and Soraya's vital fluids. Faye was playing at something dangerous.

"You're bleeding a bit," Davey said, bringing his fingertips to Faye's freshly struck cheek. "You should put something on it."

"There are literal dead bodies down here, Davey," Mary said. "I don't think it's the end of the world if she skips the Polysporin."

Faye put her own palm to her red cheek. "She's right. I'm totally fine. Umu's having a bad trip; you need to do something."

"You're the sober one," Davey said. "You said that you could do something."

They were bickering about Umu as if she weren't there. They were bickering about trivialities as if one of them or all of them weren't coming for more throats. Umu stepped sideways toward the stack, inching closer toward where Ro lay. Ro who had come here to protect her. Who had known all along that something about this night wasn't right.

"She's clearly not responding well to me," Faye said. "I'm only making it worse. One of you needs to talk to her, to hold her, to do something to bring her back to earth."

They'd put her in the earth if they had their way, Umu thought. She wasn't cold but she shivered. Shivered like she was in the middle of a frigid lake, looking for a rescue.

"I'm not doing any better than she is," Davey said.

Umu leaned against the bookshelf, longing for Ro. No one was coming to help her.

"A bad trip isn't contagious," Faye said, as though she knew anything. "She's a danger to herself and to us the longer she keeps freaking out."

She and Ro had failed each other. If she listened to him, she'd never have come and he'd never have followed her. If he were alive, he could have protected her from these monsters.

When she felt something grab her, she was too terrified to even scream. The room swam in front of her eyes, and she thought she would faint, but she fought with all her might to stay conscious, knowing if she closed her eyes it would be for the last time.

"You're safe," Davey's voice said in her ear. She writhed against his arms but he wouldn't let her go. He was behind her, his arms around her and holding her tight at the waist, pinning her arms down. His chin rested on her shoulder and he whispered in her ear. She was in the frigid lake and she'd found a set of hands, but they weren't there to save her: they were there to push her below the surface.

"No one's hunting you. I know you loved Ro but he did this. He did this and now he's gone, and I've got you and you're safe."

She stopped writhing. Davey had no weapon, only the secret he was whispering in her ear. If the booming of the books hitting the floor earlier had made the room shake, then the tone of Davey's whisper now made it vibrate. Though she'd promised herself she wouldn't, she closed her eyes. She was ready to let the water slip over her head.

"It's just the four of us standing here," Davey said. "And for the rest of the night, we take care of each other."

She had no sense of how long they stood like that, preparing to die. With her eyes closed, she let herself imagine it was Ro who was holding her. Not in a hug, they weren't friends who hugged, but that they were in that lake and after all the times she'd done it for him, this time he was the one who was bringing her back to shore.

She opened her eyes. She hadn't moved and nothing had changed, but she wasn't afraid anymore. Davey still held her but she knew he wouldn't hurt her.

"You're going to be safe because the four of us are going to take care of each other," Davey said.

He was right and he was wrong. She was going to be safe. But only because she knew exactly who had killed Kip and she was going to protect herself from them.

IV

"You can let go of me," Umu said, removing Davey from her finger by finger. "I'm better; I'm seeing everything a lot more clearly."

He was slow to unwind but he did it, and she turned to face him so she could whisper her revelation just to him.

"I know who's doing it," she whispered. She might have sounded crazy, but she wasn't crazy. She was sure. "She's right behind you. Ro's not the one who poisoned Kip. Faye is."

A murderer is a murderer is a murderer, Umu thought. She showed us who she was when she hurt Ro, but we didn't believe her.

"Umu." Davey wasn't whispering. He wasn't afraid of Faye overhearing because he thought Umu was babbling, hallucinating. "All we need to do to get through the night is to stay calm."

All we need to do to get through the night is to keep Faye's hands off our throats, Umu thought. "I'm not imagining this," she whispered.

Their back-and-forth had attracted Mary's attention. Faye, hand still on her cheek, kept her distance. "You feeling better, Umu?" Mary asked.

"She's saying it was Faye now," Davey said, and there was a sort of exasperated sigh that followed that gave Umu a chill. He didn't believe her, and if he didn't believe her, he would make himself easy prey. It was what Faye had been counting on: how easy it would be to point a finger at an outsider like Ro, how well she could hide behind her glasses.

"Listen," Umu whispered to them both. Faye was looking over. She was curious, too, but still too dumbstruck to make her way over or too self-satisfied with her deceit to bother speaking in her own defense. Umu didn't have a lot of time to make herself heard. "Ro is dead. Whether you believe me or not, admit that there's no way I'm motivated by a desire to protect him."

"Sure," Mary said. With caution, she moved closer. Umu's

newfound lucidity was rubbing off. The three were suddenly clear-eyed.

"You all blamed Ro for Kip's death, but that doesn't make any sense. It never did," Umu said. "He sold Kip the drugs, sure, but he took them himself. If he had poisoned the batch, why in the world would he have taken a tab and put himself at risk? Ro liked to get high, but there are easier ways, you know?"

"If I'm hearing you right," Davey said, practicing an active listening trick that Umu recognized from the college's mandatory conflict-resolution training. "You're saying that Ro couldn't have poisoned the drugs. So, what then? It was an accident? Or whoever sold to him poisoned them?"

She put an arm around each of their waists and pulled them so they were right against her, so her mouth was pressed in the space between their ears.

"Davey, you hid the drugs in the stacks after you got them, right?" Umu whispered. She could feel Mary's goosebumps rise up against her cheek, but she knew Mary wouldn't pull away, if only because she was wary of being struck as Faye had been. "They were down in the basement before the rest of us got down here at the beginning of the night, weren't they?"

The muscles in Davey's face tensed. Like he was beginning to understand what she was suggesting before she even had a chance to say it. Like he was finally as scared as he should be.

"Sure," he said. "You all saw me pull them out. I hid a bunch of things in the stacks over the last week so Ronald wouldn't see me bringing anything down tonight."

She wanted to give one of them the opportunity to say it, to point the finger so she wouldn't have to, but neither spoke. She could feel them coming around, those tense muscles and goosebumps saying what their words wouldn't, but neither was willing to say it.

"Who was working down in the basement today?" she whispered.

"You told me when you brought us down, Mary. You named some-one who spends most of their time working down in the basement."

"That's a bit of a leap, isn't it?" Davey asked. None of them dared look at Faye, who had to be rattled now, who had to know she'd been discovered, who had to be preparing to strike out in defense.

"If I remind you she killed Ro, you'll brush it off as self-defense, so I'm not going to go down that road, even though she quite literally has blood on her hands," Umu said. She wasn't whispering anymore. Faye started to approach them and Mary flinched, trying to pull away from Umu, but she held tight. No matter Faye's intentions, Umu knew the three of them could overpower her if they stayed together.

"Ro couldn't have poisoned Kip's drugs, because Ro took the drugs, too; he wouldn't have put himself at risk that way." Mary wrenched free and Umu let go of Davey, too, so all three were stand-ing to face Faye. "Doesn't that mean that the person who poisoned the drugs has to be the person who refused to take them?"

V

They grabbed hold of Faye without telling each other they were going to. Umu took one of her arms and Davey took the other and Mary went for her waist and there was a sickening bit of doubt that came with the fear creeping over Faye's face. Umu was able to ignore it as just another hallucination. This was the murderer in their midst. She knew it to be true.

Faye's protestations came out in a low and steady babble as they dragged her across the floor in the dark. She fought against their hold, but not too hard. They were three, and if she couldn't overpower them, she tried to reason with them. Faye said they were wrong, or that they were confused, or that they were hallucinating all the way across the basement floor as they dragged her, and Umu wouldn't let herself hear a word of it. There had been enough lies tonight.

One of them, she couldn't remember who, maybe it had even been her, suggested taking Faye somewhere she could be put behind a door, keeping her separate to keep themselves safe, and there was only one place any of them knew of in the basement where that could be done. It was the room where Umu had started her evening with Ro.

It was when they got to the door of that side room, where Umu and Ro had hidden under a table and waited for the library to close, where Faye had joined them with full knowledge of the terrible thing she was planning to do, that she really began to fight. If she was saving her energy or she hadn't really believed that they were prepared to lock her up, then she believed it now. A gurgling cry came from her throat, and she began to thrash against them. The girl they'd dragged all the way across the library floor wasn't a killer, but this girl trying to escape them was, and as Umu struggled to keep her grasp, she was also relieved to see Faye fight. She was letting the others see her for what she really was.

Umu knew the room itself was secure. She'd had plenty of time to look around it when she and Ro waited down in the basement, but she also knew there was no lock on the door. Why would there be? The room was a quiet place for a librarian to do the work of preparing an exhibition. The basement itself was a vault, as they'd learned that night, so the room didn't have to be.

The library was preparing for an exhibition from their map collection. The long, delicate sheets were laid out on a giant table in the center of the room, and Umu had passed the time by flipping through them while she and Ro waited earlier. Her favorite was a portolan chart showing the Red Sea that was labeled as having been drawn in 1505. It was illustrated in brilliant greens and reds with palm trees and church spires and, in an unscientific detail, it included the land bridge that parted the Red Sea in Exodus. Had that really only been a few hours ago? Umu's energy was occupied with keeping her grasp of Faye and with forcing her through the doorjamb. Her earlier awe at the maps was quickly forgotten. She was worried about that door, about how they'd keep Faye in the room once they forced her in.

Umu's arms were burning with the effort of keeping Faye contained. She didn't know how much longer she could hold out and she knew that Davey and Mary must be feeling the same. Mary had blood dripping from her nose, the shins of Davey's trousers were blackened from Faye's repeated kicks. This was enough now. Faye had proven who she was; now they needed to be rid of her.

The wooden skid to the side of the exhibition room door fell into view like it was under a spotlight. Once, it held a stack of book boxes, but now it was neatly standing against the wall, waiting for someone from facilities to come and discard it. For their purposes, it was made of strong wood and was just slightly taller than the handle of the door that it stood next to. They had their cage, now here was their barricade.

"Throw her," Umu said. The sight of the skid had renewed her, and the confidence with which she spoke rubbed off on the others. In a reversal, she felt Faye's fingers turn to claws and try to dig into her arms, to keep grasping and avoid the inevitable. Umu would allow no such thing. This girl, this *animal*, had poisoned the batch of drugs for a group of people she scarcely knew; she'd let Ro stand accused of her own crime and then had brutally killed him herself; and then she'd crushed Soraya, poor Soraya, who had already been so terrified.

They didn't give count to announce when they would throw her. It was like they were all thinking with one brain. They heaved back and then the three gave a mighty push that sent her into the room and onto her hands and knees, her glasses skittering against the dark concrete. Davey slammed the door shut and held his body against it while Umu grabbed the skid and pushed it under the door handle. Whatever Faye had already done, they could be sure they were safe from her now.

CHAPTER 19

FAYE

I

When Faye first moved to Vermont, that very first week, she'd woken up in the middle of the night, certain she heard a sound from inside her single dorm room. When she reached for her nightstand to get her glasses, she couldn't find them. She'd leaped out of bed, but the room was all strange shadows and at that moment she was sure, every cell in her body was sure, that there was someone in her room who was going to kill her. She lunged across the room at the light switch and with the light on saw there was no killer.

She crawled around on her hands and knees for twenty-five minutes before finally finding the glasses slipped behind a bureau. Faye didn't sleep at all for the rest of the night. Her worst fear had always been the loss of her glasses. When she stood on a balcony high on a tall building, she would feel pins and needles in her legs, but the fear wasn't falling, never falling. The thing she could picture happening was her glasses sliding off her nose and tumbling down to the distant sidewalk, leaving her blinded. Her mother had suggested contact lenses when she was younger—"they'll make sports easier"—but that was so silly; what did she care about sports?

Now, the door shut behind her and she was on her hands and knees in perfect blackness and the others had convinced themselves she'd killed Kip and Soraya, but none of that was as terrifying as not being able to see.

"She'll get out of there eventually and then she'll come for us," she could hear Umu say. The walls of the room didn't go all the way up to the ceiling. Faye remembered that now. They were high, ten feet maybe, but the concrete ceiling was higher, and the space was filled in with more metal grating. "If we do it now, we'll know we're safe."

"We don't have to do anything right this second," Davey said. "Let's all take a minute to get our heads straight. I'm still stuck back at science girl being a murderer."

"If anyone is going to know about poison, it's going to be science girl," Mary said.

Faye crawled forward, sweeping her hands in front of her in a wide arc. She had her phone in her pocket, so she pulled it out and turned on the light. It was no use. Shadows and blurs. She reached for something that could have been her glasses and found it was a darker spot on the floor, nothing more.

"But she's only a *physicist*," Umu said, in a voice that was meant to imitate Faye's. She paused from her searching and sat back on her heels. She was wrong. Her worst fear wasn't losing her glasses. Her worst fear was learning that everyone really was mocking her behind her back, the way she always imagined they were.

"Let's keep our focus here," Davey said. "How would we even do it? Who would? You won't catch me volunteering."

That they were talking about her—about ending her life—with all the seriousness of an argument about who would take out the trash was almost enough to make her give up entirely. To go to the door and offer her throat.

If Beans were here, he'd have barked and growled in her defense. He was too little for any real impact, but she'd have had someone on her side. Faye came down here to make friends, but these people weren't her friends. She had no friends. For a long time, she'd had Beans but since April, she hadn't even had him. When he was dying, Faye begged her mother to lend her the money for a plane ticket home, but her pleas were refused.

"He's a dog, Faye. We all love him, but he is just a dog."

A few days later, her mother sent her a picture of a gray-bearded Beans (when did he get so gray?) sleeping on his big red pillow. Or, not sleeping, as it turned out. So, since April, Faye had no one to protect her from the big dogs.

"I don't love the idea either, but it's us or it's her," Mary said.

Faye reached up to wipe a tear from her face. Crying wouldn't get her anywhere, but how could she not cry? She lay down on the floor. She was so hungry her head was wobbling, she was exhausted, and she didn't want to battle anymore, but there was nothing to do but to keep listening to what they said. Knowing their plans might be the only way to protect herself in the end.

The cold concrete against her cheek was a relief. A small pleasure. The floor was filthy with dust and dirt, but she didn't care. She'd be no worse off than she already was if she allowed herself to get dirty.

"This is insanity," Davey said. "Which is saying a lot because this whole night has been insanity. Obviously, we're not going to kill her."

Faye raised her head. Had he said it? Was he on her side?

"Are you working with her?" Umu said. "Is that why you're—"

"Stop it, Umu," he said.

Faye sat up so she could hear better, and when she put her hand down to shift her weight, she felt it. The cool familiarity of steel and polycarbonate.

She hugged the glasses to her chest before putting them back on her face, and she was suddenly awake again, her head unclouded and her will to make it out of this basement restored.

"She's secure in there," Davey said. "There's no opening the door against the barricade unless she suddenly gains a hundred pounds of muscle. It's a few hours until morning."

Faye put her glasses on and swept the light across the room. There was so much power in clear vision. If she'd been born in another time, her nearsightedness would have been a death sentence, but she was certain now she'd survive this place.

"The police will come in the morning," Davey said. "We don't have to do anything or decide anything because we've done what's needed. She's locked in there and all we have to do is wait."

He doesn't want to tell them that he believes me, but he believes me, she thought. He'll take my side and he'll keep me safe and he'll get me out of here.

If Umu responded, or if Mary did, then Faye didn't hear it. She heard voices, sure, but they were shrinking. There were footsteps. Someone was wearing hard-soled shoes, and the sound of them against the concrete floor announced that she was being left to herself and that whatever they decided to do with her or to her, they would decide where she couldn't hear them.

II

Faye didn't throw herself against the door once the voices receded. She had vision and she had quiet, and she needed time to figure out what to do. The room was maybe thirty feet across. It wasn't a place where she had spent any time. It was Ronald's domain, or the domain of the faculty member curating the library's next exhibition. It was the only space in the basement without bookshelves crammed in at odd angles. There were a few book trucks piled with materials, some cartons stacked up in the corner, and a giant wood table in the center of the room that held the remnants of someone's work for the day, mostly a stack of maps being prepared for an upcoming exhibition. She'd seen the selection when they were being pulled downstairs to prepare. There was one that showed a Viking settlement on Newfoundland that Faye had ridden in the elevator with, and she'd marveled at the proof that Columbus hadn't been the first of the European settlers—a piece of paper that showed it definitively. But later that night, she'd looked up the map and found it had been proven to be a forgery all the way back in 1973. The idea that she'd been so enamored by a fake made her doubt the whole mission of the library. Could they believe anything they saw on the pages here?

Soraya was dead. Faye had scarcely a moment to breathe since hearing the crash, and now that she was alone and in the quiet, the weight of the news pressed against her chest. If Kip wasn't dead, they'd all have pointed a finger right at him. It's always the boyfriend or the husband. Crime procedurals on television taught her that rule as a child, but the guilt would be especially apparent in the case of this particular boyfriend. Could Davey have killed her? Could Umu or Mary?

Faye had to put her phone down on the table. She shook her

hands to keep them from trembling. What was it about her that would ever make someone believe she could be a killer? Her fingernails were cut short and unvarnished. A necessity of her job. A flake of polish could damage a sample, a long fingernail risked piercing a glove. Soraya's nails were a soft pink. Mary's were long and rounded and painted navy blue. She didn't remember what Umu's looked like, but she'd bet they were pretty, too. Maybe they wouldn't hate her so much if she were groomed and beautiful like they were.

Her hands wouldn't stop shaking. She balled them into fists and held them against her cheeks. Kip and Soraya and Ro are dead and there'll be more if you don't get yourself out of this room, she told herself. If she let herself dwell on the fact that the next body might be hers, that they might be coming back to kill her from some misguided sense of self-preservation, that Soraya's killer was setting her up to be the next to go, then she'd never get her head straight enough or her hands steady enough to even shine her light forward. No, the truth was that Kip and Soraya were dead because someone had killed them and Faye needed to get out of here to make the blood stop flowing.

There had been quiet long enough, and she was filled with enough resolve that she got herself up and finally went to try the door. It was old, like everything in this place. Had it been installed recently, she might have been able to bust right through it. Everything new was cheap and disposable, but this door had been built to last forever, and when she pushed her weight against it, it gave slightly against the doorjamb, but then held fast.

Maybe they don't think you killed anyone, the pernicious voice inside her head said. Maybe they hate you so much that they locked you in here to be free of you.

Once, in the second grade, a group of girls invited her to play a game of hide-and-seek in the schoolyard. One of the girls, Christina, who had beautiful hair that was always in a perfect braid, whispered a suggestion that she hide behind a storage shed, so Faye gleefully did just that and she stayed there, hidden, for the full lunch hour before realizing at the bell that all the other girls had been playing jump rope instead and no one ever had any intention of coming to find her.

But that wasn't what was happening here. If she discounted Davey's ridiculous suggestion that it had been an accident, then at least one of them, whoever had killed Soraya, knew her to be innocent of that crime. It wasn't simple teasing that had her trapped in this room. She needed to act. She'd seen Umu grabbing for something before they'd pushed her into the room, but she had no idea what was blocking the door. If she could see what she was up against, she stood a better chance of getting past it.

That big, heavy table beckoned to her. She got behind it and gave it a push. Nothing happened. She was so hungry, so tired, that she might as well have been pawing at the thing like a kitten. She stood back, took a breath, shook her shaking hands again, and then heaved herself against the table.

The table jolted forward so radically that Faye was momentarily frightened it had come alive. The work materials on the tabletop, some acid-free cardboard, a professional-looking pair of scissors, and even a giant steel paper cutter, were displaced and clattered to the floor. The stack of giant maps slipped off more slowly, but they hit the floor, too. Good riddance. The paper cutter hit with such violence that Faye leaped back from the sound, but she caught her breath and everything was quiet again. Her phone had fallen and when she picked it up, she picked up the scissors with it. A tool, she told herself. They weren't a weapon, they were a tool. A ten-inch-long insurance policy should she need to cut a string or pop a balloon to get out of the basement. Nothing more.

The work wasn't nearly done. She'd succeeded in sliding the table a couple of feet forward and had made a terrible mess and a clatter in the process, but something about it had enlivened her and the rest was easier. She wasn't any less hungry or tired, but knowing for certain that the table would move for her, that it wasn't impossible, meant she got some distance with every push.

She was horribly thirsty by the time she got the table against the wall. She'd been so fixated on her hunger all night that she'd scarcely had time to think about her thirst, but the exertion brought it to the fore, and she thought again about that ear of corn and how satisfying it would be to pop the kernels between her teeth and suck the juice from them. Maybe this is nearly over, she thought, and there'll be food and drink waiting for me back in the arena.

Her sense of accomplishment at having moved the table was dulling her senses. The ordeal was nowhere near over.

Faye tucked her phone into her back pocket with the scissors so she could hoist herself up onto the table. It was exactly as high as she needed it to be, giving her just enough lift to peer over the edge of the wall through the grating to the other side. Once up at the top, she found she didn't need the light from her phone at all. There was an exit sign just on the other side of the grating, illuminating an out-of-reach stairwell that she'd never noticed because she'd never before been in the basement in an emergency. The sign gave off just enough red light to see the floor below it, and at her angle, she could see that the others had crammed a shipping skid underneath the handle of her door and it was only that awkwardly placed piece of wood that was keeping her captive.

That wasn't all she saw. Sitting on the floor by the door, arms wrapped around her knees, was Mary.

III

In the red light, Faye could see the shine of Mary's hair, the outline of her profile, and the steady movement of her breath. Where were the others? Why was she alone? If they'd decided that one of them should guard the door, then they did so without saying a word where she could hear them. Or it wasn't too late to seek a newer world. They hadn't shut her in here because they thought she was a killer. It was a long prank, all a signal of their new friendship, the blood and the bodies no more real than in a movie, the harm no more severe than a second-grade prank about hide-and-seek.

A foolish idea. Painfully foolish. Of course the blood was real. She could smell it on herself.

"Why aren't you with the others, Mary?" Faye whispered, but Mary couldn't hear her, so they stayed as they were, observer and observed, each in possession of their secrets.

Faye had hardly thought about Mary all night. Davey had been running around trying to stay in control of his event, Soraya needed hand-holding through her bad trip, Umu had been screaming bloody murder, and Mary hadn't needed anything at all, which made it especially strange that she had separated herself from the others. Faye tried to see the night through Mary's eyes. Was she keeping guard of the door? Was she sitting on the floor because she'd hallucinated some monster out in the stacks? Was she trying to block out the sights and sounds of terror like Soraya?

There were no clues. She sat there, silent, and Faye would have called out to her if not for the possibility that Mary's intention when she chose the seat was to follow through on Umu's promise that they would kill Faye before the night was through.

Would she have stayed there the rest of the night, watching Mary, unmoving? Perhaps. The fear and sense of self-preservation were

strong enough that she might have timed her breath to coincide
with Mary's and gone into a sort of trance. If Mary had never moved,
it might have been easier. But eventually she did. She shifted her
weight to retrieve something from the back pocket of her jeans.

Mary, Mary, quite contrary, your secret movements make me
wary, Faye thought, and any brief respite she had from fear was over
the moment she saw what Mary removed from her pocket.

"Ro couldn't have done this." Umu had sworn it over and over
again and they'd brushed off her denials as the ravings of someone
who had taken too much, someone who was loyal to a friend she had
misjudged, but she'd been right all along. Ro hadn't done it.

There were two ways the night could have gone. After Kip died,
they could have moved slowly. They could have examined the actions
of everyone who was in the basement in the minutes and hours
leading up to his death, and they would have seen the answer plainly.
They'd still be locked in with a killer, but they might have spared two
lives. In the other version, the one that transpired in the end, they
pointed fingers and chased after the ones who were least familiar to
them, who least seemed like they belonged in the basement.

"We're all such idiots," Faye whispered to herself.

The exit sign didn't cast a lot of light. The shine of Mary's hair.
The outline of her profile. The steady rhythm of her breath. And the
little plastic baggie, still containing the square of acid that she'd told
the rest of them she ingested hours ago.

In the darkness, the weight of the realization brought Faye to her
knees. She didn't want to take her eyes off Mary, but she feared if she
didn't get off her feet she'd fall right off the table and make herself
easy prey. "Ro wouldn't have taken the drugs that he'd poisoned
himself"—wasn't that what Umu said? Isn't that why Faye stood
accused of killing Kip?

A different Faye, one who hadn't lived through three deaths in a
single night, might have tried to explain away the drugs Mary was
holding. Maybe she got an extra baggie. Maybe she was holding

the drugs for someone else. Maybe. Maybe. Maybe. But no. There was only one explanation. Mary took the backpack full of phones to the door while the rest of them were swallowing their tabs so she didn't have to take her dose in front of them. Mary didn't take her tab because Mary murdered Kip.

Faye didn't feel quite steady enough to get to her feet, but what choice did she have? Davey and Umu were off alone, and they had no idea what Mary was capable of. What she might do to Faye, or what she might have planned for them. She held the wall and put one foot on the table, hands on her knee, the way she'd been taught to get upright on a pair of ice skates as a child. When you're unsteady—her skating instructor, a beautiful teenager with curly brown hair that she wore loose under her hockey helmet, explained. When you're unsteady you don't go looking for something to grab on to. You rely on your own body. You put one skate on the ice and you put your hand on your knee and you put all your focus into staying upright.

Up she went, and she was back to peering over the wall, feeling steadier than she had been. The red light from the exit sign that had been so helpful now shone sinister. Mary's hair, Mary's profile, framed in that angry red glow. The quality of the light wasn't the only thing that had changed. Mary's breathing had, too. She wasn't slow and steady and still any longer. She was crying.

Still seated on the floor with her back against the wall, Mary held the bag in her palm and her shoulders wobbled up and down in time with her raggedy breaths. Every so often a sob would float up and over the wall to Faye's ears. The red light reflected off the tears that stained Mary's cheeks and, rather than make her a sympathetic figure, the tears made her all the more terrifying. What did she have to cry about? What she'd done? Or what she had yet to do? The hours of the night stretched before them, and Mary's tears reflected in that awful red light were an omen that the danger wasn't behind them yet.

Mary turned to wipe her tears on her sleeve and for a moment, the fullness of her face was illuminated to Faye. It was obvious now as it should have been all night; she wasn't high. She was totally clear-eyed. Even through her tears, her face wasn't fixed in a grimace like Soraya's or Umu's had been when they saw what frightened them. She was crying, but somehow she still seemed impassive. Like she knew what she had to do next.

When Mary got to her feet, Faye nearly fell off the table. Did she know she was being watched? Did she know Faye had seen her terri-ble secret? Mary might have had every reason to kill Kip and Soraya. Whatever unspeakable thing drove her to do it was the only thing that acted as protection for Faye; she had no quarrel with Mary. But if Mary saw her watching, if Mary knew that Faye could announce her guilt to the others, then there was no way Faye was safe.

She stayed in her crouch to keep her head below the top of that wall. If Mary only looked up now, if she hadn't already sensed that she was being watched, she'd see nothing. If she did know Faye was there, if she was planning to remove the barricade on the door and burst through and end Faye's life as she had already ended two others, then Faye would have no warning.

Her hands, her hands were shaking again and her heart was beat-ing so loudly she could hear nothing else. Where were Davey and Umu? If she was spared, did it mean they weren't?

The red light from the exit sign didn't make it over the wall, and she didn't dare turn her flashlight on or give any indication she was moving. Crouched on that table in perfect darkness, willing her heart to beat more quietly, she thought again about the longest day of the year and how she'd missed it. If this was the end, then she'd have spent her last summer solstice doing laundry in a basement. She thought of Ro, who would never see the sun rise or fall again because of the violent action of her hand. Mary's guilt revealed an awful truth—Ro's innocence. Faye had killed an innocent man. All that hate Umu glared at her with? It wasn't enough.

There was no rustling of clothing, no padding of footsteps, no intake of breath, no noise at all to suggest that Mary was still moving. Was she standing there, tears now dry, having disposed of her evidence? Had she sunk back to the floor to resume her contemplation? Faye slid her phone out of her pocket to look at the time. It was nearly two. Five hours at the very least before anyone came for them. Five hours was an eternity. Her terror was absolute but so was her certainty there would be more death if she didn't act. She rose from her crouch slowly so she wouldn't make a sound. She held her breath, and even the drumbeat of her deafening heart quieted as the top of her head and then her eyes crested the wall to fall back upon Mary and see what she was doing.

Nothing, the answer was nothing. The red light from the exit sign still bathed the area in crimson light, but there was no one there to see. Mary was gone.

CHAPTER 20

STILL FAYE

It took nearly an hour, but once Faye had decided to free herself, her exit from the room was inevitable. She had a plan and decided it wasn't impossible, and in the end it wasn't. She didn't have the strength to break through the barricade, that was true, but she had the patience to move it a hair's breadth at a time. It was painful, but painful and impossible were different. She needed to be out of that oppressive room; she owed it to Davey and Umu—to Umu especially—to warn them they were in danger, and the only way to do so was to free herself.

For the first fifteen minutes, she gently rocked the door handle, pushing it open as far as it could go and then closing it and repeating the process until she had shifted the wooden barricade just enough, a millimeter at a time, to allow her to slide the scissors through the gap in the door. She needed only to cut one board, the piece of the skid directly under the door handle. If she cut that one piece, the door would give enough to get her hand through, enough for her to knock the barricade out of place. There was no way to do it but methodically, so for forty-five minutes, she slid the scissors through that tiny gap in the door and sawed at the wooden skid with them. Every splinter that hit the ground was a miracle, a flicker closer to her freedom.

When it was over, her hands were blistered and bleeding and the handles of the scissors were slick with her blood. She put them back in her pocket—it was important to have a tool—and she tiptoed through the open door and out into the dark in search of the others' voices.

CHAPTER 21

DAVEY

For the second time that night, Davey carried a corpse across the basement floor. When he and Faye had pulled Kip's body out of Soraya's view, Faye had taken charge and the whole thing had been over as soon as it started. Working with Umu to carry the body of her most cherished friend was a different experience altogether.

"There's too much blood here," Umu had said. She was the one who wanted to leave Faye, who wanted to put some distance between herself and the killer, who wanted to go check on Ro, and then as soon as she got to him, she was dissatisfied.

"Too much blood," she repeated.

Davey didn't know what to do.

"There's blood in the arena, too," he said.

"Not his though."

So it was settled. They were ankle deep in torn paper, previous books made unreadable. If she was distraught at the sight of Ro's blood, Davey was distraught at the loss of all those pages.

He took Ro's torso and she took his legs, but they stopped often. With Kip they had mostly dragged him across the floor, but not Ro. Umu wouldn't allow it. They stopped often to rest and they stopped often so Umu could cry.

It brought to mind a cold November morning thirteen years in the past. The first time Davey had ever seen the movie *The English Patient*, he'd been ten. Not at all a film for children. He remembered Kristin Scott Thomas's perfect breasts from his many rewatches but from that first viewing, he remembered Herodotus.

The English Patient was the favorite film of Davey's mother, but he was the one who'd asked her to put it on that day. She was brilliant, Davey's mother. She had worked as a translator as a young woman in Ethiopia, and she loved languages. It was her work, her facility with a dozen different alphabets, that allowed her and Davey's father to come to America at a time when so many people at home were starving.

She wasn't sentimental about home, but she taught Davey to speak Amharic and to read Ge'ez so he could fully participate at church. And she taught him Greek. Perhaps she was a bit sentimental about that one.

Davey was home from school, sick. It was the last year he was young enough that his mother stayed home with him when he was ill. In any case, in four years she'd be dead. He'd asked to see *The English Patient* because he knew she loved it and he wanted her attention.

Like Umu now, though, she wouldn't let them just get through it; she insisted they keep stopping. In *The English Patient*, the hero, played by Ralph Fiennes, tells stories from Herodotus's *Histories* to the woman he loves, played by Kristin Scott Thomas and her wonderful breasts. Davey's mother was so overcome that she repeatedly paused the film to retrieve her own volume of Herodotus and read those stories to her son in Greek. They were on their blue couch, sharing an ivory blanket. Davey had a fever. His Greek was not yet good enough to follow the stories. He didn't care. More than once that day, his mother was overcome with emotion, and like Umu, she wept.

Davey's mother died of acral lentiginous melanoma the year he started high school. Diagnosed to dead in the space of six months. After she was gone, he threw himself into the study of Greek. He wanted to know the language as well as she had, so the stories could move him as they had moved her.

Davey's father kept attending church, but Davey stopped. At home, his father continued to speak to him in Amharic so he wouldn't forget the language, but Davey always replied in English.

It was a coincidence that the library had acquired the collection of Ge'ez prayer books the year before Davey started at the college. He hadn't read the language since his mother's funeral service. He was desperate to work at the rare books library. The library had the first-known printed edition of Herodotus's *Histories*. It was printed in 1474, in Venice, in Latin translation. There were only seventy remaining in the world.

So Davey applied. He delighted his father, delighted Ronald, when he played up his language skills on the application. He wrote descriptions of prayer books and everyone was satisfied but every so often he snuck down to the basement to lay a palm on that 1474 Herodotus, and it felt like being on that blue couch with his mother.

"This is far enough," Umu said. They lay Ro down at the edge of the arena, not in the center of it. "No more nonsense with ointments or rituals, okay?" she asked. "I just want to let him sleep."

Davey didn't think it was nonsense. To stop mourning was to disrespect the dead. To be on the safe side, so he didn't risk disrespect, Davey took the thumb of his right hand and tore the nail across his cheek until he felt the blood come.

CHAPTER 22

MARY

I

"Did something happen with the barricade?" Davey asked, his voice squeaking, when Mary rejoined him and Umu just before two in the morning. His fear, it seemed, was still of Faye, his attention still on Faye, just as Mary needed it to be, just as it should be.

Mary followed the sounds of their voices back to the arena. When she arrived, she found they'd dragged Ro's body over. It was so morbid. She could imagine Umu and Davey sweating over that beautiful dead boy, determined to bring him somewhere more comfortable to rest, and she sent a silent prayer of thanks into the universe that she hadn't been with them so she hadn't been asked to help.

Mary was self-conscious about having to walk in front of Umu and Davey. The walk was when she worried they'd spot the lie. Even when they weren't speaking, there was a languid sort of quality in the way they both walked that made it clear they were on something. She could stare into the middle distance with the best of them, but she couldn't duplicate that walk, so she sat on the floor almost as soon as she came into their view.

"The barricade's fine," she said. She kept her eyes on the ground in front of her. She'd found that not speaking at all was the safest way to avoid notice, but if it couldn't be escaped then a lack of direct eye contact was helpful. "She made a bunch of noise right after you guys left, but the door didn't move and then it was quiet for a pretty long time. She might even be asleep."

"Sleeping like a baby with blood on her hands," Umu said. She was sitting by Ro's head again, absently stroking his hair.

Mary nodded silently. Nodding was good, too. The up-and-down bobbing of a head in lieu of speech could hide so many faults. Davey was pacing around the arena. It was littered with torn pages and empty book covers that had made their way over, stuck with blood to someone's feet or body, and he occasionally had to kick one aside to make his way through in his slow, loping stride. He wasn't faking anything. That was the walk of a man who was high as fuck.

She was surprised when Davey first invited her to—whatever this was. He'd never describe himself this way, but he was as straitlaced as Soraya. It just wasn't as obvious on him because he didn't have the severely smooth bob as a signifier.

"You want to do what in the what?" she'd asked.

"It's from the myth told in the Homeric *Hymn to Demeter*," Davey said.

"I wouldn't say that's a helpful description."

"If you'd read the Homeric *Hymn to Demeter*," he said, holding up a hand to block her protestations, "then you'd know the ritual involves the consumption of kykeon. Or in our case, acid. Drugs, Mary. You love drugs almost as much as you love your phone."

They were weeks from graduation. Everyone knew Davey was getting the one permanent job the library had salary money to offer, and Soraya was going somewhere she'd wear a well-cut suit in exchange for a million dollars a year, but Mary was in the job application trenches. Her long shot, the only thing she really wanted to do, was a social media director position with a growing community museum in New York. New York! A director job for a fresh graduate, even a graduate from a master's program, was a stretch, but she had her history of viral posts from her time at the library. The job application for the museum wasn't due until the week after graduation, and if she had one more banger, she was sure they'd have to consider her.

"Why the basement?" she asked. The library proper was a more handsome backdrop from the point of view of a content creator. She was sitting on the pretty library steps when he'd asked her, so she had aesthetics on the brain.

"The ritual requires we reenact the story of Demeter getting Persephone from the underworld. The basement's the underworld."

"I guess the basement's cool. People love a behind-the-scenes vibe."

She didn't ask, exactly, if she'd be able to take photos or video because she'd thought it was implied that where she went, her camera went. If she was being asked to fast for nearly twenty-four hours, she wanted something out of it.

"Who else is going?" This part she remembered asking. It mattered to her.

"A few people from the library, but not everyone. No one who might tell Ronald and get the whole thing canceled."

That was when she had suggested Faye, and Davey had ignored her.

What she remembered was that Kip wasn't in that first batch of invitees. He'd only been added to the group later. Mary didn't know why or how. Maybe Davey had always planned on inviting him but didn't say, or maybe he'd weaseled his way in, but she knew that she wasn't the only one who wouldn't have committed to coming if she'd known Kip would be there, too.

After a long while, Umu stopped stroking Ro's hair. "If she's sleeping, then isn't it the perfect time to go over there and take care of it?"

Mary kept her eyes down and Davey kept pacing. Umu wasn't in a place to be ignored. The ear of corn that had survived the night far better than the humans who might have eaten it was by Umu's left foot. Umu grabbed the corn off the floor and lobbed it at Davey. It hit him square in the back of the head.

"What is the matter with you?" Davey screamed at Umu. Mary sat with her eyes down. There'd been so much violence already that evening, but she hadn't yet figured out how she was supposed to respond to it. Every time there was violence, she found herself fixated on the person being attacked, and not on the others, whose behavior she was meant to be emulating.

"Didn't you hear her?" Umu said. "Faye's sleeping. If we're going to do it, we should do it now."

"Do what?" Davey said. He'd picked up the ear of corn that had struck him, which really undercut any sense of seriousness and authority he was trying to project. Corn was like bananas. It made the holder a bit ridiculous.

"Take care of her," Umu said. "The door might not hold all night. She's coming after one of us next unless we do something about it."

"The door will hold," Davey said.

"The door will hold," she said in a mean imitation of his baritone solemnity. "Don't be such a pussy and just do it. It's only going to be harder once she wakes up."

Mary looked up.

"You want *me* to do it?" he asked. Mary didn't have a part in their quarrel, but even she had to admit Umu was being stupid. "You're the one who wants it done; you do it yourself. Why would I ever do it?"

"Because you're the reason we're down here in the first place!" Umu said. "Your stupid fucking ritual that you called a party, but it was never anything like a party because parties have somewhere to go to the bathroom!"

Mary wished they would both shut up. If they were arguing, their attention was off her, but it was exhausting hearing them scream at one another, and she was already exhausted.

"You were excited enough to come when Kip invited you," Davey said.

Umu had the head of the lifeless body of her best friend in the world on her lap, and they were bickering about whether she'd wanted to come to Davey's party in the first place. Mary didn't know a lot about the world, but she was certain that once she got to New York, the people wouldn't be this inane.

Davey stopped pacing and sat on the floor. Were his feelings hurt? There were bodies down here, and he had hurt feelings. The wicker basket he'd brought out hours ago was still here in the arena with him, and he scratched his nails along the wicker. He looked like he might cry.

"Oh my god and your props. Your props!" Umu wasn't prepared to let this go. She gently put Ro's head on the floor, and then she went over and crouched in front of Davey, the basket between them. "There's a murderer in a half-assed jail cell across the basement from us who might wake up at any moment and come finish what she started, and you're here crying over your props?"

He put a hand on the lid of the basket protectively. "I'm not going over there to kill her. Enough is enough. The way I see it, there are three of us and one of her, and as long as we keep together, we're safe."

"And until then, you'll sit here and play with your toys." Umu reached for the basket and he yanked it back. Mary was irritated they were arguing, but she was curious about the basket, too. *A basket of secrets*, he'd called it. What kind of secrets were supposed to be revealed at the end of his ceremony?

"We can't open it if we haven't done the ritual," Davey said.

"The basement is littered with human sacrifices." Umu swept her arm around and pointed at what was left of Ro. "I think Demeter will be cool with the fact we skipped some chanting." Hard to argue with a body. Davey took his eye off the ball for just long enough that Umu was able to yank the basket out of his hands. It seemed the lid wasn't as tight as she expected and the contents weren't as heavy as she expected, so when she pulled back from him, the lid flew off and the contents of the basket flew behind it.

Mary almost laughed. She would have laughed if it all weren't so tragic.

Corn. It was an ear of corn.

"What in the fruit of the loom?" Umu said.

Now they were going to argue about corn. Mary wasn't high, but she was tired enough to hallucinate, and she was just now building an elaborate fantasy world where she had a needle and thread and was able to keep each of them still long enough to sew their lips closed in a choppy crosshatch.

"The mystery is a metaphor," Davey said. "You're seeing corn because we didn't complete the ritual."

"I'm seeing corn because it's an ear of fucking corn!" Umu held up the hateful thing. "One wasn't useless enough; now we have two. You couldn't have made your metaphor a couple of bags of Skittles?"

"I didn't bring the first ear of corn!" Davey succeeded in snatching the basket back from her, though she held fast to the corn. "Kip brought the first one, even though no one asked him to."

Duct tape would do, if she couldn't have the needle and thread. She wouldn't just cover their mouths with it. She'd wrap it all the way around the back of their heads so they'd know she was serious.

"I'm going to check to see if the barricade held," Mary said. She might have risen too fast or spoken too clearly but she didn't care. She needed to get away from these two. It felt like she'd been back here with them for hours, but her phone said it was only now three o'clock.

"The barricade didn't hold," a voice said from the dark stacks.

Umu dropped the corn and Davey dropped the basket. Faye stepped out of the dark, holding the longest, shiniest pair of scissors that any of them had ever seen. Her hands were slick with fresh blood, and her eyes were as wild as any of them who had actually taken the drugs.

"Faye," Davey said. To the surprise of all of them, he was back on his feet, approaching her first, without being asked. "Put down the scissors. Whatever you've decided to do, you don't have to go through with it."

She held them wrapped in her fist like a knife, and there was no doubt in anyone's mind that they'd wield as much damage as a knife if plunged through someone's skin. That was the thing about working in a place like this. They always kept the scissors well sharpened.

Davey took small slow steps toward Faye, his hands up and open to show he meant her no harm. Though Davey was the closest to her, though Davey was the one trying to reason with her, he wasn't the one who had Faye's attention. As Davey tried to get her to hand over the scissors, Faye only had eyes for Mary.

"I'm not here to hurt you," Faye said to Davey, though the scissors threatened otherwise. "I'm here to protect you."

Mary went cold. She was still sitting on the concrete floor, cross-legged, but she put the fingertips of both hands down so she could spring up if she needed to. Faye looked wild, thirsty for blood, and Mary was beginning to understand that it was her blood that Faye had come for.

"We don't want anyone else to get hurt," Davey said. "We're going to sit here until morning and let the police sort out the rest."

Mary had the advantage of familiarity with Davey. Faye had the disadvantage of having killed Umu's best friend. The seesaw was tilted in Mary's favor, yet she couldn't think of a way to shove Faye off the other side.

"I don't want anyone else to get hurt," Faye said. "But she does." She pointed at Mary with her free hand, and Davey and Umu both looked back at her, bewildered. "Check her pockets, Davey," Faye said. "Check her pockets and you'll see."

"We'll see what?" Umu asked.

Mary began to pull herself up.

"That I didn't kill Kip," Faye said. "She did."

II

"A killer saying they're not a killer, how novel," Mary said. She had risen to her feet slowly. Jumping up would arouse suspicion or, worse, would startle Faye and those terrifying scissors. Getting up a little bit at a time was cautious, sensible.

"You think I killed Kip because I'm the only one who didn't take the drugs, right?" Faye said. She moved toward Mary, and she had enough of Davey's attention now that he let her. "The person who poisoned the drugs wouldn't eat the drugs, right? That's why you all dragged me into a cage like an animal even though all I've been trying to do all night is help you?"

"You killed my best friend," Umu said. Mary could have kissed her. "In front of all of us, you killed him in cold blood. Is that helpful?"

"It was self-defense," Faye said. "I'll regret it for the rest of my life but at the time, I swear, I thought he killed Kip and was about to kill Davey. I didn't think I had a choice." She had eyes only for Mary. There were four of them standing there in the arena, four of them speaking, but this showdown was for two.

"We should have killed you when we had the chance," Umu said, though it was unconvincing. She didn't sound bloodthirsty. She sounded sad.

"Maybe." Faye took another step toward Mary. Mary stayed where she was. To move away from Faye, or toward her, would be to admit some sort of culpability. "But if you'd killed me when you had the chance, then there'd be no one here to warn you."

"To warn us about what, Faye?" Davey asked. There was a softening to his tone Mary didn't like.

"About Mary," Faye said. "You said I had to be the killer because I didn't take the drugs, but I told you all I wouldn't. There's insufficient research available about the long-term effects of LSD on brain function."

"The fucking physics again," Umu said.

"I didn't take them, but I told you I couldn't. Mary didn't take them, and she lied about it."

Mary wasn't one to sweat and she wasn't one to blush, but when Faye revealed her secret, it was all Mary could do to keep from vomiting.

"What's she talking about, Mary?" Davey asked.

"Check her pockets; the tab's still in there."

Someone smarter would have abandoned the baggie and the uneaten tab somewhere in the stacks, but Mary wasn't smart when she was sober. She held the cross on her necklace, zipped it back and forth against the chain. She'd bought the thing as a sobriety present to herself. In just the past year, she'd gotten high in the middle of the night and bought a collection of thirty-five Beanie Babies, an inflatable kayak that she'd shipped to her mother's house, a mint-green adult onesie, a $400 mounted light for a fish tank (she didn't own a fish tank), and a crate of $50 strawberries that rotted before she ever had a chance to eat them. She was a master of immediate gratification via retail when she was high, but when she was sober, the best she'd been able to do was a necklace with the charm of a religion she didn't even practice.

"Is she telling the truth, Mary?" Davey asked again.

"I saw her," Faye said. "I saw her when she was over by the barricade and the two of you had left. I saw her with the uneaten tab."

"And I saw Goody Proctor with the devil," Mary said. She swallowed bile and managed a laugh. No one laughed with her. Faye still held those blood-soaked scissors and now they were pointed right at her. Umu and Davey seemed to have forgotten that Faye was the one they were meant to be afraid of.

"I don't want to search your pockets, Mary," Davey said. He turned his back to Faye and her scissors. Mary had lost him. "Can you tell us if she's telling the truth?" he asked Umu.

If it had just been Davey, Mary thought she could have talked her way out of it. They'd worked together for two years, they knew one another, he trusted her. There would have been some machinations necessary to explain things, sure, but she could have done it. If not for Umu, the whole thing would have ended differently. Umu was a stranger to them, she had no idea what it looked like when Mary lied, but she had one distinct advantage over Davey. She spent a lot of time with someone who liked to get high.

Umu stalked right up to Mary. Mary didn't move. She kept her body rigid and worried that if she dared even breathe she would begin to shake and the whole thing would be over. They were almost nose to nose, neither girl saying anything, Umu only staring at her. There was a disbelieving sneer when she first approached, but it melted into something else. Still disbelieving, but then confused, then angry, then finally, terrified. It was Umu who began to tremble.

"Faye's telling the truth," Umu whispered. She took a horrified step back from Mary. Her hatred for Faye had been the one unwavering thing that night. Without it, she looked unmoored. "I don't know what else is going on, but I know for certain she's not high."

"You don't have to—" Mary started. The energy of pretending, or of disappearing into the background, that night had been exhausting. If Umu was suddenly unmoored, then Mary was the opposite: anchored, in control.

"Did you kill them?" Umu asked.

"I'm sober!" Mary said. She threw her hands in the air like it was the simplest explanation in the world. Like the real crime was that they hadn't noticed. "For, like, twenty days now, I'm sober."

"You're not sober," Davey said. "You run on Adderall the way most of this state runs on Dunkin'."

"I used to," Mary said. "That used to be true."

Faye was still standing there with those scissors, and all Mary wanted was to walk over and smack her across her smug face the way Umu had done earlier. What did she know about any of them, about anything? She'd come and made this grand declaration, and now she stood there, waiting to be hailed as a hero.

"I *just* saw you snorting crushed Adderall off the Caxton in the elevator, like, last week," Davey said.

"That was three weeks ago." That he remembered her doing it and didn't think it sounded like a big issue seemed to Mary to prove her point.

"Isn't the first step admitting you have a problem?" Faye said. She made a sarcastic gesture with the scissors, as though the danger were gone now that the others had come around to believing her. "Does it count as being sober if you don't tell people you're sober?"

"It counts as being sober if you don't snort amphetamines off priceless fifteenth-century manuscripts, you smug cunt, the other parts are 'nice to haves.'" Like she needed this farm-bred physicist telling her what counted as sobriety.

"Were you sober when I invited you to come?" Davey asked.

"I've been overdoing the Adderall, and I'm chilling with it for graduation. The whens and hows are no one's business."

"It's our business if the withdrawal led you to murder a couple of your coworkers," Faye said. "It can take months for your dopamine levels to return to normal after you stop using."

Mary pounced. That Faye was a killer was one thing. But she couldn't do it. She couldn't hear Faye say one more time that she was a scientist.

Mary had been prescribed the Adderall in high school. At the private girls' school she went to, the Adderall prescription was as much a rite of passage as a set of car keys for a girl's sixteenth birthday. Mary didn't think she had ADHD, nor did her parents. The Adderall was a competitive advantage, akin to private tutoring, and who were they to deny their daughter something that would keep her at the head of the class? It was all a bit of a cliché, the private school girl popping pills to keep up her productivity, but clichés get to be that way for a reason. The stuff worked marvelously.

In high school it meant she finished her homework, ran the student council, edited the yearbook, and started a Cantonese Club. In college the stakes got higher, and so did the dose. It made her social enough to create excellent Instagram content and focused enough to catalog rare books in Cantonese at the William E. Woodend Library.

Before graduation, when he learned he had funding to fill one permanent role, Ronald insisted that all his graduating students interview for the position. Mary had three finals that week and even though she'd decided she needed to get out of Vermont, even though she didn't even want the job, there was no way she could allow herself to do anything but excel at the interview.

So she might have overdone it on the Adderall.

Ronald let her get through the whole day. The presentation, the interview, the lunch with library donors, until finally at four that afternoon, he'd called her into his office, closed the door, assured her she'd done a wonderful job on the interview, and asked her how frequently she used amphetamines. He wouldn't let her leave his office until she promised to give it a rest, and she'd kept the promise she made him for twenty miserable days.

So when Mary pounced at Faye, it was as much about the built-up rage from the last three weeks of private withdrawal as it was about a sense of self-preservation.

"A murderer is always going to point fingers at everyone they can, and that's all you're doing," Mary yelled. She tried to grab Faye's arm that was holding the scissors, but she reared back and then they were both on the floor, Mary on top of Faye.

Davey and Umu both had their lights on, shining down at the two girls as they struggled. Theirs was an impossible quandary. Fifteen minutes ago they'd been certain they'd captured and contained their killer, Faye. Now they had a credible claim that Mary was the real danger. Mary yelled at them to come and help her, but she knew they wouldn't.

"I know it was you," she said to Faye, loud enough for Davey and Umu to hear. Still, they didn't come to her aid. She lunged up, crawling over Faye's body, and got two fingers on the scissors and that was all it took. "If you can get a finger on it, you can catch it." Her high school boyfriend said that when he tried to teach her to catch a football. Wasn't true in that case, but the scissors weren't a football. Faye's hands were so blistered, so bloody, she didn't stand a chance. Mary wrapped the sharp scissors in her fist and jumped back to her feet to face the others.

III

"Acid and Adderall," Umu said. "Those have nothing to do with one another."

Faye was on the floor, struck dumb by having lost her one advantage. Umu didn't move to help her, so Mary knew it was still possible to get Umu on her side. She was confused, but not convinced in either direction, afraid, but not sure of who. Mary held the pair of scissors in front of her, the only one of them with a weapon, but made an effort to sound gentle, lest she send Umu running in the wrong direction.

"What do you mean they have nothing to do with each other?"

"You said you were taking a break from Adderall," Umu said. "I get that. Who among us hasn't occasionally overdone it? But it's not like we're smoking meth to summon the gods. It was acid. That's about as far from Adderall as it gets."

How to explain to someone who doesn't intuitively understand that she hadn't so much as taken a Tylenol in the last three weeks for fear of triggering some impulse related to the action of swallowing a pill?

"And why hide it at all?" Davey said, rehashing ground that Faye had already tread. Mary was convinced he just needed to vocalize something so they wouldn't forget that he was meant to be in charge of the whole show. "Faye told us she didn't want to take the acid, and she didn't take the acid. You could have gone the same route. No one gave her a hard time about it."

"Until you used her abstention as proof she had killed a bunch of people!" Mary said. She was tiring of walking in circles, but now she was holding these scissors and wasn't quite sure how to get the others to go away.

"Right," Umu said. Her voice was shaky and she was holding

on to one of the stacks to keep herself upright, but her tone was more thoughtful than Davey's, and that made her more dangerous. "But at the time you should have refused the drugs, at the time she did"—she stuck her chin out at Faye, not at a place yet where she could use her name as anything but an accusation—"you couldn't have known that abstaining would make it look like you had done anything. Kip was alive."

"So unless you knew someone was going to die from taking those drugs, there was no reason to keep it a secret that you didn't want to take them!" Davey finished Umu's thought. There was a triumphant moment when he looked like he'd solved a puzzle until he absorbed the full weight of what he'd said and his shoulders dropped at the implication.

"You're all so selfish, it's like you're cartoon characters," Mary said, waving the scissors back and forth to make it clear she meant all of them. "I'm standing here telling you I have an addiction, and not one of you asks how I've been doing. This one"—she pointed at Umu—"says, 'who among us' hasn't been here. Who among you? Most sodding people, Umu!"

"Respectfully, Mary," Davey said, in a tone that wasn't at all respectful, "there are three human corpses down here with us, so you'll excuse us if we didn't pivot quickly enough to making this about Mary and her problems. Promise not to kill any more of us, and I'll bake you a cake myself when you get your one-month chip."

"This is the shit I'm talking about!" Mary said. Umu flinched a bit when Mary waved the scissors, and the flinch was a relief. Finally, they were hearing her. Finally, she had their attention. "I've been clean for almost three weeks and I've been *miserable*, and not one of you has even noticed."

"Is that why you killed Kip?" Umu asked. Only Faye was still silent. She seemed to understand, the way the others didn't, the danger of a stupid question.

"This isn't about Kip!" Mary could have exploded, she was an overfilled water balloon without any give left. "I've barely slept in three weeks. My eye bags have eye bags. At any point did one of you look at me and say, 'hey Mary, you feeling okay?' The first week I was throwing up three times per shift, and I know you must have noticed because there's only one staff bathroom, and I definitely always noticed when Soraya would go in there to throw up her lunch, but did any of you ever check to see if I needed a cup of tea or a breath mint or any help?"

"I thought you were stressed about finals," Davey said.

"You didn't think about me at all," Mary countered.

Umu, who didn't work at the library and was innocent of these accusations, put her hands up in defeat. "So is that it, Mary? It was all a sort of revenge?"

"What was all a sort of revenge?" She was past the point in her withdrawal where she constantly needed to vomit, but there was no normalcy in her emotions.

"Kip and Soraya," Umu said.

"For the last time, I didn't do anything to Kip and Soraya," Mary wailed. "What do I have to do to get you to believe me?"

"You have us at knifepoint," Davey said. Davey, who hadn't even bothered to apologize for his total lack of concern about her sobriety. "If you stopped threatening our lives, it would be a good start."

She let the scissors drop a little. She still held them tight but pointed at the ground now, instead of sweeping back and forth between the other three. If she showed herself softening, maybe they would believe her.

"I didn't do anything to Kip and Soraya," Mary reiterated. The darkness of the basement seemed somehow more consuming than it had been all night. Her palms ached from gripping the scissors so tightly, but she didn't dare readjust them or move them to the other hand. Umu was still leaning against one of the stacks, and Mary envied her that little bit of comfort. "Faye did, or Ro did, someone did, but not me. I think you're all awful, every one of you, but that's not enough motive to kill anyone. The only thing I wanted was to get clean and to put Vermont in my rearview mirror. I'm supposed to go to New York next week. You idiots might have ruined my chance to go to New York. I was motivated to leave Vermont behind forever, not to kill some of its residents."

"So what's a motive then?" Umu said.

Mary let the scissors drop even lower as she turned to her. She still held them tight, she still didn't trust any one of these three, but Umu spoke with some kindness in her voice, and Mary had a little bit of regret about lumping her in with the others when her situation was so different.

"You hated them, you said so yourself," Umu continued. "But hating someone isn't motive enough to kill them? According to you, it isn't. So what is motive enough?"

"Ask her," Mary swung the scissors up to point at Faye, but then again, let them drop. "I haven't killed anyone, so I wouldn't know."

"What if they took something you really, really wanted?" Umu said. "Would that be motive enough?"

There was a weird flickering quality to the light as one of their phones, Davey's maybe, dipped or twisted or changed position somehow. And then the light began to quiver, and Mary followed the quivering back to its source, and it was indeed Davey who was holding the light that was making the space tremble. Umu took a step back from him.

"I know something," Umu said. "I forgot all about it. I'm not sure how, but if we're talking about Kip and Soraya and what they could do to motivate someone to kill them, then I guess I do know something."

"What are you talking about?" Davey said, and Mary didn't understand what was happening, why he was trembling.

"Kip told me," Umu said. "He wasn't supposed to, but like you all keep saying, I don't work here so it's not like it mattered. I saw him last week in the humanities building when I was dropping off a paper for another class, and he told me something about Soraya and, I guess indirectly, about Davey." She backed up again, moving closer to Mary and away from Davey. Taking her lead, Mary moved the point of the scissors so they pointed at him, though she didn't know what Umu was going to say.

"You all interviewed for a job here, right?" Umu said. "Everyone who was graduating had to interview, even if they didn't want the job, or even if they didn't stand a chance at it. Kip thought that was weird. He thought it was weird when Soraya was getting ready for the interview because he said he knew she wanted to work in tech or something, and apparently everyone knew that the job was supposed to go to Davey."

When had they all come to understand the job was Davey's? Mary couldn't remember but she'd always thought so. When she prepared for her interview, she strove to do her best because it was in her nature to do so, but she always felt like she was preparing to interview for Davey's job.

"But the job didn't go to Davey," Umu said. "Kip told me it was offered to Soraya. He was super confused about why and even more confused because after mulling the job offer over for a week, she was planning to accept it."

"What does that have to do with anything?" Davey said, barely above a whisper.

"Because of what Kip said when he told me," Umu replied. "He said, 'Davey's going to kill Soraya when he finds out.' And I laughed when he said it, but he told me I shouldn't because he was serious: that there was someone at the library who he really thought would kill Soraya when he heard she took his job."

⸻

They were all liars, that was what threw Mary off-balance. Soraya had said for two years she was just passing through the library, and then she lied about taking the thing Davey desperately wanted. Davey set up this whole elaborate party or ritual or whatever he wanted to call it and lied about bringing Soraya down here as a friend. Even Kip, who doubtless had promised Soraya he'd keep the news about her job secret, had gone on to share it with one of his students. Mary had lied, too, but compared to everyone else's lies, hers was noble or justified or in some way not as terrible.

She watched Umu's pronouncement play out on Davey's face. He opened his mouth to speak in his own defense and then closed it. He looked around the remaining participants, the surviving participants, and she could hear the wheels in his head turning to craft a strategy, having to work terribly hard as they fought against the chemicals he'd juiced them with that very night.

Faye was still on the floor, where Mary had left her when she'd grabbed the scissors, and as Davey stood there, not responding to the accusation, Faye did something strange. She slowly scooted herself backward, creating distance between herself and Davey. With tiny steps and slithers across the floor, they'd repositioned themselves so Umu, the only one of them who hadn't been credibly accused of murder, stood in the middle of this triangle of terror, formed by the three potential assailants.

Why would Faye move? Mary tried to sort out a motive from the girl's face. If she believed Davey was dangerous, then it meant she herself wasn't guilty of anything. If she was putting on a show—wanting them to believe she believed Davey was dangerous—backing away from him was the clearest symbol.

We can't all make it out alive, Mary thought. If there hadn't been so much lying already, it might have been possible. If everyone had been honest about what they knew and why they were doing what they were doing, then the bodies might have stopped falling after Kip, but there'd been too much lying and there was no getting out of it now. Someone else would have to die. The hunger and the fear and the fatigue and the withdrawal had turned into a headache, and the dull pounding in her temples kept her from any sort of clear thought.

"You don't kill someone over a job." There it was. Davey's weak opening serve in his own defense, issued more as a whine than as a statement. Umu faced him, meaning she had her back to Mary and Faye, and Mary could see her discomfort, the way she held her shoulders near her ears. She hadn't yet decided who to believe.

"People have killed over a lot less," Umu said, easily sending Davey's argument back over the net at him.

"What you're saying makes no sense," Davey said. "Soraya wasn't even the first one to die. Kip was. We're down here because Mary poisoned Kip." Mary went cold at having her name invoked. She wanted the focus to stay on Davey. "In your version of events," Davey continued. "In your version of events, I knew Mary was going to poison Kip and I planned to use being trapped in the basement after she committed murder as my opportunity to take out Soraya so I could steal back the job she took from me? Seems like there would be an easier way to go about that."

It made for a much stronger return.

"But you're admitting you knew about Soraya?" Umu said.

"I—" Davey stammered. He'd been expecting her to hit back right down the middle, but this was an unexpected lob skyward. Mary was as curious to hear the answer as Umu was. Had Davey known Soraya was hired instead of him? If so, when had he found out? And who had told him?

The scissors were heavy in Mary's hand, but the point didn't droop toward the floor any longer. Her weapon was pointed squarely at Davey.

"I had no idea," Davey finally said. Mary didn't believe him. "If you're telling the truth and Soraya was hired over me, then this is the first I'm hearing of it."

They were all liars. In trying to return Umu's lob, he'd managed only a weak hit that didn't even clear the net. It rolled pathetically back to his own feet. When none of them replied, Davey did the only thing that could make the situation worse for himself: he kept talking.

"How could I possibly have known?" he said. "You all know Ronald." Though of course, Umu didn't. "He's fair and moral to a fault. If the rules say he can't tell the candidates until all the paperwork has been approved, then he won't tell the candidates until all the paperwork has been approved. I asked him about it today! Or yesterday, or whenever it was that I last saw him, but he said he couldn't make an announcement yet, so we had to keep waiting. I didn't know. Ronald didn't tell me."

Davey seemed smaller then. He was six feet tall and had big broad shoulders left over from his high school swim team, but he shrank an inch for every minute he kept having to explain himself, and if he kept going for much longer, Mary would be able to hold him in the palm of her hand. He was a liar, but she pitied him. She pitied him, but she couldn't look away from him.

Mary understood that Umu had been lobbing balls at more than just Davey only after the full weight of Umu's body came hurtling at her midsection. It occurred to Mary that Umu was smarter than most undergraduates at the precise moment she hit the concrete floor, with Umu on top of her, giving a warrior's wail. Mary had been so fixated on Davey she hadn't felt Umu's fixation on her. Clever girl.

Umu grabbed for the scissors, but Mary would relinquish those over her dead body. It was a clumsy grab and Mary pulled back easily from it. Umu was smarter than Mary gave her credit for, sure, but Mary had an advantage in this fight she knew was unconquerable. She was sober and Umu wasn't.

"Please stop," Faye whined, from somewhere by the stacks. Too much had changed for Mary to name the villain among them with any certainty, but she knew that Faye was a real threat, if only for her sobriety. If Faye didn't intervene, it was only because she was still skittish after Umu's earlier attack on her.

Davey said nothing. He didn't move toward them; he backed away to be near Faye and to let their fight play out. Mary could see he was blinking rapidly, and she had to assume he was in the midst of some sort of hallucination, perhaps uncertain whether or not this altercation was occurring at all.

"Give them to me," Umu said through gritted teeth. Mary got herself halfway up and then with all her might, she pushed Umu to the side and jumped back to her feet.

Umu wouldn't let it be over. She lunged again, grabbing for the scissors with her left hand and leaving Mary with what felt like no choice. She raised the scissors above her head to keep them away from Umu, and then brought them down on that interfering arm.

CHAPTER 23

FAYE

I

In her entire life, Faye couldn't have imagined that she'd see as much bloodshed as she'd seen in that one night.

"She cut me!" Umu cried. Mary made a quick escape into the dark and left the three of them with the consequences of her attack.

"You're bleeding," Davey said. "You should really put something on that."

It seemed to be a reflex Davey had, recommending antibiotic cream for a scratch, even as he stood next to a bomb that was about to explode.

Umu held her forearm up to the light from her phone. The gash ran from her wrist to her elbow. It wasn't deep, but it was ugly. There was some blood, but it didn't spray or gush, so it made the whole thing anticlimactic. Mary's rubber-soled shoes gave no clue where she'd run to, but she'd taken the scissors with her. Umu and her wound were the immediate danger, but Faye had equipped the killer with a weapon, and there was little chance they'd be safe from her until the morning.

"Can I take a look?" Faye said. She had to approach Umu slowly. Even with evidence that Faye wasn't the villain, the air between them was uneasy. Umu hated her, and with good reason, and Faye knew to stay away from girls who hated her if she didn't want to be subject to unnecessary cruelty. The moment called for something bigger than Faye's instincts, though. Umu needed Faye's comfort more than Faye needed Umu's kindness. Umu's big eyes were wide, and if Faye had hoped for praise for warning them that Mary was dangerous, she saw now it wouldn't come, but it didn't matter, not while Umu stood there and bled.

Umu shivered and looked between Davey and Faye and the darkness where Mary had disappeared. Any or all of them were killers, and she looked like she didn't know who to be most afraid of. But at least for now, Faye had no weapon. There was no sign of immediate danger, so Umu extended her bleeding arm for Faye to see.

Faye was wearing a loose blue T-shirt over a tank top. Both were stained with blood, and in an ideal world, she'd have liked something sterile to put on Umu's arm, but there was nothing in the whole basement that wasn't covered with human fluids. Faye pulled off her blue shirt and wound it tight around Umu's arm to create a makeshift bandage. When she first touched the girl, Umu flinched, but then she let herself be helped. She may not have trusted Faye, not yet, but there was evidence of some softening as Faye tucked the ends of the shirt in on itself to hold it in place.

"I'll bet you don't even need stitches for it," Faye said, and when Umu only nodded instead of snapping something about Faye not knowing what she was talking about, Faye counted it as a win.

An ear of corn, now one of two, was by Faye's foot. If Davey hadn't been there, if she'd been alone with Umu, she might have picked it up, pulled off the husk, and suggested they break their fast.

II

"Hello?" Davey said. Faye stepped back from Umu like she'd been caught doing something illicit. "If you're done playing nurse now, we have to go after her."

"Why?" Faye said.

"You're the one who came here to warn us about her," Davey said. He was speaking as though an accusation hadn't been made about him after one had been made about Mary. Like that part had been erased. "Do I really have to explain this to you?"

"She's dangerous and she has a weapon," Umu said, holding her blue-wrapped arm to her chest.

"Which is why we should stay here," Faye said. "We're together. We're in a space that's pretty open. This is the safest we can be."

"We can't be safe while she's still out there with a weapon," Davey said. "What we need to do is find her and restrain her so she can't do anything to us between now and morning."

It wasn't funny, but Faye laughed. They were moving in circles. "Davey, that's what you tried to do to me. How did that work out?"

He was surprised to be second-guessed. "It was Mary who told us the barricade was secure. And it was Mary who it turns out we shouldn't have trusted. This will be different. Can we go, please?"

"I can't stand here and wait to be attacked again," Umu said, and then she surprised all of them when she turned to Faye. "You should come with us."

Did she want Faye to come because she was afraid to be alone with Davey or because she was afraid of what Faye was capable of if left alone? When Faye looked at Davey, she could see him clearly with his hands on a wobbly bookshelf, pushing it down over Soraya.

She couldn't take instruction from him; she couldn't run after him into the dark.

"We're going," Davey said. "With or without you."

She shook her head. They went without her.

III

"You'll be sorry if she comes for you," Davey said. But wouldn't she be just as sorry if she disappeared around a dark corner with him and felt hands on her throat? He and Umu were moving to the edge of the arena. Davey was wound up like he wanted to sprint, but Umu moved slowly. She was tethered to Ro's body and, newly, to Faye, who she might have preferred to tie herself to for safety, if that had been an option.

"Umu?" Faye said. "You don't have to go. It's not safer out there."

"She could be right behind that stack, watching us." Umu waved her blue-bandaged arm at a dark bookshelf. "I won't stay here and be hunted."

Faye understood. There was no level of comfort she could provide that would compete with Umu's fear. She only hoped she was wrong about Davey. She hoped she was somehow wrong about both Davey and Mary, and the whole thing could still be explained away. There was too much blood to make that possible now, but she felt she owed a debt to Umu, and allowing her to run off with Davey was no way to repay her.

Any patience that resided in Davey had evaporated, and he walked out of the arena, with Umu behind him.

"Be safe!" Faye called after them, but neither gave any indication of having heard her. When she was alone again, she was worried for Umu but also relieved. Faye was good at being alone, used to being alone, and she knew she was no danger to herself. She sank to the floor and put her head in her hands, finally with some time to think. It was almost four. It would be three hours at the very least before someone came to find them. The battery life indicator on her phone said she was down to 15 percent, so she turned off the light. The darkness was absolute but what had seemed to be quiet was suddenly deafening. She'd expected to hear Umu's and Davey's footsteps, or whispers, but any distant noise was drowned out by the sounds around her. The loose sheets of torn-up books on the floor that rustled any time she moved. The air conditioner that must have been running all night but now roared like a jet engine. She'd insisted she was safer here but with all the noise, she'd never hear if someone crept up on her. Faye turned her light back on.

There were still half-burnt candles scattered across the floor, and she lit one and then reperformed the ceremony of creating a little wax pool as a candle stand before, again, turning out the light on her phone. The candle added another noise. The hiss of the wick burning down. The occasional pop of the flame. It was all so loud, but at least she wasn't in the dark anymore. She sat and she waited. It wasn't long before she finally reached for that ear of corn. After she picked it up, she paused again. No footsteps. No breathing. Only the hiss of the wick, the rustle of the paper, the roar of the air conditioner. She pulled off the husk. As she did her mouth filled with saliva, every cell in her body hummed in preparation for the most delicious thing it had ever tasted.

The candle beckoned and she imagined the aroma, the flavor, of those perfect yellow kernels licked by the flame. There was no butter or salt, of course, but the sugars in the corn would caramelize and release their juices.

In the end, she couldn't wait for the corn to cook. She needed it and she needed it immediately, so as soon as she'd removed the husk, she took a hungry bite of the raw kernels. The pleasure of hunger satisfied! She chewed slowly, a necessity after so many hours of fasting, but the corn was so sweet that she might have been floating three feet off the floor. The cob in her hand promised so much more to eat. She could have devoured the whole thing in seconds, but she took her time, decided on twenty-five chews before she would let herself swallow and while there was a sense of denying herself something, there was also such pleasure each time she chewed and extracted more sugar from the corn in her mouth.

She had finally counted to twenty-five, she had finally allowed herself the ecstasy of sending calories down to her depleted body, and was raising the cob of corn to her lips to take that next, ecstatic bite, when she locked eyes with Ro.

It was an illusion. Ro's eyes were closed. Ro was dead. Ro was dead because she had killed him. He would never enjoy sweet summer corn again and here she was, basking in the euphoria of perfect food. She put the corn down without taking that second bite. She wasn't hallucinating, she knew he wasn't watching her, but she also knew that she couldn't disrespect him by eating in his presence. She smoothed the husk she'd torn off the corn in haste and wrapped it back around that perfect yellow fruit—the wrapping on a gift she'd had no right to open in the first place.

"We want to talk!" Davey's voice rang through the basement. "Come out so we can talk to you!"

It sounded to Faye like he wanted to do more than talk. She could hear the spite in his voice, and she was sure Mary could, too. There was a promise in his tone that if she emerged from her hiding place it would be a death sentence. The only thing she could do to break that promise would be to wield the weapon she was still carrying.

"Mary!" Davey yelled again. There wasn't any reply. Of course there wouldn't be. Faye didn't hear anything from Mary, that was expected, obvious, but she didn't hear anything from Umu either, and she wondered what she might be doing, how she might be feeling. Did she have the same fire in her blood as Davey did? Was she following him because she was afraid? Was she following him despite the fact she was afraid of him?

"There's hours before the sun comes up," he said. His voice was somewhere different now. Not in the direction of the exit but coming from the exhibition room. "You're only making it harder for yourself. Come out and talk to us."

Was Mary cowering in a corner? Or was she poised and ready to pounce when they came upon her? Faye couldn't conjure a picture of her. She thought only of Umu.

When the night started she hadn't had anything in common with Umu. Stylish, beautiful, laughing, confident Umu. But that changed because Faye changed it. Now they had one significant commonality. Neither Umu nor Faye had a best friend. Faye imagined taking Umu back to her house for the summer holidays a year from now. On the longest day of the year, they would sit on her porch for the annual summer celebration. The sky would stay pink until ten o'clock, but they wouldn't mind because they'd have so much to talk about that maybe they wouldn't even notice the moment when the sun finally slipped below the horizon.

Across the basement she could still hear Davey's voice, but it wasn't a shout any longer, so she couldn't make out what he was saying. Was he still in pursuit of Mary, or were he and Umu talking about Faye? Even thirty minutes ago she'd have worried that they'd turned on her, that they were planning to harm her, but she knew now that wouldn't happen. Umu wouldn't allow it.

Umu would help Faye's mother with the baking. Her family wasn't much for sweets, but her mother made exceptional breads. Sourdough, brioche, baguettes, croissants. She treated them as science experiments and they came out perfect—gleaming and crackling every time. Faye had never had much interest. She preferred her science experiments bound to a lab. She could tell that Umu would be different, that she'd delight in the weights and measures and in the pleasure of watching a loaf slowly rise and take on a perfect brown. Faye couldn't be certain, but she thought that Umu's joy in baking with her mother might be the thing to finally turn her on to the activity, so maybe by the second summer they spent with Faye's family, it might be something that the three of them indulged in together.

She wasn't sure what Umu's family might be like, but she looked

forward to being brought home to meet them. She let herself fanta-
size that they'd think her an improvement over Umu's most recent
best friend, but she felt guilty for thinking that. It was enough that
he was gone. There wasn't any need to be thought better than him.
In any case, she'd make a real effort with Umu's family. If they were
gardeners, she'd garden with them. If they liked to hike in the woods,
she'd do that, too. She'd play video games, go to sporting events, do
whatever it was they liked to do as a family so they knew how much
she valued Umu's friendship.

She'd been trying to avoid him, but of course her eyes came back
to Ro.

"I suppose that's the whole reason you're here," she said to him.
"You were making an effort."

If he'd sat up from his dead sleep and looked her in the eye, he
couldn't have made her feel as guilty as she felt at that moment. This
boy she was so eager to replace only needed replacing because of the
work of her hand. The rest of them had been selfish, in one way or
another, in their motivations for spending the night in the basement,
but not Ro. He came to be with his best friend, to protect his best
friend, and he'd given his whole life in the process.

"I'm so terribly sorry," she whispered, but there would be no abso-
lution. He couldn't say he forgave her, no one could, and so she'd
never be forgiven and she'd carry his weight for the rest of her life.
The only thing she could do was carry on his purpose. She went to
him and took his hand. It was cold and stiff.

"I'll take care of her," she said, and then she kissed his knuckles
and went to find Umu and Davey.

<hr />

"Mary!" Davey called from across the basement. "Mary, we know
you're in here."

Asinine. Unnecessary. Where else would she be?

His voice was still coming from the area by the exhibition room, and then Faye understood. Davey meant that Mary was using the room as a refuge. And why not? If they had thought the room secure enough to lock Faye in, then Mary must have judged it appropriate to keep the rest of them out.

Faye followed the sound of Davey's fists against the door. Her candle blew out almost as soon as she started jogging with it, but she didn't dare turn her phone back on. It was only four. There was too much night left to go and too little battery to go with it, and besides, she was intimate with the basement now. She could find her way to them in the dark.

She knew she was getting close when she saw the faint red glow of the exit sign. It had illuminated Mary for her a short while ago, and now it illuminated her path back to her. She was right upon them, Davey's voice, Davey's fists, they were right around the corner, but before she reached them, she saw something else that she'd been seeking for hours. The exit sign pointed to a door that was behind the grate and out of reach, but on the wall inside the grating, there it was. A fire alarm. She exhaled in absolute relief and pulled it and the alarm began to scream.

IV

"You've pulled the wrong pig, Mary. Open this door!" Davey screamed as she came around the corner. The door to the exhibition room swung out and there was no lock on it, so Mary must have been keeping it closed by sheer force, pulling it in while Davey tried to pull it out. She was half his size, so it should have been impossible, but nothing is impossible when someone is desperate.

"Is there a fire alarm after all?" Umu said when she saw Faye. She was standing by Davey but offering no help. Only holding the fabric of her skirt with her uninjured arm and swishing it between her anxious fingers again. The alarm wailed. When you hear a siren like that, you're supposed to flee, and it was a disconcerting sensation, hearing the warning but remaining fixed in place.

"You'll be sorry if I have to break down this door!" Davey took a break from pulling at the handle and went at the door with his fists.

"I found a fire alarm and pulled it!" Faye said. She went to Davey and put a hand on his shoulder. "We can stop this now. Someone is going to come and rescue us. The fire department is going to come."

He took Faye's hand off and grabbed the door handle and, maybe he was imbued with new strength or maybe Mary's was depleted but, in any case, the door flew open and Mary stumbled back from it, deeper into the room. She clutched for her scissors and then got herself into a fighting stance.

"Put down the scissors," Davey said.

Faye could see the muscles in Mary's forearm tighten as she clutched the scissors harder. One thing was clear. She had no intention of putting them down. The fire alarm was the old sort; it sounded like a desperately clanging bell or a screeching telephone. It rang for three seconds and then paused for one and then rang for three seconds again and so on.

"I want to talk," Davey said. "We can't talk if you're holding a weapon at us, so put down the scissors and let's sort this out."

"The second I put down these scissors, you grab them and you kill me," Mary said, and if the only evidence under consideration was the murderous look in Davey's eyes, then she was right. If she put down the scissors, she didn't stand a chance. But if she held on to them, it might be another one of them who perished.

To be heard over the sound of the alarm, they had to scream, but Davey went to Umu and whispered something in her ear. Umu looked uncertain. Faye thought she knew the girl well enough to be able to say that now—what she looked like when she was uncertain—but Umu nodded.

The alarm shrieked and Mary clutched the scissors and then Davey and Umu, in time with one another, ran at Mary.

V

Mary laughed the way people do when something is wholly unexpected and they aren't sure how else they're meant to react. I have to stop this, Faye thought. I have to stop it. But she couldn't move, so she only watched. Umu was a step or two behind Davey, and Faye was sure it was because she still wasn't certain which of the two, Davey or Mary, was the real threat in the room. Davey threw his whole body on top of Mary's and pinned the arm that held the scissors to the ground above her head.

"Umu, grab them," he said, and she tried, but Mary wasn't going to go down without a fight. Three seconds on, one second off, the siren continued to wail. Mary rolled onto her side and managed to get herself out from under Davey's arm and then she was back on her feet.

"End this," Davey said, and all Faye could do was stand in the doorway with her hands over her mouth, willing them all to stop, though she knew it had gone too far now: they'd never stop. One of them would run out of strength, and their body would be the next offer for the waiting gods.

The problem was that the three of them were so tangled in one another. Davey got back to his feet after Mary did, but Umu was now somehow in between the two of them—she'd remained upright all along—and in the heat of the moment and over the shriek of the siren, he didn't tell Umu what he intended to do. He lunged for Mary, lunged for the scissors, and Mary held them up, either because she had the taste of blood in her mouth or because a person will always defend herself. But there was Umu, caught between them, and it was no one's intention that it should end so, but those impossibly sharp scissors caught on Umu and plunged right into her beating heart.

All night Faye had been hanging back, waiting for permission to give a comforting touch, allowing Davey to reach out and grasp her hand but not daring to give that same outreach herself, but at the moment before Umu realized what was happening, she turned her head and locked eyes with Faye and though the alarm drowned out her words, Faye could read them clearly on her lips.

"I'm scared," Umu said, and it was all the permission Faye needed. She threw herself toward the fray so she could grasp Umu's hand and promise her that things would be all right.

Her own breath, her own heartbeat, drowned out by the sound of the siren, Faye waited for Umu to shake off Mary and Davey, but she didn't. When Faye got to her, when she took hold of her lovely hand, Umu fell, face-first to the ground, and the impact of that concrete floor forced those long scissors all the way through so the gleaming tip peered out by her lifeless shoulder blade.

VI

Did Mary rear back in horror, or did Davey push her away from Umu's body? Impossible for Faye to know; it all happened too quickly. Mary was scrambling back across the floor and Davey was scrambling after her and Faye's heart was broken. She knelt by Umu's body and put her fingertip on the end of those scissors. The summer nights watching the sun go down, the laughter in the kitchen as they baked with her mother, the shared secrets, the shared jokes, they all vanished when she touched the weapon that had killed her would-be best friend.

Davey and Mary were at the far end of the room, where the big table had been before Faye moved it. Now there was dust and their rolling bodies. They swore and grunted and banged at each other and the siren shrieked, three seconds on and one off, and Faye's only relief was that they were far from any sort of weapon, that the only implement of murder in the room was through Umu's heart, so at the very least, they would be spared more blood.

During one of the second-long pauses, Faye heard the back of a head smash against the ground, but when she looked over at them, they were both still moving, still fighting, so she kept her attention on Umu's body. There was an indecency to letting her stay face down, but Faye wasn't yet prepared to see her face in death, so she stroked her back and offered her apologies and assured Umu that she would be reunited with the friend that she would have missed so terribly if she'd stayed in the living world.

VII

"Please!" Faye yelled at Mary and Davey during one of the pauses in the alarm. They were disturbing Umu's rest. The endless fighting, the endless violence, was a disrespect to the dead. "Please, I'm begging you to stop this. The fire department will be here any minute; what's the point? Please stop."

Davey yelled something in her direction, but he didn't wait for a pause in the alarm so she didn't hear him. Faye recalled where the campus police building was, close to the largest of the residence halls, but had never seen a fire station. She imagined the fire truck would have to come from a nearby town but even still, it was summer, it was the stillest part of the night, it would be there in minutes.

"There's no one coming!" Davey yelled. Maybe he repeated it when he saw that Faye still looked hopeful. The alarm rang for another three seconds and then Davey yelled over to her again in the next pause. "It's just noise. The alarm doesn't call anyone."

Some part of her must have known that. In a building so old it didn't have working smoke detectors, in a building so old it didn't have fire exits, she must have known that the fire alarms wouldn't have a link to the fire department. It was a noise, a warning that someone should call the fire department, but they were the only ones who could hear it. She hadn't freed them. She'd only caused a racket.

VIII

'Tis not too late to seek a newer world, Faye thought as she watched Davey and Mary wrestle. He was stronger; she was faster. He had the intensity of the intoxicated; she had the focus of the sober. They were evenly matched. It might go on all night. There was no one coming to stop them. Only Faye and a pile of bodies to wait for the outcome, and the truth of the matter was that one of the two who were grunting and shouting across the floor from her had killed Kip, which could only mean that when they finished with each other they were coming for her. Tennyson was wrong. It was too late.

The alarm, that terrible alarm, kept at it. Three seconds on and one off, and she might have had the clarity to find a way out of it if not for the noise, but she couldn't think of anything but her fear and her despair in all that clamor.

"Please stop," she said, her voice little, her sentiment half-hearted. Did she want them to stop? If they stopped, wouldn't they come for her? "Maybe Soraya was an accident," she offered, weakly. Repeating Davey's claim that she hadn't herself believed. She didn't wait for the pause in the alarm that time. In the next pause she heard another crack of a body part against the floor. A head again? A knee? What did it matter? They would tear each other apart.

Outside the library, in the world they had no access to, the sun would soon begin to rise. In these endless sunny days, the sky turned purple well before five in the morning and the pinks appeared not long after. The raccoons and skunks would soon be heading for their rest. It was too close to morning for a late-night reveler to be passing the library and hear the alarm and too steeped in night for an early morning runner or cyclist to be passing. The alarm shrieked. Mary and Davey struggled. One of them had killed Kip. They would soon finish their battle and then they would kill her.

"What is the matter with you?" Davey yelled, and it was clear he was yelling at Faye, not at Mary. "How can you sit there? She's going to kill me!"

Was she? Faye supposed it was possible. Hadn't she been the one who had exposed Mary's lie? Hadn't she blistered and bloodied her hands so she could warn Davey and Umu about the danger Mary posed to them? That felt like days ago.

"The scissors," Davey panted when the alarm next paused. "Help me." Three more seconds of shrieking. "Get the scissors and hand them to me."

The scissors, the weapon, the thing they were too far from to reach themselves, were still buried in Umu's chest and sticking through her back. To get him the scissors would mean disturbing Umu's rest. Turning her over to see her face in death, grabbing the scissors in her fist, and yanking them out of her body. It was an act so violent it made Faye physically ill to think about it. Could anyone but a killer ask her to inflict such violence? Could anyone but a murderer ask her to defile a body in such a manner?

"The scissors!" he called again, and he sounded so bitter, so angry. How could she consider him anything but a threat to her safety? "Stop with this pathetic turtling and give them to me!"

He had Mary pinned to the floor, held so securely that he was only using one hand to hold her arms. The other was stretched in Faye's direction, certain that any moment she would hand him the scissors, certain that she would do what he asked, certain that she was so desperate for his approval that she would aid him in a murder. If he wanted to restrain Mary for safety, he'd done so. Faye would take this no further. She sat with Umu's body and hugged her knees, waiting for the violence to end.

They both looked terrified, Mary and Davey. Someone's phone, Mary's perhaps, was face up on the floor, and it illuminated their features. They were frozen in place. Davey atop Mary with no means by which to advance the fight and Mary under Davey with no means of escape. One of them was a killer, Faye reminded herself, and she kept her place by Umu's body.

It might have ended there. They might have been locked in that impasse until morning. Until the sun sat high and the door swung open, but Mary's impulse for flight was stronger than her impulse to remain as she was, and Faye heard a groan of pain during one of the pauses as Mary managed to free her leg and jam her knee as hard as she could at Davey's groin. It only took a moment, but a moment was all Mary needed. She rolled out from under his arms and then she was atop him. There was a metallic clatter as they struggled, some forgotten object out of Faye's view. She didn't want to look, she didn't want to see any more violence, but she looked because she knew she was next. She moved to a crouch, her toes flexed so she could flee if she needed.

Mary pressed her forearms down on Davey's throat as he writhed to get his arms out from under her chest. His eyes bulged, he gurgled something unintelligible. She was going to kill him. And with the act, she would dispel any doubt Faye had about the identity of Kip and Soraya's killer. Death is the end of life, ah why, should life all labor be? The chant from earlier in the evening, a lifetime ago, played in her head. Without joy, without amusement, with only good grades and sterling graduate school recommendation letters to show for their years. This is where it would end.

Like she had been about so much else that night, Faye was wrong. It wasn't the end. Davey let out a desperate gulp for air and in doing so, summoned some hidden strength. There was another metallic clang and then he rolled Mary's body off his. Mary gasped in surprise, and then there was that metal sound again, louder now, the sound of Mary's head against something hard that sounded different from the concrete floor, and then Davey roared so loud that Faye didn't have to wait for a pause in the alarm to hear him, and he brought the curved steel arm of the paper cutter down, the heavy green paper cutter that dropped to the floor when Faye moved the table, the paper cutter Mary had rolled onto, the paper cutter that Davey used to cleanly sever Mary's head.

CHAPTER 24

STILL FAYE

I

She had planned to run but Faye found she couldn't. Davey's roar turned into a whimper the moment he got the blade all the way down and Mary's body, detached from her rolling head, continued to twitch in the dim light. Faye planned to run, but her terror made it so the electrical signal from her spinal cord to her muscles, telling them to contract, telling them to move, failed somewhere along the way.

The room was lit only by that one phone. The phone had an attachment it wore like a backpack, an extra battery. It had to be Mary's. Who but Mary would need such a device, would exhibit such forethought about her device? For the rest of them, it was just a phone; for Mary it was a window to the outside world, a window for the outside world to see into her. That flashlight could shine for hours longer. It could shine until morning, though Mary no longer had any need of its light.

If anyone saw Mary's face, just her face, not her neck or the strands of her hair that were sticky with blood, but her pretty features, they might think she had been surprised by a birthday party in her honor or by the sound of a popping balloon. It wasn't horror, it wasn't pain, but her lips were parted and shaped into an *O*. If one couldn't go peacefully, then surprise wasn't the worst outcome. Faye supposed that Mary had never seen the blade of the paper cutter coming. She'd been wearing a delicate gold necklace with a cross on it. Faye wouldn't have guessed her as religious. It stayed with Mary's head. Intact, clinging to what remained of her neck.

Davey was on his knees over Mary's body, which was finally, mercifully, lifeless. Her head had rolled some distance, and her face was turned to Faye so he couldn't see her expression of happy surprise. If he was imagining anything, it was sure to be a snarl of horror.

"Faye?" he whispered across the room. The alarm continued its work and when it paused, he said it again. "Faye?"

She shook her head. What could he possibly have to say to her? Was there a speech he planned to make? An admittance of his guilt and his intentions, the way a villain might speechify in a film before carrying out his last terrible deed? The alarm blared. It probably hadn't grown louder since Faye first pulled it, but it felt that way. She didn't answer him, but she did meet his eye. She wasn't sure what she expected, but it wasn't tears. His face was wet with them.

Davey put his hands up. Like she was the firing squad rather than him. "It was self-defense," he said. "You know that, right? That I wouldn't have hurt her, but she would have killed me?"

If there was a wilder claim he could have made at the moment, she couldn't think of it. Self-defense was a matter of proportional response, and Mary's head was rolling across the floor. Entirely unproportional, she would say.

"She was going to strangle me," he said. "She had her full weight on my throat and I was starting to see spots. Faye. Faye? You have to believe me."

Had Mary been in any position to speak in her own defense, she might have pointed out that she was half Davey's size and that all he had to do to subdue the threat of being strangled was to get out from under her arms, which he'd done successfully before chopping off her lovely head.

"You have to believe me," he said again. He lowered his hands, slowly, to make clear he was no threat, and rested them on his thighs.

"Tell me the truth, okay, Davey?" This cursed library had seen so much bloodshed. The place would need to be burned. That was the only image that gave her any comfort, the idea of the whole place up in smoke. "It doesn't make any difference now anyway." The subtext—because he was surely about to kill her. "Why did you poison Kip?"

She could begin to understand Soraya. That Davey felt ill will toward her. While Kip was hardly a lovable character, his death had been so ugly that it could only have been inspired by a deep hate. The alternative, the one she hardly dared consider, was that Kip's death was incidental. That any of them, including her, could have been the recipient of the poison. That it had started as a game.

"I didn't poison Kip," he said. "I didn't poison anyone!" He added that as though he were following her line of thought. That he needed a body for his ritual and Kip hadn't been guilty of anything, only unlucky.

The scissors Davey had asked her to grab for him were still in Umu's chest, and she was ashamed to find herself considering them. When Davey had asked for them, the idea of disturbing Umu was abhorrent, but for the sake of self-preservation, it didn't seem so terrible.

"Then tell me the truth about Soraya," she said. Every second she kept talking was a second he wasn't upon her; it was the second before the next terrible event. "Did you plan it, with Soraya? Or was it in the heat of the moment? You were high, there was so much emotion…"

"She was climbing the stack and it collapsed. Accidentally. That must be what happened. I didn't kill anyone!"

A lie. Mary's body there to prove it. His swollen eyelid looked like it was throbbing. They were still apart. She, by the door, he, by the back of the room. She didn't dare even look at Umu, should he follow her eyes to the scissors.

"But you knew about the job? That she was hired over you?"

That swollen eyelid, throbbing in time with his heartbeat.

That alarm, giving him a moment to consider his answer.

"No," he said after a time. "No. I thought the job was mine until Umu told us otherwise tonight. I didn't know anything until after Soraya was dead."

They were all liars. How could she know if anything he said was true?

"Faye," he said. "Faye." Like saying her name over and over would get her on his side. When they'd worked together in the library, while the rest of them chatted over coffees in the break room or gathered around a desk to look at a recent acquisition one of them was working on, she'd longed to be invited in. She'd longed to hear her name spoken. She could go days, weeks in a row without hearing it. Sometimes when she called her mother, she asked specifically to hear her name said aloud. And now he said it, over and over, now that she didn't want to hear it from him anymore. "I didn't kill Soraya. I didn't kill Kip. I didn't kill anyone."

Except Mary. Again, the elision. She didn't say that though. She wouldn't dare anger him.

"You think she did it?" Faye asked, turning her attention to Mary's body. "Kip, I mean?"

He shook his head and wiped a fresh tear from his nose. "I have to think that, don't I?" In wiping his tear he'd smeared blood on his face. His swollen eye, his bloody face. More and more he looked like he'd been in a battle. "If I didn't believe she did it, I'd never sleep again. I killed a killer. I need that to be true."

If he hadn't moved they might have coexisted that way through to the morning, but from that stillness, he moved quickly to get to his feet and every ounce of adrenaline left in Faye's body screamed at her to flee. She had her back to him before he was fully on his feet, and after a split-second consideration of the scissors, it was her body that ultimately decided for her what she needed. Why was Davey rising? To kill her? To embrace her? It didn't matter. Faye ran. She was finally able to run the way she should have as soon as Mary was killed, the way she should have when Davey invited her here in the first place.

When she ran into the arena, she was greeted by her own ghost. It was perfectly dark—there was no time for candles and she didn't dare turn on her light, but she didn't need it because she could see her own specter, she could see all of them, pushing the shelves out of the way, dancing, chanting, full of anticipation for the night ahead of them. The people they'd been only a few hours ago weren't yet monsters, and she wished she could stay here and remember how they sang and laughed.

She was out of breath by the time she got to the arena, but she couldn't stop there. Of all the places in the basement, she'd least like Davey to kill her here. She couldn't bear to have to look at Ro's body in her final moments of life. "I killed a killer. I need that to be true." That was what Davey had said of Mary and that was what Faye had thought of Ro, but she knew now she'd taken a life for no reason.

"I'm sorry," she whispered to Ro. There wasn't any light, she couldn't see him, but she knew he was there. The screaming of the siren made it impossible to know whether Davey was right behind her. If there were footsteps, she'd never hear them; if he was panting, she was deaf to it. She felt something against her foot and reared back, terrified she'd misjudged the distance and done Ro even more disrespect by walking into him. But no, this wasn't the fleshy firmness of a human thigh. It was the corn, the corn! She had to flee but before she did, she took that blessed fruit. She held it to her chest and she ran away from the evidence of her own crime.

"Faye!" Davey screamed for her during a pause in the siren. She stopped her running and crouched right where she was, pulling her knees into her chest and daring not even to breathe, lest he hear her. "Faye, I only want to talk. Where are you?"

Hadn't he only wanted to "talk" to Mary? Hadn't he called for her in that exact same tone? Hadn't he hunted for her in the basement with that exact same urgency? They were all liars, there was no doubt of that now, but only Davey was alive to continue lying.

"It's safe," he called. "For the first time tonight, it's safe!" She let the siren drown him out. He would come to the arena looking for her, but she refused to be his prey. She didn't rise to her feet; she stayed on her hands and knees so that her eyes wouldn't reflect in his flashlight if he swept it across a section of the basement as she was crossing. She shoved the ear of corn into her tank top for safekeeping, and she crawled only when the siren was screaming. When the noise paused, so did Faye, and she listened for breath or steps or any clue to where he was during those second-long reprieves.

"You're making it harder on yourself!" he called, and she preferred it when his voice dipped into anger. When the pretense of friendship or comradery or whatever he was playing at gave way to his frustration with her, she felt like she was really able to see him for who he was. She made terrible time, crawling that way, but it didn't matter. She had all night. Sometimes his voice drew nearer and sometimes it was further. A couple of times she thought she saw a flicker of a flashlight come across the top of a row of books, but it always disappeared quickly, and then she wasn't sure she had seen it at all. He was never near enough that she could hear him breathe.

As soon as it began to feel easy, this pattern of siren and pause and crawling away from the sound of him, it turned on its head because he stopped calling, and then she had no idea where he was. She managed almost no movement at all then, not daring to move in any of the silent moments, making sure she was perfectly still well before the siren paused for breath.

Then, after he was no longer yelling for her, she began to hear him whisper. "You won't survive me," his voice said in her ear. He dared her to disagree, to answer back, to make a noise, to reveal herself, but she held firm, stayed still during those silences. "You'll die tonight, with blood on your hands."

She found she couldn't crawl any longer, once he got into her head, so she got to her feet and ran through the dark to the one place he wouldn't come to look for her.

Soraya's body lay half-covered with books and splintered lumber, just as they had left it. One of the stacks in the collapsed pile was at a diagonal, with just enough space underneath for a person Faye's size to fit under. The shelf had been relieved of its books in the crash, so even if it gave way onto Faye, she didn't think it could do very much harm. In her little crawl space, she was near enough Soraya that if she'd reached out, they could have touched fingertips. It was how she knew Davey would never seek her here. Much as she couldn't risk her last moments being within sight of Ro, she knew Davey wouldn't come anywhere near Soraya's body. Had he pushed the stacks that had fallen and killed her? He swore he hadn't, and Faye didn't think she'd ever know the truth. In the case of Soraya, the truth didn't matter. Even if he hadn't taken her life with his own hands, Faye could tell that Davey would carry Soraya's death forever, whether he died tonight or in sixty years. She took something that was his, or that he believed to be his, but that didn't mean he cared for her any less. No, Davey wouldn't come here. He'd leave a wide berth around Soraya's broken bones.

When Faye came to rest in the crawl space, she was reminded of the needs of her mortal body. She waited for the siren to wail, and then she shifted position to lay her weary head on the concrete. In the short silence she paused, listened, heard nothing, and during the next wail, she removed the ear of corn from inside her shirt. She needed rest and she needed food. It was easy to forget her body when she'd been running for her life but now, with just the tiniest bit of safety, her body remembered.

The siren blared and she tore off one part of the husk. This wasn't the ear of corn she started earlier; this was the second one, the one that had tumbled out of Davey's basket of secrets. She was grateful. It meant one more mouthful of food than she would otherwise have. In four or five turns of that siren, she got the husk off, but still she didn't begin to eat. It was only about four thirty; that left so much time in the basement. She removed one single kernel with her fingernail and while the siren was blaring, she placed it in her mouth and began to count to one hundred. Only when she finished her count did she allow herself another.

She didn't keep count of the kernels; that wasn't the point. She didn't need to know how much or how little food she was consuming. All she knew was that it was bliss. The sweet corn on her tongue and between her teeth for one hundred perfect seconds at a time. It was time when she felt safe, time when she didn't feel hunted, time when she had control, and she kept at it, not daring to break the cycle until she found she had no corn kernels left, and still, it was not morning.

Faye didn't reach for her phone. She didn't dare shine any light, she didn't dare exhaust the battery and, besides, what was the point? If she had eighty minutes left in the basement or two minutes, did it make a difference? It would take Davey only seconds to kill her if he came upon her.

She wasn't a person who had ever struggled to sleep, but no level of fatigue would have allowed her to close her eyes that night. Once the corn was done, she played with the cob, stroking it like it was a doll, and still the night wasn't over. What would she say to her mother, she thought, if she lived. She could think of nothing. She hadn't learned anything; she wouldn't emerge from here a changed person. The best she could think of was to never tell her mother or any other soul any of the things she'd experienced. It was as she pondered that, the possibility of forgetting, that the impossible happened.

The lights came on. It was morning.

II

However much blood Faye had imagined or expected, she had vastly underestimated it. Her only experience of a crime scene, a death scene, was from movies and television, and the scene in the library basement under the glare of fluorescent lights was too much for any rating board or decency panel to ever put on-screen. There were ugly smears of blood across the floor from where the dying or injured had tried to drag themselves to safety, there were footsteps, large ones and small ones, since it seemed that since Kip's death early in the evening, no one had taken a step without blood on the soles of their shoes or bare feet. There were abandoned garments, destroyed books.

Faye took her phone from her pocket. There was 4 percent battery remaining. It was seven o'clock in the morning. She might have been more relieved at the time of day, at the idea that there was someone else in the building, if not for the chaotic scene around her. It was like waking up from a nightmare only to find yourself in a nightmare. The light hurt her eyes, and the brightness somehow made the alarm sound louder. That was the opposite of what was supposed to happen. The loss of one sense was supposed to sharpen the others. Now that there was light and she had full vision, she would have expected her hearing to have dulled, but there was no such relief.

Still, the horror of the scene and the volume of the siren didn't matter, not now. If there was someone who had turned on the lights, then there was someone in the building. If there was someone in the building, then they had heard the alarm. The help she'd thought she'd be able to summon all those hours ago was finally coming. Faye slid herself out of her crawl space. She still used the sound of the siren to conceal the sound of her movements. Help was in the building, but it wasn't downstairs yet.

When she got to her feet, the room spun and tilted sideways, but she wouldn't let herself succumb to the sensation. She put her hands on her knees to take a breath, and then she began to tiptoe forward, toward the door she'd come through the night before. Her tank top was stained yellow from the corn, and as she moved forward, she tried to brush off any kernels or pieces of husk that might have remained on her clothes or her face. It was embarrassing that she'd taken the time to eat while others lay dead.

Wherever Davey had spent the last couple of hours, it was closer to the door than Faye's crawl space. Or maybe not. Maybe he'd arrived at the door more quickly because he hadn't bothered to tiptoe. If he'd moved quickly and unafraid once the lights turned on, then his position in the basement didn't matter at all. Because she was slow and cautious, Faye saw him before he saw her.

He had his back to the gate, facing not the elevator that would be their salvation but the direction he thought Faye would greet him from. He had his arms stretched up, palms facing her. He surrendered.

"I didn't hurt Kip or Soraya," he said to Faye when he saw her. The condition of his face, like the condition of the basement, had been concealed by the darkness. He'd smeared blood from his hands onto his mouth and cheek, sure, but it mingled with his own blood from the gashes he'd torn out of grief or theatricality. His eye was swollen all the way shut. He was a monster. "You have to believe me," he said.

Faye laughed. How pathetic she must seem to him, that even now he was still asking for something from her.

"I don't have to do anything," she said. "Those doors are about to open and the fire department or the police or the fire department *and* the police are going to come get us out of here and they can decide who you did or didn't hurt." She wanted to say more: how she thought they'd be friends by the end of the night. How she felt tricked into coming. How he could have done the ugly things he did without trapping her in the basement to witness them. "Get away from the gate," she said.

He looked behind him, surprised, but then he did as he was told and moved a good distance from the exit. The alarm sounded even louder right by the door, but Faye didn't let herself appear bothered by it. When Davey was a sufficient distance from the gate, she went to stand by it.

"I didn't hurt anyone," he said again.

"Tell me this," Faye said, and then waited for a pause in the alarm. She wanted to ask him again what she'd already asked him. She wanted to know if he was capable of telling her something true. "The job. Did you know Soraya was getting the job and not you?"

The alarm gave him the opportunity to think about his answer, but she saw it in his face before he said a word. And he knew that he'd hidden it poorly, that he didn't have the dark as a mask any longer so he didn't bother to lie. Not this time.

"I found out tonight," Davey said. He paused for the alarm. "Soraya told me herself, just before she died."

They were all liars. She couldn't decide whether telling the truth now, after everything that had happened, made him less culpable.

"You found out just before you killed her?" Faye said, though his woe looked so real, she was beginning to doubt.

"It was after Kip was dead," Davey said. "I didn't come down here with any motive…"

The alarm drowned out the rest of what he was trying to say and, behind it, another noise. The ding of the arriving elevator. While they'd been speaking, the orange light indicating that the elevator had reached the basement flicked on. Davey lowered his arms and they both turned to see the old elevator door clatter open.

III

Faye saw Ronald first. Rumpled and concerned, he wasn't wearing a sport coat, he hadn't shaved, and there were thumbprints on his glasses. Behind him in the elevator were men she didn't recognize, but they were dressed in navy and had gleaming bronze badges pinned to their chests. Her nightmare was over. Help was here.

She would have wept with relief if there was time to do such a thing. Instead, things began to happen quickly. Ronald ran to the gate and unlocked it, and Faye pushed through, desperate to get out, and Davey followed right behind her. Ronald and the police eyed them with horror, and before she could get into the elevator, one of the officers had the wherewithal to stop her. "You're bleeding," he said.

She had to shout to make herself heard over the screaming of the alarm, so she did. She screamed, "the blood isn't mine," at the top of her lungs, but as she did so, the alarm went quiet, so it was only her words that rang through the now-quiet basement.

"Did someone hear the alarm?" Davey said. An officer had taken him by the arm and he, too, was getting a once-over to try to identify the source of the blood on his hands and face and clothing. "Is that why you brought the police?"

Faye caught his eye and she felt vindicated. That screaming alarm that had been such a part of their torture that evening, could it have been the thing that summoned the police? If the alarm had brought them to the library even fifteen minutes earlier than they might have come otherwise, then it was worth all the noise.

"The police came with me," Ronald said. He touched a smudge of blood on Faye's shoulder and then pulled his hand back, horrified.

"I don't understand," Faye said. "Did someone tell you we were down here, so you brought the police to look for us?" There were three officers with Ronald, but they were still all standing between the elevator and the gate. There were more bodies than there was help. "You're going to need more resources," she said.

"We're not here looking for you," Ronald said. "The police and I…" He finally moved past the others and went through the gate. He looked at the concrete floor, at the bloody footsteps. Too many, too great a variety, to have been made by only Faye and Davey. "The police are looking for Kip," Ronald said. "They have reason to think he's in some danger."

———

Faye told them where to find Kip's body, and then the locations of the others came tumbling out, too. She said they thought Kip had been poisoned, and Davey blurted out that they hadn't done it, that he hadn't hurt Kip. Ronald put a gentle hand on a part of Davey's back that wasn't stained with blood, and he told Davey he knew that no one had hurt Kip. The apparatus of law enforcement came into place so quickly that there was no time to ask questions. They had done so much damage, to each other, to the library, but they weren't treated as suspects in anything.

"We didn't get to do it," Davey said. He was talking to himself. The police were too occupied to concern themselves with him. "Demeter didn't show us her secrets, and now we'll never get to do it."

"People are *dead*," Faye said.

"The whole point was to emerge free from fear," Davey said. "Now we'll be terrified for the rest of our lives."

Someone from the fire department, because it turned out the fire department had also arrived, was summoned to the basement with two blankets to escort Davey and Faye out. Riding up in the elevator, an itchy gray blanket covering her stained tank top, Faye couldn't stop shaking. In the elevator she had to stand almost shoulder to shoulder with Davey and what was worse, when they got upstairs, the firefighter took them to the coatroom to wait together.

"They're going to have questions for you," he said. "But you'll want to be out of the way as they start to carry out the…" He didn't want to say "bodies" to a couple of blood-soaked kids barely old enough to buy their own beer, so he let their imaginations fill in the rest. He turned to leave, but Faye grabbed his arm. She couldn't be left here alone with Davey. Any danger he posed to her in the basement still existed here if they were left alone. The firefighter put a hand on hers, kindly, but then he peeled her fingers back. "I'm sure you've seen some stuff, kid, and we'll find someone for you to talk to about it. But there's a lot to clear up down there. So wait here with your friend and try to get some rest until the police are ready for you, okay?"

"If you weren't looking for us," Davey said, "then what are you doing here?"

Davey didn't look like he was eager to be left alone with Faye, any more than she wanted solo time with him.

"I really have to get back. The police will be able to answer any questions you have," the firefighter said. "We've been looking for that graduate student, Kip, most of the night."

"For Kip?" Faye asked. "Why were the police looking for Kip?"

"There was some evidence last night that he'd ingested arsenic," the firefighter said. He looked over at the elevator. "Looks like that turned out to be true."

Faye let her hand fall away. "Arsenic?" she repeated.

The firefighter left and Faye was alone with Davey, the two of them wrapped in those blankets that bit at their skin, but it didn't matter: there was no reason to be afraid any longer because the morsel of information the firefighter was able to offer was enough to flip a switch. She knew how Kip had been poisoned, and it hadn't been by Davey's hand.

"Did he say arsenic?"

The answer didn't come to Davey the way it had to Faye. He clutched his blanket around his shoulders and looked to the door for the disappeared fireman for answers. "Where does someone even get arsenic? We're not in an Agatha Christie novel."

The coatroom had a small lost and found box filled with abandoned articles: a scarf left over from the winter that would never be reunited with its owner, a handful of pens, forbidden in the reading room, no fewer than five cell phone chargers. Faye pulled one out and plugged her phone into the wall. Letting Davey stand and shiver, she sank to the ground next to the outlet.

"From the books, Davey. He got arsenic from the books."

There was a clatter from outside. A couple of paramedics wheeled a stretcher past the coatroom to the elevator, with no particular urgency.

"There was arsenic hidden in the books?" Davey said. He didn't understand. He pretended to know so much about this place, his pedantry on display during those tours for graduate students, but he had no idea.

"What is it you think I've been working on here?" she asked. He'd passed by her workstation, seen her protective goggles, gloves, the plastic sheeting draped over the shelves of books, barely twelve hours earlier.

"You're doing X-rays of the books," he said. "What does that have to do with anything? Are you going to talk about physics again?"

"I'm testing the books with X-ray fluorescence spectroscopy," she said. "I'm not checking them for broken bones. Aren't you curious at all?" There was no attempt at kindness in her tone. "No wonder Soraya got the job over you."

Faye's phone, fueled by a refreshed battery and connected to the cell service it had sought all night, began to buzz, over and over, as the messages from her mother and push notifications for services she didn't remember signing up for, all that chatter that had eluded her for hours began to arrive. She left it face down.

"Okay," Davey said. "You come here and you do X-ray fluorescence spectroscopy. Great. What does that have to do with Kip?"

It wasn't that he thought science was worse or less important than what he did, Faye realized. He just wasn't a curious person. He didn't understand her work because he'd never thought to ask a question about it. She felt sorry for him. It would be terrible being so indifferent. 'Tis not too late to seek a newer world. She could never be friends with someone who had so little curiosity. He wasn't the type of person she wanted in her life. She deserved someone better.

"I only take samples of the green books to the lab. Have you ever wondered why?" Her work area, surrounded by that protective plastic, had only a single hue. "When you came by with your students last night, did any of them ask? Did you wonder? Why green?"

"I assumed you chose to start there so you could do all the green ones at once," Davey said. "Like those idiots on Instagram who organize their bookshelves by color rather than by subject or author."

"It's called Paris green," she said, and she thought that she really was quite a bit smarter than him. "This library has one of the world's largest collections of books in Paris green. It's one of the things that makes us special—or strange. You should know that if you profess to be an expert on the place."

"I'm an expert on the contents of the books," he said. He didn't like being talked to this way, not by an undergraduate physics student, no matter the circumstances.

"Sometimes the form is more interesting than the content," she said. "Paris green gets its distinctive green hue from arsenic. That's what we're testing. We cut slivers from the book covers and take them to the lab to test for poison to see if it's safe for readers to ever touch those green books again."

CHAPTER 25

AND WITH THE LAST WORD, FAYE

When Faye flipped over her phone, she found she'd been sent the link to the video by a classmate, Frankie, she of the study group, who knew Faye worked at the library.

"Faye!" the message read. "Don't you work at this library? Do you know this fool?"

After she'd declined Frankie's study group invitation, the girl had continued to say hello in class, continued to invite her to things, sometimes even G-chatted her in the middle of class with jokes that were only funny if you were deeply rooted in the study of physics.

Before hitting play on the video, she sat for a time with Frankie's message. She typed and deleted, then typed and deleted, then finally retyped, "It's a crazy story if you want to hear it. Lunch?" Then she hit send before she could think about it for even another second.

The link in Frankie's text wasn't to Kip's original post; that wasn't the one that had thousands of views. It was a repost by someone whose name she didn't recognize that added a skull-and-crossbones emoji and a succinct explanation of the problem with Paris-green books in a split screen with Kip's original.

Faye didn't need the background information, though, and neither did Davey when they got around to watching the clip together, so they focused their attention on Kip. In his video, he was wearing the shirt from that very night, the one that was stiff with dried blood now. He stood, smiling gleefully against a background of brilliant green books. It did make for a handsome setting for an online post. When Faye squinted, she could see that the volume she'd worked on the afternoon before was still on the shelf. He'd snuck into the basement in the early morning and filmed himself before she'd come in. He turned his back to the camera briefly and retrieved a Paris-green copy of *Little Women* from the shelf. Then he moved to a side profile and ran his thick, wet tongue across the cover before smiling into the camera and saying, "I hate America. I hate Americans. That's disgusting."

READING GROUP GUIDE

1. If you were invited to Davey's ritual, how would you have responded? What might have motivated you to participate?

2. Why does Davey find Mary's outward silliness and interest in attention "distasteful"? Why do we see seriousness as a necessary attribute for intellectual rigor?

3. The Eleusinian Mysteries ritual is meant to banish fear from its participants. What would you do if you had no fear? What might some of the unintended consequences be?

4. How does the dynamic of the group change when they realize Kip was poisoned? If they hadn't been fasting for the ritual, would that detail have sown so much chaos?

5. Persuasion becomes the most dangerous weapon in the story. Which character do you think is the most persuasive? What happens when the person who's most persuasive is different from the person who's most right?

6. At the end of the book Davey assures himself repeatedly that he didn't kill anyone. As Faye points out, he continuously forgets

Mary, but do you hold him responsible for any of the other deaths?

7. In the world of the book, the revelation of Kip's death by arsenic absolves the other characters of guilt. In the real world, how do you think the story of his death would be reported, and what would its fallout be considering that it involved both re-creating a viral meme and licking an extremely rare book?

A CONVERSATION WITH THE AUTHOR

What was the inspiration for *That Night in the Library*? What are the first decisions you make when you start writing a new story?

This story came to me as two lightning bolts, and it was almost fully formed in my head before I sat down to write it. First, I saw a couple of movies, a couple of takes on the locked-room mystery format that were modern and irreverent and reminded me of how much I loved that form. I was working on another project, but I started to say to others, "Wouldn't it be cool to have a locked-room thriller with a bunch of students partying at a rare books library?" I wanted someone else to write it because I wanted to read it. Right around the same time, someone shared an article with me about arsenic in green books, and it immediately clicked in my head as a murder weapon or, I guess, a tool for accidental poisoning. Once I had that ending, I couldn't not write the book. As soon as I committed to writing the story, I got to start in on my favorite bit: populating the cast of characters that I was going to trap in that library.

Your previous mystery, *The Department of Rare Books and Special Collections*, is also set in a library but takes a very different story-telling approach. How did the writing experience differ between the two books?

I can only describe the writing of the first draft of this book as feverish. My first book, *The Department of Rare Books and Special Collections*, is a bit of a slower read. Not in a bad way, but it's focused on character, and it takes its time to unfurl. It was slower to write, too. But this book, particularly the second half, barrels forward, and the experience of writing it was almost exactly like the experience of reading it. I couldn't stop once I'd started, I knew exactly where I wanted the story to go, and I was so excited to get to the next twist, to drop the next body. It changed a lot over several edits, of course, but writing that first draft was a delirious exercise.

Faye's loneliness is one of the biggest driving forces in the book, but this particular attempt to make friends is utterly disastrous. What do you hope is next for her?

I view Faye's loneliness as a bit of a self-inflicted condition and largely driven by her fear of being embarrassed. There's a vision of friendship that she's seen in films that she desperately wants, and she doesn't recognize the early steps of friendship in the advances that people have made toward her over time. And then, in her desperation to resolve her loneliness, she dives in with both feet with this group of near strangers. I think, in this one terrible night, she's seen good and bad friendships modeled up close. If nothing else, Faye now knows what she doesn't want out of a friendship, and she's seen such terrible things that there's not much left to be afraid of. I have hope for Faye! I think she'll accept a couple of invitations, keep reaching out to others, and finally make those friends she wants so badly.

Which of the characters was the most fun to write? Why?

The pairing of Ro and Umu was my favorite to write. I love the sound of smart people talking, and Ro and Umu are both bright and sharp but in different ways from each other and from the way you might expect people to be on a college campus. I also love long relationships, and these two have inside jokes and a shared language that stretches back to their childhoods. I also like how imperfect they are, as individuals and as friends. They're insecure—I was so insecure at that age. I'm still so insecure, but I was *really* insecure at that age, and it's nice to have a safe space to explore those feelings of wanting to be something or someone but not quite knowing what or who that is yet.

If you were trapped in the library basement along with these characters, do you think you would make it through the night?

Like Leonardo DiCaprio, I have a strict "no hard drugs" rule that I think would have served me well had I been trapped in the basement of the William E. Woodend Rare Books Library. In the Rudyard Kipling poem "If—," he writes: "If you can keep your head when all about you / Are losing theirs…Yours is the Earth and everything that's in it." I am no more clever than any of the characters in my story, but I "Just Say No" to hard drugs so I'd have kept my head about me and, I hope, survived. Knowing myself as I do, I would have snagged the corn by ten p.m. and disappeared into a corner somewhere with my snack as soon as the rest of them started chanting.

ACKNOWLEDGMENTS

My sincere thanks to Erin Clyburn for finding a home for my crew of characters and to Anna Michels for welcoming me back to Poisoned Pen Press/Sourcebooks. The entire Sourcebooks team—editorial, design, my beloved marketing team—is a joy to work with, and I'm thrilled to be getting back on this roller coaster with you all.

In a very real way, this book would not have been possible without my Team Cly-Fi comrades, and I owe particular thanks to Taylor Tyng, who shared the *National Geographic* article from which my murder mystery draws its culprit.

For their inspirational scholarship, I'd like to thank lead conservator Dr. Melissa Tedone, lead scientist Dr. Rosie Grayburn, and the rest of the team at the Winterthur Poison Book Project, as well as George Mylonas and R. Gordon Wasson for their wonderful books about the Eleusinian Mysteries.

Thank you, as always, to my colleagues at the University of Toronto Libraries for your good humor and support of my double life.

Sincerest thanks to Bronia Jurczyk for indulging my childhood love of Christopher Pike novels and never asking too many questions about the age appropriateness of my reading materials.

And finally, to the two great loves of my life, who make writing harder but living better—Matthew and Henryk Valentine—you are forever my dudes.

ABOUT THE AUTHOR

Eva Jurczyk was born in a mining town in Poland and wound up halfway around the world in a Canadian city that often masquerades as New York in the movies. As her day job, she buys books, building library collections for the University of Toronto Libraries. Her first novel, *The Department of Rare Books and Special Collections*, was a Canadian bestseller as well as a LibraryReads, IndieNext, and Loan Star selection. She travels to Paris whenever the wind is good but currently lives with her husband, son, and collection of books in Toronto, Canada.